Titles by Jaci Burton

Hope Flames

JACI BURTON

B

BERKLEY SENSATION, NEW YORK

THE BERKLEY PUBLISHING GROUP
Published by the Penguin Group
Penguin Group (USA)
375 Hudson Street, New York, New York 10014, USA

USA | Canada | UK | Ireland | Australia | New Zealand | India | South Africa | China

HOPE FLAMES

A Berkley Sensation Book / published by arrangement with the author

Berkley Sensation Books are published by The Berkley Publishing Group.
BERKLEY SENSATION® is a registered trademark of Penguin Group (USA)
The "B" design is a trademark of Penguin Group (USA)

ISBN: 978-1-62490-795-1

PRINTED IN THE UNITED STATES OF AMERICA

Cover photo of "Guy" by Claudio Marinesco; "Background" by Andreytiyk/Shutterstock.
Cover design by Rita Frangie.
Interior text design by Kelly Lipovich.

This is a work of fiction. Names, characters, places, and incidents either are the product of the author's imagination or are used fictitiously, and any resemblance to actual persons, living or dead, business establishments, events, or locales is entirely coincidental. The publisher does not have any control over and does not assume any responsibility for author or third-party websites or their content.

For Ashley. I've seen you grow into a beautiful young woman of fierce dedication and determination. No matter what roads you've chosen to travel, I'm so very proud of where you've ended up.
Love you!

Acknowledgments

To Maya Banks and Shannon Stacey, who held my hand and acted as cheerleaders when I needed it most. You're the best friends I could have ever asked for.

Chapter 1

EMMA BURNETT COULD have never imagined that going hundreds of thousands of dollars in debt would be so exhilarating.

She could barely contain her excitement as she looked over every aspect of her just-about-to-open new veterinary practice with a heavy dose of pride and more than a little trepidation.

It was six-fifteen in the morning. Her staff would be arriving soon. She grinned at the thought. She had a staff now.

"We're here, Daisy. We made it."

Daisy, her yellow Labrador retriever, thumped her tail and looked up at her, dark eyes filled with adoration. You had to love a dog because no matter what happened, they'd always love you back. You could have an awful day, be grouchy and in the worst mood, and your dog would still sit at your feet and be there for you.

Emma rubbed Daisy's head and locked up her bag in her office, then closed the door, moving into the lobby. Daisy followed along, sniffing every square inch of gleaming tile Emma had spent the weekend polishing to perfection.

Sure, she could have had a cleaning service do that, but this place was hers and she wanted to do it herself. Then, after she'd cleaned, she'd inventoried, going over every scalpel, pair of forceps, IV pole, and thermometer. She'd inventoried all the drugs—twice—from antibiotics to pain medications, making sure everything was in order.

This place was hers. She still couldn't quite believe it.

She swept her hand over the pristine reception desk, tapped her finger on the desktop computer she hoped was filled with appointments for the day, then moved on through the double doors leading to the back room where the sparkling instruments awaited her first touch.

Cages were ready, and so were the exam rooms. The OR was prepped. Everything was spotless and sterilized.

She was in debt up to her eyeballs, but, come hell or rising water from the creek down the road, this place was all hers now. It had taken years and more than a few major detours, but Hope Small Animal Hospital was now owned and operated by Dr. Emma Burnett, DVM.

She inhaled and exhaled, letting the dual feelings of satisfaction and utter terror wash over her. At least this time it was a healthy dose of terror. Not like before.

It would never be like *before* again. She'd lost five years of her life on that mistake, and now, at thirty-two, she was making a late start. But after going back to school and working with a veterinary group in South Carolina, she was finally home and on her own with a practice that was all hers.

A knock on the front door made her startle. She curled her fingers into her palms.

"Calm, Emma. This is your big day." She hurried to the door, grabbing her keys out of her lab-coat pocket.

It was Rachel, her receptionist, along with Leanne, her tech. Her two assistants were the gas in the engine that drove this clinic. She smiled and unlocked the door. "Good morning."

"Mornin', Dr. Emma," Rachel said with a grin, her arms laden with donuts and coffee. "Thought you could use these."

"It's so good to be back here again," Leanne said, her

long blond hair braided into two pigtails, her purple scrubs decorated with tiny paw prints.

Totally adorable.

"You're my lifesavers. Both of you. Thank you."

They sat in the tiny break room together and ate donuts, drank coffee, and went over the appointments for the day.

"You have a full day, Dr. Emma," Rachel said.

"Really? That's great." She wanted to leap up and pump her fist in the air, but that would be so unprofessional.

"Doc Weston always had a full waiting room." Leanne licked donut icing off her fingers. "Everyone was disappointed when he had to close so suddenly. So were we."

"No kidding," Rachel said. "Leanne and I were lucky to hook up with the Barkley clinic on the north side of town after Doc Weston closed, but Barkley sucks."

"Understatement," Leanne said. "The doctors there are dicks."

Emma would not smile about that. Really, she wouldn't.

Leanne nodded. "I've been spreading the word about the reopening. It's like *Field of Dreams*, Doc. People will come."

Emma let out a hopeful sigh. "That's so good to hear." She wanted to be busy. She needed to fill this place up with clients.

Since Dr. Weston had retired six months ago, the clinic had been closed and Hope residents had to go to the other clinic for animal care. Bruce Weston had been a wonderful veterinarian. He'd taken care of Emma's terrier, Soupy, and her collie, Max, when she'd been a kid, and she'd loved him. She'd always been eager to come here and look at all the pictures of animal breeds on the wall of the exam rooms, check out the charts and the models of the insides of dogs and cats. She'd been curious and he'd always been more than happy to answer all her questions. Besides her utter love of animals, Dr. Weston had been one of the primary reasons she wanted to become a veterinarian. He was kind and patient, and had taken just as much care of the owners as he had of the animals.

She'd been sad to hear about his heart surgery and sub-
sequent retirement, but happy for him now that he and his
wife, Denise, were moving closer to their grandchildren in
Colorado. She'd been ecstatic that he'd been amenable to
her buying out his practice. It had taken a whirlwind trip
from South Carolina back to Oklahoma so she could meet
face-to-face with him to iron out the particulars once she'd
learned his practice was for sale. He'd been generous in his
price and had helped her work out the loan details so she
could get it done.

Maybe her luck was finally changing.

At six forty-five they cleared out the remnants of donut
nirvana and Rachel, ever efficient, booted up the computer,
while Emma and Leanne set up the rooms and instruments,
ready for the first patients to start rolling in.

And did they ever. The first clients started coming in as
soon as they opened the doors at seven. The clinic offered
drop-off service for people on their way to work in Tulsa.
Since they were on the main road leading to the highway, it
was convenient. People could drop off their animals, Emma
would diagnose and treat them throughout the course of the
day, and their owners could pick them up on their way home
from work. She charged a minimum boarding fee to house
them for the day.

By eight o'clock, the appointment customers started piling in, and Emma reacquainted herself with the people in
her town. She'd been so busy renovating the clinic, updating
inventory, and working with her staff since she'd come home
that she'd had no time to visit with anyone. She wished she'd
had a chance to see her sister, but Molly didn't come home.
Ever. Period. If she wanted to see her little sister, she had to
first track her down because Molly was as mobile as they
came. And then she had to fly or drive to whatever location
Molly called home that particular month.

They talked on the phone at least once a week, and that
would have to be good enough for now.

At the moment she had her hands full with a hundred
and forty pounds of very exuberant Newfoundland, who

was happily slobbering on her neck as she performed an exam.

"He's very healthy, Mrs. Lang," she said, as she and Leanne wrangled King, who was determined to play with them. He stuck out his tongue and slurped her face.

Good thing she appreciated dog drool.

"He's eating my pear tree. Bits of bark at a time." Mrs. Lang did not look happy.

"Do you take him out for walks? How big is your backyard? Do you have other dogs for him to play with?"

"King is our only dog, and the yard is small. And well . . . he's kind of a lot to handle. It was my husband Roger's idea to get him." Mrs. Lang looked mournfully at King. "He was such a cute little puppy."

Many people thought puppies were so cute. The problem was, cute puppies often grew into giant dogs. Like King. She glanced over at King's chart to check out the Lang's address. "He needs exercise and stimulation. There's a great park over on Fifth near your house. Does he walk on a leash?"

"Yes. Very well. I made Roger take him to those classes."

"Excellent. If you walk him twice a day and take him to the park, it will help work off all this energy he has. Also, I highly recommend neutering him. You don't want him to get out and father a bunch of unwanted pups, do you? And it will help settle him."

"Oh, of course. Let's do that." She smirked. "Roger won't like that. Men and their . . . equipment, you know. They take it so personally. I'll tell him it was your suggestion and he'll do it. And I'll make sure we walk him." She patted her stomach. "We could all use the exercise."

The morning flew by in a blur of shots, exams, worming, and one tiny and filthy pit bull puppy someone had found in a ditch. She was a mass of flea-bitten adorable, a brown-and-white baby who'd either been abandoned or lost. The person dropping her off said she couldn't keep her because she had two rottweilers at home and couldn't possibly handle one more dog, but she couldn't leave her shivering in the morning cold, either. Though it was late spring and the days were warming, the nights were still cool.

Emma assured the woman they'd clean her up and find her a good home. She examined the pup, and other than needing a serious flea bath and a good meal, she was healthy, thankfully. She gave the pup to Leanne, who took her away to give her the flea bath and her first round of puppy shots.

She only had time for a quick bite of the peanut butter and jelly sandwich she'd packed for lunch when the second round of afternoon clients came in. Daisy wound her way around the clinic, checking in on Rachel and Leanne as they did their work, too. Emma was so thankful to be this busy, she had no complaints. They were jammed all afternoon until the last pickup at closing, when her staff finally left.

It was quiet. She swiped her hair out of her eyes and breathed a sigh of utter contentment as she walked around the clinic.

It had been a good first day. This is what she'd wanted, what she'd worked so hard for. She'd lost sight of it for a while and thought she'd never have it.

"Hello? Is anyone here?"

Daisy's ears perked up, and she bounded out of the office at the sound of the deep, booming voice in the lobby.

Emma thought she'd locked the door.

She hurried out to see a man holding a German shepherd by the leash who sat regally while Daisy tried to play with it.

"Daisy, come here."

Daisy came over and sat dutifully next to her, tail whipping against Emma's lab coat.

"Can I help you?"

"Yeah. I saw your lights were on and was hoping you'd still be open. My dog hurt his leg."

He came toward her, and she took a wary step back, until he walked under the overhead lights and she saw he was wearing a cop uniform. She breathed a sigh of relief.

"You scared me there for a second."

"I'm really sorry. Luke McCormack. I'm local police here. This is my dog, Boomer."

McCormack. Last name sounded familiar, but she couldn't quite place it. She would definitely remember a guy who looked like him. Tall, broad-shouldered, wearing a uniform that fit him—very well. Dark brown pants, lighter brown shirt. Gun strapped to his hip. Very dark hair, cut short, full lips. Serious expression, which only made him look . . .

Hot. Sexy. Though she didn't think about men being sexy these days. She didn't think about men at all, and hadn't for a very long time.

As he approached, she noticed the dog was limping. "Oh. What happened?"

"We were chasing a perp—uh, a suspect. Boomer must have twisted his leg in a hole or something because he yelped and came up limping. I was headed toward the Barkley's vet clinic and saw Doc Weston's office was open again, so figured I'd stop here first. If you're closed, I can—"

"No. Of course, I'll look at him. Bring him on back." He walked side by side with her, and she noticed how very tall and broad he was. Daisy wound between them, licking the officer's hand and staring adoringly up at him.

Yeah, some watchdog you are, Daisy. Daisy wasn't exactly what one could consider a personal bodyguard, unless excessive licking and an overabundance of affection counted as weaponry.

Emma led the officer into the exam room and flipped on the lights, then turned around and knelt down, trying to calm her stupid, raging heartbeat. She smiled at the dog. "Okay, Boomer. Let's take a look."

"Boomer. Sit," the officer said.

The dog sat and she examined his leg. He whimpered as she pressed on it. After finishing the exam, she lifted her gaze to the police officer. "Officer McCormack, I'd like to get an X-ray of this leg. I don't think anything's broken, but I want to be sure."

He nodded. "Okay."

"You can come with me. It'll calm him to have you there."

She brought them back to the X-ray room, and he helped
her get Boomer on the table while she got his leg in place
for the X-ray.

"So, you bought Dr. Weston's practice?" he asked.

Again, that voice of his. Deep and seriously . . . unnerv-
ing, but not in a bad way. It was doing something to her
nerve endings she found decidedly . . .

Uncomfortable wasn't the word. She just noticed his
voice. And so did her body. "Yes. I bought it right after he
retired."

"I'm sorry, but I don't think I got your name."

She looked up at him and frowned, then realized she'd
been a complete moron and hadn't bothered to introduce
herself. "I'm so sorry, officer. I'm Emma Burnett."

"Nice to meet you, Emma. Are you new in town?"

"Actually, I grew up here. My parents live over on
Willow."

He nodded. "Did you go to Oakdale High?"

"No. I went to Hope High."

"Oh, okay. The Burnetts on Willow. Your sister is Molly
Burnett, then, right? She dated my friend Carter Richards
in high school."

Hope was such a small town. Everyone knew everyone
else. "Yes, Molly's my little sister. Did you go to Hope
High, too?"

"No. I went to Oakdale."

That's why she didn't recognize him right off. He'd gone
to the high school nearer to the county line. "Your name
sounds familiar to me, too. Did you play football for
Oakdale?"

"Yeah. Wide receiver."

Now she knew why she recognized his name. He'd been
some kind of football star. She remembered reading about
him in the newspaper. He'd been good. But they hadn't
known each other back then.

"So this is your clinic now?" he asked.

"Yes, sir."

She grabbed the film and slid it in.

"Luke."

She looked up. "Excuse me?"

"Call me Luke. Not officer, and definitely not sir. Too formal."

He'd cracked a smile. He had a quirky, kind of off-kilter smile, and greenish-blue eyes that went really well with his dark hair. He had a rugged face, a square jaw, and, again, that really sexy mouth.

Not that she was looking at him in *that* way, because she didn't do that anymore. She and men were definitely off-limits. She'd learned her lesson the hard way.

But that didn't mean she couldn't be nice to her clients. "Okay, then, Luke. Let's get this X-ray going. I need you to position his leg here for me, then if possible, ask him not to move."

"No problem. Boomer—stay."

Boomer lay perfectly still as they went behind the screen so she could take the shot.

"Good boy." Luke said to Boomer after the X-ray was taken. He swept his hand over the dog's back and neck, showing care and affection.

She liked seeing that in a dog's owner.

"Just one more film and that should do it. I need to turn him this way."

Luke helped her, and she couldn't help noticing his hands. Strong. Big. Masculine, with a fine sprinkling of dark hair on his forearms. He hadn't worn a coat inside, and he had some serious upper arm muscles peeking out from the sleeve of his uniform shirt.

But she wasn't looking, and she definitely wasn't interested, despite the pinging in her nerve endings that conveyed otherwise.

Chemistry couldn't be denied. But that was biology. She had a choice, and she already knew what her choices were these days regarding men.

She took Luke behind the screen and captured the second X-ray.

But he did smell really good, though it wasn't cologne.

Shampoo, maybe? Or soap? Did they make scented soap for men? She had no idea.

But she wasn't interested, so it didn't matter what kind of soap he used.

"Are we done?"

She looked at him. "Yes. Yes, we are." She turned one way and he went the other, so they bumped into each other. He reached out for her arms to steady her, and she found herself staring up into those amazing eyes of his.

"Sorry," he said with a deep laugh that Emma felt all the way down to her stomach. And maybe even a little lower.

"No. It's my fault." He took a step back and she moved around him.

He had her acting like a teenager all filled with raging hormones. Ugh.

"Just wait here a second with Boomer so I can make sure we don't need to retake any shots."

She hurried out of the room and took a deep breath when she got into the reading room.

What was wrong with her? She'd had male customers all day long. Some had been really good-looking, too, yet none of them had affected her like Luke was doing now.

Likely because she hadn't been alone with any one man all day. That had to be it. She never put herself in a position to be alone with a guy. And though Luke was a police officer, owned a dog, and seemed all nice and trustworthy, she knew better than to trust any man.

She'd been naïve and trusting once, and it had cost her dearly. She was never going to be that stupid again, no matter how gorgeous a man was, or how nice he seemed.

Or how good he smelled.

Besides, this was the year of her career and nothing else. And so far, day one had been spectacular.

Chapter 2

LUKE HAD BEEN a cop long enough to know two things were certain. One, when things were at their worst, more bad shit tended to pile on, and two, never judge a book by its cover.

The first came true tonight when he'd been chasing the crackhead he'd pulled over for a speeding ticket, only to have the moron bail and run on him. He and Boomer had taken off on foot in pursuit, and Boomer had ended up wrenching his leg in a hole in someone's front yard. Good thing he'd called in for backup—the suspect had been located hiding in someone's shed. Asshole.

The book with the pretty cover was currently taking an X-ray of Boomer's leg. Dr. Emma Burnett was beautiful, but not in that fashion-model, take-your-breath kind of way. Her dark brown hair was pulled back in a ponytail, though some of it had escaped and framed her face. Her eyes were chocolate brown, framed by thick, dark lashes, and she had those full kind of lips that a man would want to spend hours kissing. She also had a body he'd be more than eager to pat down. Nice curves in all the right places, for sure, if a guy was in the market for a woman, which he wasn't.

He had plenty of women popping in and out of his life these days, which was just the way he liked it. In one day, out the next. The out part was the best part.

Though right now the only thing that mattered to him was his dog. Dogs were the only creatures that were truly faithful. Women? Fun to play with. Definitely not fun to spend the rest of your life with. He'd tried that once.

Epic fail.

"The X-rays took just fine," Emma said when she returned to the room. "I just need a few minutes to review them. I'll be right back."

"Sure."

She led Luke and Boomer back to the exam room.

He watched her walk out, disappointed the lab coat hid her backside. Based on the front of her, he'd wager she had a great ass, though he didn't see someone like Emma Burnett as a one-night-stand type. Too bad.

Hell, he hadn't seen her in town at all before today, hadn't even realized the clinic had opened up again. Good timing.

She came through the door a few minutes later. "I have good news. Nothing's broken."

He finally relaxed. "That's great."

"Boomer does have a sprain, though. I'm going to give him an anti-inflammatory injection and suggest you keep him calm. Which means no heroic police-dog activity for at least a week."

Luke looked down at Boomer and scratched his ears. "He's not going to like being off duty that long."

Emma squatted and ran her fingers through Boomer's fur. "I'm sure he won't, but it's a short period of time for recovery, compared to what could happen if he hurts himself while he's still trying to heal."

"Understood, Doc. I'll make sure to take good care of him."

"I'm going to wrap his leg, which will offer him some

stability and ward off swelling. You can take it off after twenty-four hours. I'm also going to give you some anti-inflammatory meds. Give those to him once a day. They'll help ease any discomfort he might feel."

He watched her work. She was competent, and Boomer lay there like he was at a spa, his tail thumping while Emma talked to him in that soft, sweet way that females spoke to dogs. Boomer was eating it up, especially when Emma gave him a treat.

"He's going to want to come here every day now," Luke said.

Emma laughed, and Luke felt the twist of that sweet laugh all the way down to his balls.

"Yeah, I'm very popular with the canine crowd."

"I imagine you're very popular with every male, human and canine."

She lifted her lashes, and he saw the blush creep on her cheeks. Surely she was used to being complimented, but she looked away just as quickly and got down to business.

Interesting. He didn't see a wedding ring, but maybe there was a boyfriend and she thought he was hitting on her. Who knew? He was the last person to understand women.

After the shot and bandaging, Emma walked him to the front desk.

"What do I owe you?" he asked.

She looked over at the computer. "You know what? I have no idea. Rachel handles all the accounting." She turned to him. "We can send you a bill."

He frowned. "I can drop by tomorrow and settle up."

"All right. Thanks."

"No, thank *you*. You saved me a trip farther north to the other clinic. Boomer was in pain, so I'm glad you're open and running."

"It was my pleasure." She went to the desk and pulled one of her cards. "If you have any problems, or Boomer doesn't seem to be getting better, give me a call, or bring him back in."

"Will do. Thanks again, Emma."

She blinked, looked at him as if there was something she wanted to say, then nodded. "You're welcome . . . Luke."

EMMA BALANCED THE dog carrier in one hand while nudging away Daisy's excited attempts to push through the door leading into the house from the garage.

"Daisy. I know. I'm hungry, too. Just give me a second to turn the knob, and it'll be dinner time."

Her purse drooped off her shoulder, the carrier tilted sideways, and Daisy barked. The pup whimpered.

"Hang on, guys." She turned the knob and Daisy bolted inside, her toenails tapping on the wood floor as she disappeared into the darkness of the house.

She hit the switch and the hallway was bathed in light. She laid the carrier on the dryer long enough to punch the button, dropping the garage door closed. Daisy came bounding back to lick her hand and give her a hopeful stare, and the puppy cried again.

"I know, kids. I feel exactly the same way. I could use a bath and a glass of wine, but I'm sure that's not first on your agendas, is it?"

Emma could have left the puppy at the clinic. She'd been cleaned up, inoculated, and fed, and she would have rested for the night. But she would've been the only guest at the clinic, and Emma couldn't stand the thought of Annie— which is what Emma decided to call her because she was little and orphaned—being left at the clinic all alone.

Emma headed into the kitchen, placed the carrier on the counter, and grabbed some dinner for Daisy. Now that the dog was occupied chowing down, she turned to the puppy.

She set the carrier on the kitchen floor and opened it. Annie sniffed at the carrier opening for a few minutes, then not so gracefully tumbled out. Daisy, having already gobbled her bowl of food in about two bites, scrambled over to give Annie a sniff. She licked Annie's face, which caused the pup to fall flat on her face.

"Daisy. Gentle," Emma admonished. "She's just a baby."

Though she wouldn't be for long. Emma scooped Annie up and gave her some love. She was trembling. "Poor little thing. Who would abandon you?"

Sometimes, people just sucked. Emma knew that from experience.

She fed Annie, brought her and Daisy outside. While the dogs were out doing their thing, Emma took a few minutes to admire the stars and take a few deep breaths to relax and roll her shoulders.

It had been a good day. She hoped they were all going to be like this.

The dogs came running back, so she let them in and locked the door. Emma put the pup back into her carrier. Annie curled up onto the blanket and went right to sleep. She was totally adorable. And Emma was not going to keep her, no matter how much the cute little thing pulled at Emma's heartstrings. She hoped someone coming into the clinic would adopt her. She made a mental note to have Rachel post Annie's picture and a notice on the bulletin board in the waiting room tomorrow.

In the meantime, Annie's carrier could sit next to Emma's bed tonight.

After heating up a rather unappetizing frozen dinner, washed down with a cheap glass of chardonnay, she grabbed the bottle and glass and headed into the bathroom, poured some great-smelling lavender gel into the tub and turned on the water.

Daisy came into the bathroom, sniffed at the steam rising up from the tub, looked up at Emma, and burped.

"Love you, too, punkin," Emma said as she undressed and climbed into the tub. She grabbed her glass of wine and sank into the water up to her neck with an audible sigh.

Now this was the way to end the day. She took a few sips, and even though it wasn't the finest vintage, it tasted good going down, relaxing her tired, stressed body. She set the glass on the edge of the tub and closed her eyes, replaying the events of the day.

She'd had a lot of clients—more than she thought she'd have. She'd been afraid they'd go elsewhere for veterinary care, but with only one other clinic in town, it was comfortable to stay with the familiar, even if there was a new doctor running it. Though she'd been gone a lot of years, she wasn't a stranger—she had at least grown up in Hope. Her family was known. That helped.

And then there'd been Luke McCormack, the very attractive police officer.

No. She was naked in the bathtub and thinking about a hot man in uniform. What the hell was wrong with her? She did not want to go there.

She paused, about to shut down the thoughts, and sat up in the tub, reaching for her wine to take a long swallow.

How long had it been since she'd even thought about a man, let alone been out with one? How long had it been since one had even interested her?

She thought back to the practice she'd worked at in South Carolina. She hadn't dated anyone there. No one had even remotely sparked her interest. Even further back, there'd been school. Who had time to date while in vet school? It was like living a nightmare. Nonstop classes and tests and clinicals and no sleep. There'd definitely been no men in her life then unless they'd been study partners, and they'd been as exhausted and stressed as she'd been.

The last time she'd had a man in her life had been . . .

Ugh. That was so long ago, and he'd been her nightmare. She refused to think about him ever again.

But today . . . now . . . she'd thought about a man. A very attractive, very sexy man. Was that such a bad thing?

She might not want to have a man in her life, and she might not have one in her master plan for right now, but that didn't mean she shouldn't allow herself to think about one. She was human, after all. And a woman.

She had the right to fantasize, dammit. A sexual reawakening was a good thing.

Her phone rang. She wrinkled her nose, pondered ignoring it, but knew better. It would just ring again. And again, until she picked up. She wiped her hand on the washcloth and grabbed the phone from the edge of the bathroom counter, already knowing who it was.

"Hi, Mom."

"You knew it was me, didn't you? How was your first day? I was going to drop in, but when I drove by, the parking lot was full so I didn't want to bother you. I'm so excited for you, Emma. I knew you were going to be a huge success. Dad says hi, by the way."

So much for relaxation. Her mother was a tornado of energy, both physically and verbally. "It went great."

"We should have had balloons and a big grand opening."

"It's not a retail establishment, Mom. It's a veterinary clinic. No balloons. When they pop, the animals will swallow them. Bad for the intestines."

"Oh, that's right. Still, I think you need a grand opening. It won't hurt to draw in more customers. You need to advertise, Emma. I already told you we'll help with that. You have to push, push, push to be successful."

Push was her mother's middle name.

"And I already told you that Dr. Weston had plenty of customers. Let me see who we get back first. Word of mouth is the best way to draw in clients."

"Whatever you think is best. For now. We'll talk more about that when you come over for dinner on Sunday. Tell me all about your day."

Emma stared longingly at her empty wineglass while she filled her mother in on her first day. She loved her mother, but Georgia Burnett was a force to be reckoned with and rarely took no for an answer once she had an idea in her head. She was opinionated, stubborn, and one of the strongest women Emma had ever known. They'd butted heads from the time Emma was a child.

She'd thought long and hard before coming back home to set up her practice, but buying out Dr. Weston's practice had been a deal she couldn't pass up. Plus, she'd wanted family in her life again, needed the comfort of familiar places and faces. It was scary enough going into debt, even though her parents tried to help with the loan for the practice, which she didn't want. She'd been dependent before, and she'd never be that way again. This time she was doing it all on her own. But she was doing it with family close by.

"Do you need anything?" her mother asked.

"No, I'm good, Mom."

"Your dad and I are worried about you, Emma. All the money you've poured into the business, plus your college-loan debt. It's too much. We can help—"

"I'm going to be fine. You know I used some of the money Grandma left me in her trust to help fund the practice. It'll start making money right away."

"But it's going to take years to pay off your college loans. It's just you by yourself and it's a huge burden. Why do that alone when you don't have to?"

She took a deep breath, and let it out. "Because I have to do this myself. And you know why."

Her mother was quiet for a few seconds, which Emma knew was a rare thing.

"I understand. Of course, I do. But, Emma, we're here for you if you need us. No questions asked."

Tears filled her eyes and she blinked them back. She'd already cried enough tears for a lifetime. Never again. "I know, Mom. That's why I came home."

Chapter 3

LUKE DROVE DOWN the main highway. It was after rush hour, so the streets weren't full of cars like they'd been an hour ago.

There wasn't a lot of crime in Hope. It wasn't a large town. Big enough to have a city council and a police force and a mayor, which Luke was glad about. It had given him a job and a purpose and a chance to show off what he was worth, but sometimes it got downright boring.

He wrote a lot of traffic tickets, and because the state highway ran through town, there were a lot of fender benders. He worked those, sometimes side by side with the highway patrol, which meant he often got to hang out with his friend Will, who was a state highway patrol officer.

But major crime? Yeah, not so much. Meth labs were big in Oklahoma, and small towns bred them, so there was that. A few drug arrests, break-ins, drunk and disorderlies, and kids doing shit they shouldn't do, but the opportunities to use his gun were rare. Which was a good thing, although he did continue to hone his shooting skills at the firing range or out at the family ranch.

Someday he'd end up on a big-city police force. Tulsa didn't have openings, and with the current budget cuts he was damn glad to have the job he held, so he wasn't complaining. But he kept his eyes and ears open to the possibilities. Will often suggested he move over to HiPo, but he enjoyed being a city cop and it looked like that's where he was going to stay for the moment.

Which was fine. He liked being in this town. This was home, and protecting it meant something to him.

The past few days he'd made some drive-bys around Dr. Emma Burnett's place. Each time her parking lot was full of cars.

Good for her. He was glad to see she had customers.

"She seems to be doing fine so far, Boomer."

Boomer, asleep in the backseat of Luke's patrol car, had no comment. Likely because he was still pouting about not getting to run the past few days.

"You'll be back in action soon enough, Boom."

He should stop by the doc's office and have her take a look at Boomer's leg. Luke was due for his break anyway. Not that there was anything wrong with the leg, but it was almost closing time and she didn't seem to have any clients right now. No point in not being diligent about his dog.

Yeah, and you want to see the hot doctor again.

No, that wasn't it at all. Emma seemed like someone a guy dated more than once, which wasn't at all his type. He pulled in and turned off the engine. Boomer's ears perked up.

He called in to dispatch that he was taking a break, and he'd be temporarily unavailable.

"Come on, buddy," he said, grabbing Boomer's leash.

He remembered Rachel from the other day, when he'd stopped by to pay the bill he owed for Emma treating Boomer's injury. He hadn't seen Emma at all that day. She'd been in the back with patients.

"Hi, Officer Luke," Rachel said with a wide smile.

She was good at remembering names. "Howdy, Rachel."

She frowned and glanced down at the computer. "I don't have you on the books for an appointment. Did I miss one?"

"No. And I know you're about to close. I was just driving by and thought if Emma—if Dr. Burnett had a second, maybe she could do a recheck on Boomer's leg."

"Oh. Sure. Let me find out for you." She picked up the phone and hit a button. "Hey, Dr. Emma. Officer McCormack is here with Boomer. Do you have a second to take a look at Boomer's leg?"

She waited, smiling up at Luke the whole time. The girl was adorable, couldn't be more than twenty-one or so, with short dark hair and glasses that only added to her appeal. She probably had ten boyfriends.

As it should be at that age.

"Okay, thanks." She hung up the phone. "She's finishing something up in the back. She told me to take you into one of the exam rooms, and she'll be right there."

"Great. Thanks."

Rachel led him back to one of the rooms and he took a seat. Boomer, always happy to get out of the car, wagged his tail and paced around the exam room.

"You're just bucking for another treat, aren't you?"

Boomer showed his teeth in a wide smile and wiggled his butt.

"Yeah, some fierce police dog you are. Some burglar will wave a cookie at you, and you'll let him run right by."

Luke grinned. He knew better than that. On command and on duty, Boomer was as good a cop as any of them out there.

Emma opened the door and her dog Daisy came bounding in behind her, greeting Boomer with a fierce wag of her tail and a sniff. Boomer did the same.

Emma smiled at him, and he felt the gut punch. Not sure why someone in pink scrubs and tennis shoes with her hair messily piled up on top of her head could spark his libido, but there it was.

No. Not your type, remember? You're here for the dog.

"Hi, Luke," she said as she closed the door behind her. "Is something wrong with Boomer's leg?"

"Honestly? Not a thing. He seems to be healing up fine,

and I'm taking him on walks every day. But I had a free minute while I was on my shift tonight, and I saw you hadn't closed yet, so I thought I'd drop by and have you take a look."

"Oh, I'm glad you did. I've been thinking about . . . him."

He couldn't help but smile and wonder if it had really been Boomer she'd been thinking about, because there were those telltale spots on her cheeks again.

She was gorgeous when she blushed.

Okay, she was gorgeous without needing to blush.

She took Boomer with her and left the room, Daisy following behind them. He went, too, watching as she walked all around the clinic with Boomer, testing his leg strength. When they came back in, she moved Boomer's leg back and forth, pressing on various parts of it. He tensed, waiting for Boomer to show signs of pain.

She looked up at Luke, her easy smile relaxing him. "He's healing very well."

He breathed out a sigh of relief. "That's great news. He seemed to be doing okay, but I'm glad to hear it from you."

But then she frowned. "You said you were on duty?"

"Yeah."

"Why's he with you?"

"Oh. He goes everywhere with me. But he's not on duty. If I get a call, I keep him in the back of the cruiser. He's just riding along so he doesn't have to stay home."

She nodded. "I'm glad to hear that. He's doing great, Luke. His leg is steady. He's putting all his weight on it like it's not causing him any pain at all, so you're doing a fine job with his rehab. Give it another couple days of rest, then I think you can start running him again."

She bent and petted Boomer and Daisy simultaneously, not seeming to mind at all when they both licked her face.

You had to appreciate a woman who didn't object to a little dog spit. A lot of women didn't want to be mussed up. Obviously Emma had no problem with it.

"Thanks. I'm relieved to hear that, and I appreciate you

taking another look." He dragged his fingers through his hair. "I worry about him. It's stupid, I know."

She stood and laid her hand on his arm. "It's not stupid at all. I treat Daisy like she's my kid. Animals can't speak for themselves, so they rely on us to be both their caretakers and their playmates. I'm so happy you're doing such a good job of caring for Boomer."

He looked down where her hand lay on his arm. Just as quickly, she jerked it away, then reached into the jar on the counter and gave Boomer and Daisy a treat.

"Anyway, I'm glad he's rehabbing so well."

She walked him out front. "I'm sorry to say that everyone's left for the night again. Rachel had a date so I let her leave, and Leanne had already taken off."

"So . . . alone together again, huh? This is getting to be a habit."

She looked at a loss for words. She wrapped her arms around her chest, then shoved her hands in the pockets of her lab coat.

Huh. Interesting. "Emma. Do I make you uncomfortable?"

"Yes."

Well, at least she was honest. "I'll take off, then, and drop by tomorrow to settle up my bill with Rachel." He led Boomer to the door.

"No. Wait."

He paused and turned.

"It's not you, Luke. It's nothing about you."

"Okay."

She shook her head. "It's . . . nothing. It's me." She smiled. "Honestly. I'm just not comfortable around guys."

He popped up an eyebrow, then it hit him. "Oh. I get it. Sorry."

Her eyes widened. "No. You are not getting it at all. That's not it." She took a few seconds. "I'm not explaining myself well. Look. It's been a long time."

He cocked his head to the side. "Huh?"

"Um, you know."

"No. I don't."

She bit down on her lower lip, then said, "First, there was four years of vet school, and after that I had to dive in and work with several doctors at a practice. Getting my feet wet, you know? It was nonstop work. There was no time in my life for the whole dating thing."

Now he really did get it. He came toward her. "So, you're saying you're . . . rusty?"

This time, at least, she didn't back away like he had the plague.

"Yes. That's it exactly. I haven't dated anyone in years."

He found that hard to believe. "Years?"

She tilted her head back and looked up at him. "Yes. Years. It's a little embarrassing."

Up close, she was more than the pretty face he'd first thought. Her eyes were wide pools of whiskey brown, her lashes so long she'd never need makeup, and her lips—damn, she had a sexy mouth. "You need to get back in the game, Emma."

She sighed. "Tell me about it."

"With someone you can trust."

She looked toward the door. "Easier said than done."

"Let me take you out."

Her head jerked up and her gaze met his. "What?"

Yeah, what exactly. He couldn't believe he'd said that. But now that he had . . .

"You heard me. Let me take you out. We'll go out somewhere and eat. Use forks and knives. Have a nice conversation and a drink. Then I'll take you home, walk you to your front door, and call it a night."

She had this wary look on her face that would have made him laugh if he wasn't sure she was taking this so seriously.

"That's it?"

He grinned at her. "Well, that's not how I usually do it, but for you, sure. That's it."

She frowned. "How do you . . . usually do it?"

"Look, Emma. I'm not the dating type. But I like you.

And I can see you want to ease into this. I want to help. I want to be your friend."

Her gaze narrowed. "My friend."

"Yeah."

"But I'm not your type."

"I didn't say that."

"You implied I wasn't the type of woman you typically did . . . whatever it is you do with women, since you just said you're not the dating type."

He resisted rolling his eyes. This was why he didn't like having extended conversations with women. It usually led to him getting in trouble for something he said that he didn't really say, but the woman thought he meant what he didn't say in the first place.

Women drove him crazy.

"I didn't imply anything. I just asked you out on a date."

She crossed her arms, only this time it was in irritation, not defensiveness. "I don't need a pity date, Luke."

Shit. Foot-in-mouth struck again. "I don't pity you. I like you."

"You already said that. As a friend, of course."

He clenched his jaw. "Is there something wrong with that?"

"No. I love being your BFF. It's exactly how I want you thinking of me. Thanks for the offer, Luke, but I'll pass. If you have any more problems with Boomer, don't hesitate to call me."

She pushed him toward the door, opened it and herded him out, then locked it behind him.

With him on the outside and her inside, he could do nothing but stand there and stare at her, struck utterly dumb by whatever the hell had just happened.

She'd been pissed. Even now, she stared at him as she shuttered the blinds closed, and he could see the hurt in her eyes.

Women were one fucking mystery after another. His ex-wife had driven him batshit crazy, and he'd sworn he'd never get involved with another one.

He'd tried to be nice to Emma, tried to help her out. Hell, he'd even asked her out after hearing her story about not dating for years, figuring she'd be happy to have a night out. He found her hellaciously attractive, but he knew limits, and when a woman was skittish, he could stay hands-off. But instead of being grateful, she'd acted as if he'd insulted her.

He should have left Emma alone. He'd broken his own cardinal rule, and look where it had gotten him.

Tossed out on the sidewalk.

He looked down at Boomer, who stared up at him and wagged his tail, oblivious to what had just happened.

"Let's go, Boom. Time to get back to work."

A MERCY DATE. Mr. Hot and Sexy had asked her out on a mercy date.

The sparks between her and Luke had been out of this world. Twice she'd been alone with him, and she might have been a little wary, but she hadn't been afraid. He was nice. Luke had a good sense of humor, and he was oh-so-fine-looking. And he had a great dog that Daisy loved. If she was going to go out with someone—which she wasn't—he'd be the right guy.

But then he had to treat her like she was some poor, pitiful misfit who couldn't get a man to ask her out if she'd put a front-page ad in the hometown newspaper begging for one.

Take her on a date. As a friend. Just to help her out.

"What a colossal douchebag."

She wanted to throw something. Unfortunately, everything in the clinic cost too much to hurl across the room.

She stormed into her office to grab her bag, Daisy bumping into her leg to shove her head under Emma's hand.

There was the calm she needed. She absently petted Daisy, then sat in her chair and nuzzled Daisy's neck.

Was she really that pathetic?

She'd felt the chemistry between her and Luke, had been excited to have those feelings again. She'd thought that maybe . . . just maybe, at some point she could take a shot at having a normal life again after all the hell she'd been through. But she was obviously throwing off some kind of odd signals that screamed she was helpless and pathetic.

Ugh.

She was not helpless, and she didn't need a guy to rescue her from her self-imposed dating exile. Just because she didn't have a man in her life didn't mean she was miserable.

She was fine. Perfectly fine. She had her shiny new practice and her patients and her dog.

What more did she need to be happy, dammit?

She finished up at the clinic and took the dogs home, got them fed and settled, then wandered the kitchen, searching for something to eat.

Nothing sounded good. She felt unsettled, as if there was something she should be doing, but wasn't.

Her thoughts wandered back to Luke, which got her irritated all over again. Now she had a full steam of mad and nothing to do with all that pent-up emotion.

Since sex was out of the question, she needed an outlet. She'd already gone to the gym before work this morning, though nothing said she couldn't go again. Then again, that's not what she wanted.

Routine was her problem. She finally decided she needed to get out of the house. Too much sameness wasn't good for her, and she'd spent the past week doing the exact same thing every day—going to the clinic, coming home, and spending the night alone.

If she continued that, before long she'd have two dogs and a house full of cats, and she'd park her butt on the sofa watching one too many of those *Real Housewives* of some city or other.

She refused to let that happen, so she changed into jeans and a sweater, grabbed her keys, and drove to Bert's, the town's best diner. A bowl of chili for dinner sounded really good.

The good thing about showing up late was avoiding the normal four to six p.m. dinner crush. Bert's was a popular place, and Hope was a very small town. Tuesday was meatloaf night, and she'd had Bert's meat loaf before. It was awesome. So was his chili.

The place had pretty much emptied out, so she grabbed a table. Anita, one of the waitresses who'd been there "forever" according to her, hustled over.

"How ya doing, honey?" Anita asked, grabbing the pencil from her multicolored hair.

"Great, thank you."

"You're in late tonight. I hear the new clinic is keeping you busy."

The one thing about Hope—and Bert's diner—was that there were no secrets, and everyone knew your business. Which for Emma's business could be a very good thing. "It has been busy, which makes me very happy."

"And hungry, I hope. What can I get for you?"

"I'll have a diet soda and a bowl of chili. Can I get macaroni with that?"

"You bet. I'll bring your order right out."

She'd brought a book with her, determined to settle in and enjoy taking herself out to eat.

Who needed a guy? She didn't.

"Hey, Emma."

She looked up and smiled as Jane Kline and Chelsea Gardner appeared at her table. She'd gone to high school with both of them, and had recently renewed her acquaintance with Jane because they worked out together at the local gym.

"Hi. Are you two here to eat?"

"Yes," Jane said. "We had a very long school meeting."

"Which means we're starving," Chelsea added. "Are you eating alone?"

"Yes. Would you like to join me?"

"Love to." Chelsea pulled out a chair.

"Are you sure we're not intruding? Maybe you want to be alone," Jane said, looking unsure.

Emma laughed. "I spend plenty of my nights alone. I'd love some company."

Jane took a seat, too, and Anita came over.

"A late rush tonight, I see."

"Meetings," Chelsea said. "Ugh."

"Oh. No wonder you two look so miserable. Do they like to torture you poor teachers by making you spend all day long with those kids, then all night with a bunch of bureaucrats?"

"Yes," Chelsea said while perusing the menu. "All just perks of the job, you know."

Jane nodded. "But it's over now and we can finally eat. What are you having, Emma?"

"Chili."

"Oh, that sounds good. I'll have that, too."

Chelsea ordered the soup of the day, and Anita brought their food over within a few minutes. They all dug in.

"It's a good thing Will took an extra shift today," Jane said. "At least he's not fending for himself, alone with the kids."

"Oh, for God's sake," Chelsea said. "The guy can open a can of SpaghettiOs or make a grilled cheese sandwich, Jane. He doesn't need you to be there to cook dinner for him."

"Oh, I know. I just like to cook. I always cooked for the kids and me before Will came along, you know. It's just nice to have a man in the house again."

"Women in love. Spare me," Chelsea said to Emma with a roll of her eyes.

Emma laughed. "Will is rather spectacular-looking. It's a wonder you don't have him locked in a closet somewhere, Jane."

Jane grinned. "He is a hottie, isn't he? I don't know what he's doing with me."

"Uh, because you're a rockin' sexpot?" Chelsea said.

"Oh, sure. A rockin' sexpot with two kids."

"That just meant you know what you're doing. And who says women with children can't be sexy?" Emma said. "Look at you, Jane. I sometimes can't believe you've had two children. You have an amazing body, you're a wonderful teacher, and those blue eyes of yours are knockouts.

You're smart and gorgeous. Maybe Will should be the one locking you up in a closet so no other guy gets within five feet of you."

"Hell, yeah," Chelsea said, toasting that comment by raising her glass of iced tea.

Jane's cheeks pinkened. "If I'd known it was going to be Build Jane's Ego Up Night, I'd have dressed better. Thank you, ladies."

"Just stating the truth."

"Will tells me you treated Luke McCormack's dog, Boomer."

Emma's spoon stilled on its way to her mouth. She looked up at Jane. "Will knows Luke?"

Jane smiled innocently at her. "They're best friends. Is Boomer all right?"

Okay, dog talk she could handle. "He's doing fine. Luke brought him in for a follow-up tonight, as a matter of fact. He's healing up nicely and should be able to return to active canine duty within a few days."

"That's great news. The kids love Boomer. And I'm weakening in the get-a-dog department. Ryan and Tabby are really giving me the full-court press about one. And Will says he thinks it would teach the kids responsibility. Secretly, I think it's Will who really wants the dog."

"Dogs are great companions for kids, providing you get the right breed, one that's good with children."

"Maybe you could come over and talk to all of us about that. I don't want to make the wrong decision."

She nodded. "I'd love to."

"I'll cook for you, too," Jane said with a wink.

"Sold."

"See, I have nothing to offer. No dog advice, nothing. No wonder I don't get invited over for a home-cooked meal," Chelsea said.

Jane nudged her. "You have an open invitation to come over anytime and you know it, so quit with the false complaints."

"Fine. I'm coming over when Emma does. Maybe she can talk me into a dog, too."

"You?" Jane asked. "As fussy and as much of a perfectionist as you are? I can't see you as a pet owner."

Chelsea lifted her chin, her hair flawless and still perfect, despite the horrible lighting in the diner and after a long day at work. It was difficult for Emma to be around Chelsea because she was gorgeous, with her red hair and stunning blue-green eyes, and she was built like a centerfold. And to top it off, she had a funny, dry wit and an easygoing personality. She was quite possibly perfect. Emma had loved her from the moment Jane introduced them.

Someone like Chelsea probably went on a lot of dates. Maybe she would be the person to ask for advice about how to handle reintroducing herself back into the world of men. Not that she was looking to do that or anything, but eventually her self-imposed exile would have to end, and she hadn't exactly dealt with Luke's invitation all that well.

Then again, she wasn't sure if that was her fault or his.

"So, I sort of got asked on a date tonight. I think, though I'm not really sure."

"Really? That's exciting," Jane said, grinning. "Who's the guy?"

"Uh . . . Luke McCormack."

"Real-l-l-ly," Chelsea said. "Luke asked you out? That's so interesting."

"Well, he didn't ask me out on a date. More as a friend?"

Chelsea frowned. "What do you mean?"

She told them about her exchange with Luke at the vet clinic.

Jane rolled her eyes. "Men can be so dumb sometimes. He thought he was doing you a favor by asking you out? What an idiot."

"I'm with Jane. He's an imbecile. I'd like to kick him in the nuts."

Emma laughed. "Thank you. I thought I was being overly sensitive, or maybe I read the situation wrong."

"No, you definitely didn't read it wrong," Chelsea said. "As if you need a mercy date. You're hot, Emma. You could walk out this door, and ten guys would fight each other for a chance to go out with you. Luke's a moron, and you should tell him to shove it. Never mind, I'll tell him to shove it."

She laid her hand on Chelsea's arm. "Oh, please don't say anything to him about this. You, either, Jane. I just wanted some advice, but I'd like this to stay among the three of us."

"You're no fun," Chelsea said. "I love reading the riot act to Luke. We've been sparring for years now. I'm an only child, so I never had brothers and sisters to fight with. He's like the brother I never had."

Emma laughed. "Well, no fighting with Luke on my account, though I appreciate it. I think I made my thoughts on the matter clear enough."

"Okay. Still, I think he's a dipshit."

"Me, too," Jane said. "Why are men so obtuse when it comes to women?"

Emma wished she knew. If she'd understood what made men tick, she likely could have avoided a lot of heartbreak years ago.

But as it was, she had no more understanding about the male mind now than she had then.

Men were just a mystery to her.

Chapter 4

"I DO NOT understand women."

Luke sat on the front porch of the family ranch house sharing a beer with his older brother, Logan.

Logan tipped up the brim of his cowboy hat and stared at him. "And you're coming to me of all people with that statement? You know I don't know shit about women. That's why I live out here in the middle of bumfuck nowhere. All alone. Just the way I like it."

"Yeah, yeah. I know. You're the king of solitude. You're way better at this than I could have ever been."

"You're still part owner of the ranch."

"I told you I'd sell you my portion anytime you wanted it."

Logan looked out over the land. "It belongs to the family, and all that's left of our 'family' is you, me, and Reid since Mom up and left."

Logan always said that part about their mother so matter-of-factly, as if her remarrying less than a year after Dad died and leaving town—leaving them—was no big deal. It was as if he'd easily wiped her existence out of his life. Luke hadn't been able to do that so effortlessly.

"You ever think about her?"

Logan frowned and looked at him. "Who?"

"Mom."

"Nope. And I'm fine with you keeping your ownership of the ranch. Maybe someday one of your kids will want their share."

Luke snorted. "I'm never getting married again."

Logan looked over at him. "Is this about Becca? What's she done now?"

"No, it's not about Becca. Last I heard she was living in New York. Or maybe it was Miami. Hell if I can keep track. Some big city back east that's bound to make her happier than life with me ever could."

Logan tipped the bottle of beer to his lips and took a long swallow. "Wallowing in self-pity again, little brother?"

"Fuck you."

Logan laughed, dragged his boots off the porch railing, and stood. "You need another beer."

Logan went inside and Luke propped his feet up on the railing, looking out over the property. Boomer was lying under the shade of a giant blackjack oak, taking a nap next to Whip, one of Logan's dogs. He spanned his gaze out over the land. They owned as far as he could see. Acre upon acre of grass, trees, and green hills where cattle grazed and wild horses ran free.

Though he couldn't fathom spending the rest of his life working the ranch, he loved coming here. It gave him a sense of peace and perspective he couldn't get in town. It was quiet, the only sounds the howling wind and the occasional wails from the cattle out in the pasture. This was home to him, where he'd been raised, where he used to fight with his brothers out in the dirt, where he learned to ride a horse, rope a steer, and shoot a gun.

This was the place he'd learned all about being a man—from his father.

Being out here made him miss his dad. He couldn't stay after his father died, after his mother had decided she'd had enough of living on a ranch.

Just like Becca, his mother had been raised a city girl, and once his mom had gotten remarried to Clyde, that had been it for her. She'd been outta there faster than a sudden twister moving through.

Though had he been any better? Luke couldn't take over the legacy of being a rancher. Their youngest brother, Reid, had gone off to college back east and had stayed there, had settled and started his career. And while Luke loved the L& M Ranch, running it, living it, wasn't in his blood like it was in Logan's.

Fortunately, Logan loved the ranch, loved the cattle business, and couldn't dream of doing anything else with his life. Luke had wanted something different, and Logan had encouraged him to get out and live the life he'd dreamed of.

Logan pushed open the screen door, two bottles of beer in hand. He took a seat on one of the old wood chairs, propped his dusty booted feet up on the railing, and handed Luke a beer.

"Have you heard from Reid lately?" Logan asked.

Luke cracked a smile, thinking about their youngest brother. "Yeah. He called the other day while he was hopping a flight from Boston to New York. Said he was too busy to even get laid lately, and that he planned to call you later in the week to catch up when he got back to Boston."

Logan screwed open the top of his beer and took a long pull. "Who knew being an architect would keep the kid running so much?"

"He's excellent at what he does. Apparently his work is in demand."

"Well, good for him."

"You miss him?"

Logan let out a snort. "Hell, no. He's a pain in the ass."

"Yeah, I miss him, too."

Logan cracked a rare smile and didn't say a word.

Luke took a sip of beer, scanning the land. "How's business?"

"We're doing okay."

That was always Logan's standard answer. As part owner,

Luke had the right to look over the books and question the operation of the ranch, but hell, he trusted his brother to know what he was doing in managing the place. And if they were in trouble, Logan would tell him.

"So what woman has you by the balls?"

Luke laughed. "No woman will ever have me by the balls again. I might have been a dumb sonofabitch once, but at least I learn from my mistakes."

"Apparently not. Who is she?"

Luke grimaced and took a sip of beer. "New vet in town."

"Emma Burnett."

Luke turned to him. "How do you know about her?"

"Hey, we're not exactly cut off from the world out here. I do get into town. And the hands do, too. Heard she bought out Bruce Weston's practice. So, you dating this woman?"

"I don't date any woman. Not anymore."

"I've heard you're man-whoring your way through the single female population of Hope."

He glared at Logan. "You hear a lot."

Logan shrugged. "Yeah, I do."

"The women aren't complaining. I'm keeping them happy."

"And you're so modest, too." Logan tipped the beer to his lips and took another swallow. "So what is it about the doc that's got your balls pulled up so tight?"

He glanced over at Boomer, still asleep.

"I had Boomer in there a few days ago. He'd hurt his leg during a pursuit, so I brought him in for her to recheck him. We started talking, and she mentioned she hadn't been out with anyone in a few years. So I asked her out, told her it would be just a friends date."

Logan snorted.

"What?"

"You don't ask a woman out and say up front that you just want to be her friend. What kind of a moron are you?"

"Hey. She seemed skittish. I didn't want to scare her off."

"But you don't date women. You screw their brains out

and leave them the next day with a satisfied smile on their faces, right?"

"It's not like that. And that's not what Emma wants. I just figured she needed to get her feet wet again, so I was trying to help her out."

"I take it she didn't say yes."

He picked at the label on the beer bottle. "She practically threw me out of the clinic."

"Imagine that."

Luke pushed off the railing and stood. "I was trying to do a good deed."

"Is she ugly?"

He turned to face Logan. "Hell, no. She's gorgeous. And sexy."

Logan shook his head. "And you only want to be her friend? I worry about you, Luke. Becca messed you up bad."

"This has nothing to do with Becca. Emma's a nice woman. I don't want to start something with her, so I thought I'd just be friends with her."

"But what you really want is to get in her pants."

"No, I don't."

Logan's lips curved. He picked up his beer. "Liar. I think you need to start over with the pretty doctor, first with an apology for acting like a dumbass. Then maybe it's time you figure out what the hell you want from women."

"I know what I want from the women I see. And so do they."

"Yeah, well, eventually you're going to run out of women to have meaningless sex with. Hope isn't that big a town. Then what are you going to do?"

"What do you do? You live out here like a goddamned monk."

Logan laughed. "I do just fine. And we aren't talking about me today, little brother. This is your dog-and-pony show."

This was not helping him at all. He'd come to Logan for some clarity, and now he was more confused than ever.

But Logan was right about one thing. He'd screwed things up with Emma, and he needed to figure out how to make it right.

Maybe he wasn't in the market for a happily-ever-after, but he wasn't an asshole, either. He needed to fix things.

"I KNOW I'VE been out of touch, Em, and I'm so sorry. I've been really busy. I moved again."

Emma rolled her eyes as she cradled the phone between her ear and shoulder and listened to her sister, Molly, recount her latest adventure. "Didn't you move three months ago?"

"Yes. But that didn't work out. It turns out Memphis wasn't really where I wanted to be."

So not surprising. "Where are you now, Molly?"

"Little Rock. It's so charming here. I really like it. This could end up being the place I call home. I already have a job. It's kismet."

Emma had heard this same song and dance from her sister several times a year. There was no "home" for Molly, because Molly was a runner. She always had been and always would be. Her sister couldn't settle on one city, on one job, for longer than a few months before she'd get restless and take off again. She'd long ago stopped trying to figure out why.

"I hope it works out for you this time, Mol."

"Me, too. I really love the little apartment I got. It's so cute. I'll text you pictures as soon as I get everything in place."

"You do that." Emma sighed and put her feet up on her open file drawer, taking a breather. It was Saturday night, the office was closed, and she was catching up on paperwork, enjoying the quiet atmosphere. Daisy was running around the clinic chasing after Annie.

"Tell me about the clinic, Em. How's it going?"

Emma smiled. "It's amazing. I love it so much. Many of Dr. Weston's old clients are returning."

"So business is good?"

"So far. I'd like to get more clients in. Mom wants me to do some advertising."

"It's not a bad idea. More business is a good thing."

"That's true, but you know how she gets."

"Do I ever. But she does have really good ideas. You might want to at least hear her out."

"Easy for you to say. You're not the one who has to put up with her."

Molly laughed. "So true. Maybe you could hire a marketing genius."

"No can do. My budget is stretched tight as it is. I can't hire anyone right now. Unless you want to come home and be my marketing genius."

Molly laughed. "Yeah, sorry, sis. I love you, but there's no coming home for me. You know how it is. Home gives me hives."

"I had to try."

"You always do."

Emma heard a crash, then several loud barks.

She rolled her eyes. "Uh, oh, Mol. Sounds like the dogs have gotten into something they shouldn't have. Gotta run."

"Okay. I'll call you in a few days. Love you."

"Love you, too. Bye."

She clicked off the phone and slid it into her pocket, then opened the door to her office. "Okay, what are you guys into?"

She froze at the sound of breaking glass. More barking, then Daisy came running toward her.

Heat and panic filled her. Daisy barked frantically. Something was wrong.

"Shh." She grabbed Daisy by the collar, but she had no idea where the pup was. Then she heard sounds coming from one of the back rooms.

She listened carefully at the door, trying to pinpoint the location of the sound. It was quiet for a few seconds, then she heard the crunch of glass.

The pharmacy room.

Oh, God. Someone had broken in. She lifted her phone

from her pocket and dialed the local police, putting the phone to her ear as she backed into her office, Daisy in tow. She quietly shut the door behind her.

"Someone's breaking into my office," she whispered, giving the dispatcher her name and address.

"Are they still there?"

"As far as I know, yes."

"Stay on the line with me, ma'am. We'll have someone on the scene shortly."

Her hands were shaking as she took a seat, hoping Annie was okay out there with whoever was in her clinic. The pup was still so small, so sweet and innocent.

Please don't hurt her.

Sweat ran down her back as she opened her desk drawers, wincing at the slightest sound the left drawer made. Nothing but paper clips and a stapler, hardly a handy weapon unless she threw it at someone.

The right drawer had a pair of scissors. She grabbed them and stuck them in her pocket. She was not going to be helpless.

Never again.

She walked to the door and stood at the other side. If someone opened it, she could at least surprise them instead of sitting at her desk waiting for them to rush in and attack her.

"Still there, ma'am?"

"Yes," she whispered, her voice quavering.

"Our car will be there in thirty seconds."

She hoped she'd still be standing there in thirty seconds. Her heart pounded and her throat had gone sand dry. She couldn't muster up enough saliva to swallow, and she felt the sudden need to cough. Daisy kept growling, and she had to keep a tight hold on her to keep her from barking.

Emma shook violently, and it was all she could do to stand upright against the wall.

It had been much longer than thirty seconds. But how much longer? She was so hot.

She wanted to go find Annie. Poor Annie. She was tiny

and playful, not at all a threat. Whoever was in there wouldn't hurt a puppy, would they?

She heard footsteps, then a loud bark.

"Emma? Emma are you in here?"

Luke.

"Is the officer there now, ma'am?"

"Yes. I'm hanging up now." She clicked off the phone and opened the door.

"I'm here."

Daisy took off like her tail was on fire. So did Emma, flying through the door. Luke was there, his gun in hand, looking fierce and alert, and oh, God, she'd never been happier to see anyone in her life. Boomer was circling the room, tail up, his neck fur standing on end. She threw herself against Luke, and when he wrapped his arm around her and tugged her close, she felt safe.

"It's okay, Emma. Whoever was in here is gone now."

Even better, he didn't let go. She was still shaking. He holstered his weapon and put both arms around her, sliding his hands over her hair and her back. "It's all right. He's gone."

"Someone was in here," she said against his neck.

"I know. Your drug cabinet was broken into."

She finally pulled back, though every part of her was still shaking. "What?"

"Boomer and I did a search of the whole place before I came to find you. Looks like they were after drugs."

Her fear was quickly replaced by shock. "Seriously?"

"Yeah. Come on, I'll show you, but be careful not to touch anything. Crime scene unit will want to dust for prints."

"Okay."

Just then Annie raced toward her. Tears pricked her eyes. She picked up the puppy. "Oh, Annie, I'm so glad you're okay." She inspected the puppy for any signs of injury, found none, and snuggled her close to her chest.

As they walked through the clinic, Emma put both Annie and Daisy in one of the nearby kennels so neither of them would cut their paws on the glass, or mess up the crime scene.

She heard sirens outside but ignored them, sticking close to Luke as he led her to the room where they kept all the pharmaceuticals. Boomer followed.

The room was a train wreck. One of the cabinets had been busted open, some of the drugs were clearly missing. Everything was out of order. They'd have to do a full inventory.

"Damn."

"It was a dash-and-run, obviously," Luke said. "I don't know what kind of drugs you keep on hand, but they didn't take everything."

"I was on the phone with my sister when I heard the crash and barking. I thought Daisy and Annie had been playing rough and had toppled something over."

"Whoever broke in likely didn't expect to find a dog in here. They made a grab for whatever they could and ran out. Otherwise they'd have cleaned you out."

Two more officers came in. Luke nodded and introduced them to her. She gave them her best effort at a smile, while Luke filled them in on what happened and told them they'd need to sweep for fingerprints and other evidence. They left the room, and so did Luke and Emma.

"Come on. You look like you need to sit down."

"I have to clean this up. And replace the door and the lock. And call my insurance company." She looked up at Luke. "How did he get in?"

"Picked the lock on the back door. The crash you heard was after he smashed through the locked door on the drug cabinet."

She inhaled and let out a shaky sigh.

"Do you have an alarm?"

"Yes. I deactivated it when I came in to work tonight."

"I'm surprised they broke in, knowing someone was here. Normally they wouldn't hit a business if someone was inside."

"I parked across the street because of the road-repaving

project they're doing this weekend. The parking lot is blocked."

"That's right. I didn't even notice your car wasn't out front. So he wouldn't have known someone was in here."

Now that the adrenaline rush was over, her head had started to pound.

"You want something to drink?"

She nodded. "Water. My throat is dry." She looked in her small refrigerator in her office, but it was empty. She made a mental note to restock it, if she could even remember. Her thoughts were scattered.

"I'll go get you something. Boomer, stay."

Boomer sat with her. She took a minute to call her insurance company to report the break-in. She told them the police were there right now. They said they'd send someone out in the morning to look things over and file a report.

Luke came back a few minutes later with a bottle of water. He unscrewed the cap and handed it to her. "Raided your main fridge."

"Thanks." She grabbed a couple of acetaminophens from the drawer in her desk and popped those with the water.

"I've got the guys taking photos, and the crime-scene van just arrived to dust for prints. Chances are it was someone looking for a quick drug score."

"We keep painkillers here and anesthesia drugs."

He nodded. "I know. We see that a lot. Some of the medical and dental clinics have reported break-ins over the past couple of months."

"Great. Just great."

He took a notepad and pen out of his pocket. "You want to tell me everything that happened again? Anything you saw or heard."

Emma dragged her fingers through her hair and recounted everything that had happened from the time she came to work to the time she saw Luke.

"Thanks, Emma. That's helpful."

"I don't see how anything I just told you could help. I didn't see him. I could have gone out there when I heard the crash. Maybe I would have seen him and could have given you a description."

He frowned. "That would have been stupid. What would you have done? Yelled at him? You don't know what kind of person that was. High or desperate, and he could have had a weapon. Criminals are unpredictable. You did the right thing staying in here and calling it in. Now we'll do our job and try to catch him."

"I just hate being a victim." Again.

"You're not a victim. You did everything right." He came over and crouched down in front of her, his warm eyes sincere. "You took care of your own life. Some people are stupid. You aren't. You were very brave tonight."

He was trying to make her feel better. And he was taking care of her. In her past, someone *would* have called her stupid, would have blamed her for the break-in and the loss of inventory. Illogical, but that's the way it would have been. Luke didn't think she was stupid.

"Thank you."

"Let me go check on the crew, see how things are going."

"Okay."

She should call her parents. And Rachel and Leanne.

Not right now. She'd do that tomorrow, after she passed out and slept off this nightmare. If she called her mother right now, she'd rush right over and want to baby or pamper her, and she wouldn't be able to handle that smothering kind of love. She felt inept enough as it was.

"We're clear here. And I fixed your back door," Luke said when he came back into her office.

Her brows lifted. "You did?"

"Yeah. One of the guys ran to the all-night hardware store and bought a replacement lock." He handed her the keys. "Here are your keys."

"Thank you for doing that. I need to clean up in here."

He swept his thumb over her cheekbone. "You look about ready to fall on your face."

"Okay, you're right about that."

"Besides, your insurance company will want to come in and assess the damage before you clean up."

"You're right about that, too. I called them and they're coming out in the morning."

"Then you can clean up after they finish taking photos. Right now you need to go home and get some sleep."

She squinted at him. "Did my mother call you?"

He laughed. "Definitely not. Come on, I'll walk you out."

Everyone had cleared out, so it was just her and Luke. She grabbed her dogs, set the alarm, herded Daisy out the door, and grabbed Annie's carrier, making sure the door was set to lock when she closed it. Part of her wanted to stay there all night and guard her dream.

"It's going to be all right, Emma. He won't be back."

"The logical part of me knows this. But everything I have is tied up in this business."

"We'll make sure to drive by several times tonight."

She turned to him. "I'd appreciate that a lot. Thank you."

"Put your menagerie in the backseat of the cruiser and I'll drive you across the street to your car."

"Okay."

She climbed in the front. "I've never been in a police car before."

"Good to know," he said with a wry grin.

She laughed, and it felt good to let out a little of the tension she'd held inside. He pulled across the street, bypassing the cones that had been set there by the road crews. When he stopped next to her car, she turned to him.

"Thank you, Luke. I feel like I've said it a hundred times already tonight. But thank you for getting here so fast."

He smiled at her, that quirky, off-kilter grin that made her stomach do flip-flops. "It's my job."

"You're very good at it."

"I'll follow you home."

"Oh, no, don't do that. I'm fine, really."

"When I got to the clinic, you were terrified. So don't tell me you're fine."

"I might have been a little freaked out to think someone had broken in. But I'm better now."

"Okay. Have a good rest of the night, Emma."

She got out and transferred the dogs to her car, started toward the driver's door, then realized Luke was still there. She walked over to the police car. He rolled down the window and she leaned over.

"You're following me home anyway, aren't you?"

"Yup."

She smiled and pushed off his car. For some reason, she didn't mind that as much as she thought she would.

Chapter 5

———————

JUST AS EMMA suspected, the topic of the break-in was a popular subject at Sunday dinner.

Her mother had been frantic when Emma had called her and told her about it, even though Emma had assured her it had been a random break-in, and the guy had likely been looking for a quick drug score. But her mother worried. A lot.

Understandable, given what Emma had been through in the past and how powerless her parents had felt.

"Emma, are you sure this isn't related to . . . you know?" her mother asked as they sat at the dinner table.

"Georgia," her father admonished. "How about we not talk about the past? I'm sure that's not something Em wants to revisit."

"Thanks, Dad. And no, Mom. It's not related."

"I worry, that's all. I don't want anything bad to happen to you. Again."

The last word, spoken as a whisper, made Emma's heart clench. She reached over and squeezed her mother's hand.

"It won't. I won't let it. I wasn't smart before. I'm a lot smarter now."

"You were always smart," her dad said. "It's just . . ." He trailed off. "Well, no sense rehashing the past when I said we wouldn't."

"Good," Emma said, happy to never go down that road again. Instead, she turned to her mother and smiled. "The lasagna is awesome, as usual."

Her mother turned off her worry face and offered a bright smile. "Thank you. I know it's one of your favorites. I made extra so you can take some home and freeze it. I know you don't have a lot of time to cook."

Emma laughed. "How about no time to cook?"

"Work's going well, then?" her dad asked.

"It's going better than I expected. We've been busy every day."

"I figured you would be. I'm not all that fond of the doctors who run the Barkley clinic. No bedside manner. They're too brusque and businesslike. I think you'll bring a warmth and love of animals that's been lacking in this town since Bruce gave up his practice."

She offered up a wide grin to her father. "Thanks, Dad. I hope so. And speaking of animals, Pokey's getting fat."

"He is not," her mother said.

"He is, too. You need to bring him in and let me look at him. He's due for his annual exam and shots anyway."

As her father slipped the long-haired dachshund a piece of his bread, she rolled her eyes. "And that's why he's getting so fat, Dad. You know better."

Her father shrugged. "He doesn't feel like a part of the family if he doesn't get to eat when we eat."

"Then bring his food bowl in here and give him dog food. How many times do I have to lecture you about how damaging it is to give human food to dogs? And how bad will it be for my reputation when my parents parade their overweight dachshund through town?" She wiped her lips on the napkin and pushed her chair back, then picked up Pokey.

"Ugh. He needs a restricted diet and a lot more exercise." She turned to her mother. "Bring him in next week?"

"Yes, Doctor," her mother said with a smile.

"And you," Emma said to her dad. "Stop feeding him food scraps immediately."

"She's mean," her dad said to her mother.

"She's right and you know it."

After dinner she found Pokey's harness and they all went for a walk. The night was crisp and cool, so she grabbed a sweater from her truck.

Her father had put on a little weight as well, so it wouldn't hurt him to take Pokey on a walk a couple times a day, though she told him it was for Pokey's benefit only.

"How's work?" she asked her mom as they walked behind her dad and Pokey.

"Busy. We have a couple of new clients and some great marketing campaigns coming up, so it's pretty exciting stuff. But, you know, I'm never too busy that I can't take you on as a client."

"Thanks, Mom, but I think I'm okay for now."

"All right. But if you change your mind, you let me know. I already have several ideas that I think would boost your clientele. What if you did an adoption day at the clinic, in conjunction with the local shelter? They could bring their animals over, and you could provide reduced-fee services for like six months or a year for every animal someone adopts? That way animals get adopted, and you pick up new clients."

Emma was about to open her mouth to object, but then thought about it for a second. "You know what? That's a really good idea."

Her mother shot her a knowing smile. "Of course it is. I'm brilliant that way."

There was no doubt her mom was a genius with marketing and promotion, but Emma just couldn't afford it right now. And the last thing she wanted was her mom's fingers in her business. But that idea was a good one.

"I'll consider it and get in touch with the local shelter. Thanks, Mom."

"I can help you with the advertising. I already have some things in mind."

She laughed and looped her arm through her mother's. "I said I'd think about it. Don't go hog wild with a marketing plan just yet."

She loved her mother, but if she did go forward with this plan, she'd have to put a leash on her mom's marketing genius. The whole idea of going into business for herself was just that—to do it herself. Independence was key.

So far she was doing all right on her own, minus that night of the break-in when she'd needed Luke's help.

She'd been grateful for that, and despite being irritated with him for offering to take her out on a mercy date, she'd never been happier to see him than when he'd shown up at her clinic that night.

He'd been so sweet to follow her home, too, which she knew wasn't at all a requirement of his job. It had been him being nice to her.

And she'd been a giant bitch after he'd offered to take her out.

Maybe she should do something about that. She just didn't know how she would go about it. That, too, was going to require some thought.

After dinner, she went home and loaded Daisy and Annie into her truck, then drove to the park. Daisy would stay right next to her, but she'd been working on leash-training Annie, somewhat unsuccessfully. The pup parked her butt on the trail and refused to move.

"Come on, Annie. You'll enjoy the walk. It's nice outside."

Annie looked up at her, offended by the leash and none too happy about the collar, either. But Emma was determined, and she'd leash-trained plenty of dogs. She gave the leash some lax, and walked a few feet away. Annie followed, and Emma continued to move at a snail's pace, much to Daisy's chagrin, who was used to the two of them taking the trails at a run.

Daisy whimpered.

"I know, sweetie," Emma murmured. "But we have to do this for Annie."

Annie, who no one had claimed yet or shown interest in adopting.

Emma sighed and patiently worked with Annie for a good half hour, until the pup realized it wasn't going to win this battle. Annie finally started walking alongside Emma, who gave the pup tons of praise as she clumsily lumbered next to her.

It wasn't the run Daisy wanted, but next time she'd leave Annie at home and they could jog.

When the sun disappeared behind the houses on the other side of the lake, the temperature dropped. Emma zipped up her jacket, not wanting to head back to her car just yet, even though the trails were mostly deserted.

A few years ago, she wouldn't have allowed herself to be alone like this.

But this was the new Emma. The Emma who refused to let fear rule her life.

When she heard a car pull up slowly behind her, though, she whipped around, ready to grab Annie and make a mad dash back to her truck.

It was a police car. She leaned forward to see Luke behind the wheel. He stopped and got out, looking sexy in his uniform.

She gave up trying to be immune to the sexy. The man was hot.

"Oh. Hi, Luke," she said, trying to relax her frantically beating heart.

"Hi yourself. You do know the park closes at eight, right?"

She grabbed her phone out of her pocket to check the time. It was eight thirty. "I'm sorry. I've been leash-training Annie and just lost track of time."

She started back to her truck.

"Hang on," he said.

He let Boomer out of his car. The three dogs smelled and greeted each other with a wild wag of tails.

He started walking with her.

"You do realize your car is up there," she said after about five minutes.

He gave her a smile. "Just doing my official duty and making sure you hooligans leave the park."

She couldn't help the smirk. "Oh, now we're hooligans?"

"Well, you look suspect. Never know what kind of nefarious activities you and your cohorts could get up to without me keeping an eye on you."

"I see. Well, guys," she said to the dogs, "looks like we've been thwarted."

Annie fell off the curb, shook her head, and climbed back up. Daisy was too busy running circles around Boomer to pay much attention to anything Emma said.

"Huh. Some sidekicks you two are."

"I think you need better partners-in-crime," Luke said as they arrived at her truck.

Emma scooped Annie up and deposited her in her carrier. "Apparently."

She called for Daisy, who hopped into the front seat of the truck. She closed the door and turned to Luke. "Thanks for the escort. And for not throwing me in jail."

"I wouldn't have thrown me in jail, you know."

He quirked a smile at her that made her belly tumble. She wished he didn't have that kind of effect on her. It would be a lot easier if he were just some random guy she could be friendly with. But she remembered that she owed him, that he'd been so nice to her.

"So, about the other night?"

He frowned. "The break-in? Is everything all right? I hadn't heard of any recurrences."

"No. Not that. The other night before that night. When you were so nice and offered to take me out. My reception to that was a little . . . unfriendly."

"Oh. That." His lips quirked. "Don't worry about it. It's forgotten."

"I haven't forgotten, though. And I was rude. I'm sorry.

I told you I was rusty in the dating department. Apparently that includes my social skills. Please accept my apology."

"Not necessary. I don't think my offer was worded in the right way, either. I didn't mean you couldn't get a date on your own. Obviously, you're a beautiful woman, and you sure as hell don't need me to take you out on a date."

He gave her the once-over, the way a man looks at a woman that isn't at all insulting, just . . . intriguing. Her body fused with heat.

"Uh, well, wow. Thank you for that."

He offered up a smile. "I'll let you head home, Emma."

He was about to leave. She could have left it at that, and she'd be off the hook. But something about the way he looked at her, the fact that he'd walked her all the way down the hill instead of just telling her to hightail it out of the park—

So she let instinct take over, and she grabbed his arm.

"Luke . . . wait."

He stilled. "What is it?"

She should have let go of him, but his body felt warm. Solid. And he didn't seem to mind that she was touching him. In fact, he leaned a little closer.

Which she didn't mind at all, either.

"I'd still like to go out with you, if the offer's open."

"You would, huh?"

"Yes."

He cocked his head to the side and gave her the kind of half-smile that made her belly clench and all the female parts of her squeal with joy.

He reached out and tucked an errant strand of hair behind her ear. "Are you sure, Emma?"

Her wary mind said no. Her libido screamed *Oh. Hell. Yes.* "Absolutely."

"Okay. How about Saturday?"

"Saturday sounds great." She wasn't sure about anything, especially where men were concerned. But she'd consider this part of her reintroduction to the opposite sex. "But just as friends, right?"

"Whatever you want, Emma. The Double-A baseball team has an in-town game. Do you like baseball?"

"I love baseball."

"Great." He pulled out his phone. "If you want to give me your number, I'll call you after I figure out game time."

She gave him her phone number and put his number in her cell.

"I'll see you on Saturday, then."

"Bye, Luke."

She started to turn away, but this time Luke grasped her arm.

"Hey, Emma?"

"Yes?"

He tipped her chin and brushed his lips against hers. Her breath held and she felt that brush of a kiss all the way to her toes, and every delicious part of her in between.

He stepped away. "Just a friendly kiss. Nothing more."

He smiled at her and walked away.

She hung outside the door to her truck and watched him and Boomer make the trek up the hill, the muscles of his legs working easily as he climbed the steep incline.

He also had a great butt. Not that she noticed or anything, because she was only interested in him as a friend. Not in his mighty fine ass. Or the way he had just totally and completely rocked her world with a two-second kiss.

She grabbed her keys and realized her hands were shaking.

If he could incite that type of response with a short kiss, Emma wondered if she could survive a longer one.

She climbed in the truck and started it, then looked over at Daisy, who cocked her head to the side.

She scrubbed her fingers through Daisy's fur.

"I know, Dase," she said. "I have no idea what I'm doing."

Chapter 6

LUKE FIGURED A baseball game was as safe and unromantic a date as he could plan. Tons of people, beer and a hot dog, and lots of screaming kids.

Plus, it was Take Your Dog to the Ballpark Day. You had to love Double-A ball. Though Luke would much prefer to have a major league baseball team in Hope, there were certain advantages to having a minor league team in the city. The promotions were one of those advantages.

The game started at three, and Emma worked at the clinic until noon, so he came to pick her and Daisy up at two. He brought his truck and swung by her condo, taking Boomer with him to her front door.

She opened the door, and damn if he hadn't expected her to be low-key and kind of unattractive. After all—baseball game, right?

Yeah. She had on tight jeans and tennis shoes, along with a white T-shirt. How hot could that be?

Pretty damn hot, apparently. She'd scooped her hair up in a ponytail, and she looked freshly showered, smelled like strawberries, and his dick twitched. He'd thought a lot about that impromptu kiss he'd given her the other night. He wasn't sure why he'd done it. Impulse, maybe, because she'd been so stuck on the "let's just be friends" thing, while at the same time grabbing on to him and leaning in to him. He figured he'd test the waters and see what kind of reaction he'd get.

He'd gotten a reaction, all right. An uncomfortable one he'd had to live with in his patrol car for hours.

Emma hadn't exactly pushed him away when he'd kissed her. She'd melted just a little into him, making him want a lot more than a short kiss.

And now she had to look smoking hot.

Shit.

"Hey, sorry I'm running a little late. We had an emergency surgery this morning, and it took a little longer for me to get through appointments."

All this was said as she hurried back into her apartment to grab her bag and keys while Daisy sat dutifully staring up at him, wagging her tail at Boomer.

Pushing thoughts of kissing Emma—and more—aside, he nodded. "No problem. We have plenty of time."

"Great." She took a deep breath as she closed the door behind her. "Hey, Boomer. Daisy's really excited about the game today, are you?"

Luke couldn't help but smile at the attention she showed Boomer. "Boomer likes game day, too."

The dogs piled into the backseat of the truck, and they headed out.

"Where's Annie?"

"In her crate, and not too happy about it, either. But she's not ready for the ballpark."

"How's training going?"

"She's very smart, and oh-so-affectionate. And she ate one of my flip-flops yesterday," she added with a grimace. "She's teething."

He laughed. "Sounds like a normal puppy to me. Any takers on the adoption front?"

"Not really. We had a couple people show some interest, but then they never followed up. Everyone wants small dogs, and pit bulls are a tough sell because people think they're fighting or attack dogs, when they absolutely aren't, unless someone trains them that way. They're actually very sweet animals. I finally took the notice down."

"Which means you're keeping her."

"I guess so. If I deliver her to a shelter, she won't last there. And she's already part of my family. Daisy loves her, and honestly, how could I give her away?"

"You keep that up, you're going to need to move out of that house and buy a ranch soon."

She sighed. "Tell me about it. I've always been a sucker for animals, especially the ones no one wanted. I vowed once I became a vet I'd own several."

He made the turn onto the highway. "Then you're definitely going to need that ranch."

"Yeah, that's right at the top of my list. As soon as I pay off all my student loans and the debt from buying the clinic."

"Well, anytime you want to take the dogs out to a place where they can roam free for the day, you let me know."

"Okay, sure." She went quiet for a few minutes before turning to face him. "Why? Do you have a ranch?"

He kept his gaze on the road ahead of him. "As a matter of fact, yeah, I do."

He felt her eyes on him.

"Seriously?"

"Yeah. I own a ranch with my brothers, though my older brother Logan runs it."

"No shit."

His lips curved, and he took a quick glance at her. "No shit. And I wasn't kidding about running the dogs out there. You can bring Daisy and Annie out there sometime."

"I'd love to see it. It's my dream to own some land at some point."

"I'll take you out there. Logan lives by himself, so I try to get out there as much as I can so he doesn't become a recluse."

"Surely he doesn't run the ranch by himself."

"No, we have hands to help."

"But you don't live there anymore."

"Ranching wasn't my thing. I wanted to go into law enforcement, and Logan had ranching in his blood."

"I see."

"You two would be a good fit, seeing as how you want to live on the land someday. I should fix the two of you up."

She gave him a curious look. "That's . . . nice of you, but I'm not interested in a fix-up with anyone at the moment."

Good, since he really didn't want to see his brother going out with a woman he had a thing for. He had no idea why he'd suggested it, and had wanted to take it back as soon as he'd said it.

Not that he was interested in a relationship with Emma.

But he sure as hell didn't want Logan having one with her, either.

Christ, he was a mess.

Shoving stupid thoughts about women and relationships into the back of his mind, he pulled into the ballpark parking lot and retrieved Boomer from the backseat.

Dogs would have to be leashed, even though Boomer would likely be the best-trained dog in the ballpark today. With the leash lax in his hand, he and Emma walked side by side, the dogs on the outside of them, much to Boomer and Daisy's chagrin. He could tell Boomer wanted to walk next to Daisy, but his dog did what he was instructed to do, and that was walk on his left side, just like he always did when they were out on patrol.

He picked up the tickets he'd reserved, then they walked inside.

It was a perfect day, forecast in the eighties. Awesome weather for a ball game. There were a lot of animals in attendance, some of them freaked out by the other dogs. Boomer and Daisy did great, though, just like he suspected. They found their seats above the first-base line and settled in.

"Would you like a beer or a hot dog?" he asked.

Emma shook her head. "Not yet. I'm just excited to be here."

"Have you ever been to a major league game?"

"No. You?"

"Yeah. I traveled to Dallas and caught some of their games, and to St. Louis, too."

"How exciting. I can only imagine the difference in the stadiums."

"It's a huge difference. Bigger stadium and just a different feel. Kind of epic."

"I'll have to make it a point to get out to the 'big city' sometime and catch a game."

"Yeah. You should."

He was about to suggest they take a road trip and catch one of the games this summer, then caught himself.

What was he thinking? He wasn't going to continue this relationship with Emma beyond today. He was taking her out to show her a good time. One-time thing, and then he was done. Where women were concerned, there were no repeat performances. Because when there were repeat performances, one thing led to another, and before you knew it, you were in a relationship.

And after a relationship came marriage, and he knew what happened then.

Kiss of death to anything fun.

They settled in to watch the game while the dogs barked and wriggled and kept their eyes on the other dogs nearby. Lots of people had brought dogs, so it was fun to see them in the stands.

"I love this," Emma said, her sunglasses shading her eyes as she surveyed the stands. "I should have brought my business cards with me. I could walk row by row and hand them out."

He arched a brow. "Really?"

She laughed. "No. I'm exhausted. It's been a killer week, and all I want to do is sit back and watch the game. But it's something my mother would think I should do to drum up business for the clinic."

"She wants you to do more advertising?"

"Like you wouldn't believe."

"Do you need more business?"

"I can always use more, especially since I'm just starting out. But I'm not as aggressive as she'd like me to be. I think word of mouth spreads, and if you're good at your job, the business will come your way."

"I can see that, especially in your line of work."

"She did have a good suggestion, though. She wants me to sponsor an adoption day at the clinic. I'd work with the local shelter and offer discount services to anyone who adopts an animal."

He shifted to face her. "That's a brilliant idea. Are you gonna do it?"

"Yes, I think I am. I've already been in contact with the shelter, and they're interested."

"I could come by and bring Boomer. He's always a hit with the kids."

"You'd do that?"

"Sure. I assume you'll do it on a Saturday?"

"Yes. Jane Kline said she and Will—your friend Will? They're thinking about adopting a dog. That might be a good time for them to look at some animals."

He leaned back. "Yeah, Will loves dogs. And I know Jane's kids, Ryan and Tabitha, have wanted a dog for a while now."

"I guess I'll make it happen."

"You should, Emma. I think it would be great for your business. Your mom's pretty smart."

"She is. But if you ever meet her, don't tell her I said that or she'll come up with a hundred different marketing and advertising plans for the clinic."

He laughed. "Duly noted."

They settled in once the game started. Surprisingly, Emma knew her baseball, and she wasn't afraid to show her pleasure—or her displeasure—as the game progressed.

"Masters has a rocket arm at third base," she said, hunkered down in her seat, her feet propped up on the back of the empty seat in front of her. "He's fired off some killers to first. But they need a new second baseman. Twice now, their shortstop Alioto has scrambled for the balls that hit second, and you don't need your shortstop trying to cover both his position and second base. It's clear that he's trying to cover for how slow Trainor is."

He looked over at her, studying her as she grabbed a handful of popcorn and shoved it in her mouth, then followed it up with two very large swallows of beer.

"Is that right?"

She pulled her gaze away from the game and looked at him. "Well, yeah. Can't you tell? Trainor's either hiding an injury or needs to lose some weight. And judging from the paunch in his belly, I'd say he needs to lay off the cheeseburgers."

Luke snorted. "Maybe you should have a talk with his conditioning coach."

"Somebody needs to, or he's going to find himself booted down to Single-A ball."

"I had no idea you knew so much about baseball."

She shot him a grin. "I love sports. I played softball all through school. I'd have played it in college if I'd had the time. I was good enough to get a sports scholarship."

"But that's not what you wanted to do."

"No. I had big plans to become a vet." She stared out over the field.

"And now you've got your own practice."

"Yes. Finally." She shoved another handful of popcorn into her mouth. He wished he could see her eyes behind her sunglasses, because he could tell her thoughts had drifted.

"So you ended up changing colleges? You went to school in South Carolina?"

She focused on the game for a few minutes before she answered. "I had a hiccup in my school-and-career plan for a while. Kind of derailed me for a few years, so when I decided to apply to vet schools I couldn't get back into school here in Oklahoma. That's how I ended up in South Carolina."

She turned her head to look at him. "How did you know about South Carolina?"

"It's on your 'About Dr. Emma' page on the clinic's website."

"Oh." Her lips quirked. "You've been to the clinic's website?"

"Yeah. Have to know who's treating my dog, you know."

She laughed. "Of course. How very thorough of you. Did you run a background check on me, too?"

"Nah." He grabbed a handful of popcorn and resumed watching the game. "Not yet, anyway."

She looked at him, and he again wished she wasn't wearing her sunglasses, because there was definitely something going on. She wasn't smiling.

"I'm kidding, Emma."

She laughed, but it was a nervous laugh. "I knew that."

Okay, so the idea of a background check freaked her out. What did she have to hide?

Not that he did background checks on women he dated. He never investigated girlfriends—which Emma wasn't, and would never be, despite her sun-kissed cheeks and the way she yelled at the players and how much Boomer looked up at her with adoration.

Or how much he wanted to kiss her again.

As she watched the game, she absently petted Boomer's head. It was an unconscious act, but Boomer ate it up and leaned into her hand.

"He likes you," Luke said.

Her gaze drifted to his and she smiled, the kind of smile that punched a guy in the gut. She grabbed a handful of Boomer's fur and ruffled it. "I like him, too."

"You're so natural with animals."

She shifted. "You seem surprised by that."

"No. Well, yeah. My ex hated animals, and especially Boomer."

"Your ex-girlfriend?"

"Ex-wife."

"Oh. I'm sorry."

"For me or for Boomer?"

She laughed. "Both of you. Who wouldn't love this dog?

He's perfect." She leaned down and pressed her forehead against Boomer's. Her affection was so natural, and when Daisy came over and the dogs started to play, she stood.

"They're restless and they've both been so good for so long. How about a walk?"

"Sounds like a great idea."

They got their hands stamped by one of the attendants at the gate and took the dogs across the street to the park.

"If you don't mind me asking, how long have you been divorced?"

"Almost four years."

"Wow. A long time ago."

"Yeah. We were both too young to get married, but we met my first year in college, and it kind of stuck. We got married my junior year, and she moved out to the ranch to live with me."

"And that didn't work out?"

He let out a short laugh. "Uh, no. Rebecca was country club and lattes for breakfast every morning, and going shopping with her friends, and getting manicures and pedicures. Being stuck on a dusty ranch with a bunch of stinky cows and a husband who wanted to be a cop wasn't as romantic as it had sounded. She hated the ranch, hated the cattle and the horses, and she especially hated the dogs, especially Boomer."

Emma stopped and stared at him. "Wow. Really?"

"I'm not exaggerating, Emma. The woman I fell in love with and married totally disappeared once she stepped foot on the ranch. Rebecca was sweet and fun and full of life and laughter, but she really goddamn hated that ranch and the life associated with it."

"But you didn't end up living on the ranch, either. So why not move off the ranch?"

They resumed their walk through the park. "She knew that was the eventual plan, but patience wasn't one of her virtues. Besides, Boomer would have still come with us, and she made it clear she wanted a no-animal household. Then I brought up having kids, and she balked."

"She didn't want kids, either?"

"No, though that's not what she told me when we were dating. She wanted travel and expensive cars and a big house. Not kids and definitely not animals."

"Oh, for heaven's sake. You're kidding me, right?"

"I wish I was. There were just too many obstacles to overcome, so eventually she hightailed it back to Tulsa, and we got a divorce. It was a clean break. All she wanted was out of the marriage, and by that point I was more than happy to have her go."

Emma laid her hand on his arm. "I'm sorry, Luke. It must have been miserable for you."

"It wasn't the happiest time of my life, that's for sure. But I learned a lot from the experience, and next time—if there is a next time—I'll know better."

"Surely you want to get married again."

He shrugged. "Maybe. Someday. I don't know."

Her lips quirked. "A little skittish about that first go-round of happily-ever-after?"

She read him well. "That's an understatement."

"That's what you meant that night when you said that's not how you usually do it."

He stopped. "Huh?"

"When you were offering to take me out. You don't 'date.'"

She used air quotes around the word *date*.

"Oh, right. No, I don't. Not often."

She paused and pulled the leash around her hand. Daisy sat dutifully at her feet as Emma crossed her arms. "Well, after what you've been through, I can't say I blame you. Women must scare the hell out of you."

And that was a little too close to Emma having him figured out in one afternoon.

He wasn't sure he liked that.

Chapter 7

EMMA WATCHED THE myriad of expressions cross Luke's face as he talked about his ex-wife. A lot of anger and resentment, for sure, mixed with sadness, which she appreciated. He had obviously wanted it to work out with his ex, and it so clearly hadn't. He and his ex hadn't been well-matched.

That happened. Sometimes people weren't honest about what they really wanted in a relationship. No one knew that better than her.

Of course her situation had been different, and the person she'd become involved with had been deliberately deceptive.

At least they hadn't gotten married.

She shuddered at the thought. She'd been tied so strongly to him as it was. If their relationship had been legally binding . . .

She shook off the unpleasant thoughts and focused instead on the interesting revelation about Luke. His reticence about taking her out became so much clearer now. It wasn't that he didn't find her attractive. Not that she really cared about that—much. Okay, maybe she did, just a little, but she dismissed the thought. Her ego could rest comfortably now.

It was Luke's fear of relationships that held him back. He was obviously a one-night-stand kind of guy, gun-shy about women since he'd been burned by his ex.

Now *that* she understood all too well. They were kindred spirits in that regard, though she didn't do one-night stands.

Or any-night stands, for that matter.

She watched Luke with Boomer, his patience and affection with his dog.

Someday he'd make a great father. You could always tell. Guys who were great with animals would also be good with children.

Not that she was shopping for a father for her as yet nonexistent children. And if she was, Luke wouldn't be on her list, since he was currently living in one-night-stand land.

"You went quiet," he said, pulling her out of her thoughts.

"I was thinking about you."

He cocked a brow. "Yeah? What about me?"

"You, your ex-wife, the fact you're afraid of relationships, and how good you are with your dog."

He laughed. "That's a lot of thinking. And I'm not afraid of relationships. I'm just not in the market for one right now."

"Me, either."

"Did you get burned by an ex, too?"

And there was a conversation she didn't want to have with Luke. Not in detail, anyway. "I did. In the worst way. Who doesn't have an ugly breakup in their past?"

"True. Were you married?"

"No. It was just a bad relationship."

"I'm sorry."

"Me, too. And now I'm too busy with the new clinic."

"Oh, come on. You don't live it twenty-four seven."

"That's true, but relationships take time and commitment, and I don't have the time or the energy for one right now."

"I understand. So coming out with me today is perfect. No strings attached, but you can still get out and have some fun."

She liked Luke. "You're right. We're perfect for each other. Neither one of us has any expectations of the other."

"Yeah. Exactly."

And for some reason, that made her wish for more.

Which was the dumbest thing ever.

Damn that kiss, anyway.

After a short walk, they went back and caught the rest of the game. Fortunately, the home team won and even the dogs seemed to enjoy the day. She sure did. Luke took Emma back to her place. As he pulled into her driveway and she and Daisy climbed out of his truck, she leaned inside, not quite ready to let go of the day—or Luke—just yet.

"Without expectation, would it be all right if I fixed you dinner, or do you have a non-date date for tonight?"

He cocked a grin. "No, I cleared the whole day for you."

"Now I feel special. Come on in."

She held the door for him and Boomer.

"Nice place," he said.

"Thanks. It was my grandmother's. It's small, but it's perfect for me and the dogs."

She let Annie out of her crate, which led to crazy barking and greeting. She let all the dogs out into the backyard, then shut the slider.

"Would you like a beer?" she asked.

"Sounds good. Thanks."

She grabbed two beers out of the refrigerator and popped the tops off the bottles, then handed him one. She leaned against the counter and couldn't help but watch him as he took a long swallow. In his jeans and long-sleeved Henley, he looked lean, yet the muscles outlined against his shirt were unmistakable. If she were in the market for a guy— which she wasn't—Luke McCormack would be one hell of a man to play with.

He caught her watching him, and cast a look at her that made her body tighten in all the wrong places.

Just friends, Emma, remember? It was more important for him to think of her as a buddy, as just one of the guys.

Unfortunately, with her nipples beading and everything south screaming for her to jump on top of him and unzip those very worn jeans to get to the goods, she wasn't thinking of herself as one of the guys. She was thinking of herself as a woman who hadn't had sex in a very long time, and as Luke who was someone she'd really, really like to have sex with.

Did he have to keep looking at her? He had to have the hottest mouth she'd ever seen.

She shuddered as she inhaled. "So."

He licked his lips. She watched his tongue, and swallowed—hard.

"So. What's on the meal agenda?" he finally asked.

Meal? What meal? She wanted to devour *him* for dinner. "Uh . . . right." She turned and stuck her head in the fridge. "How do hamburgers on the grill sound? I make killer bacon cheese fries, too."

"How can I resist that offer? What can I do to help?"

It would help if she hadn't stupidly asked him to come in for dinner. Distance from men was her salvation. Or at least, distance from Luke.

"You can go wrangle the dogs while I get things started in here. Oh, and the grill is out on the back patio. Can you turn it on and get it ready?"

"I can handle that."

As soon as he left the kitchen, she exhaled, grabbed her beer, and took several long swallows, needing the cool brew to relieve her parched throat. Unfortunately, there was no help for her other throbbing body parts.

Good Lord. What was wrong with her? She'd been cool, calm, and totally immune to men ever since . . .

Well, ever since. And now there was Luke, and there was something about him that got to her in a way that no man had gotten to her in a very long time.

She wasn't ready for it. Not yet.

Though it had been a lot of years. Maybe it was time she did get ready for it.

She'd made a lot of vows once she'd escaped the worst

relationship of her life. And the number one vow was to never get involved with a man who hit all her hot buttons again. She'd only do safe and boring in the future.

Luke McCormack was anything but safe and boring. She could go up in flames with him, lose her sense of self. If he crooked his finger at her, she'd come running.

She'd done that once, and it had been a disaster.

Never again.

She set the oil on to heat, then peeled and sliced potatoes, the activity clearing her head. By the time Luke came in with the dogs, she had the distance she needed.

Until he came up behind her, and she inhaled the scent of him. He smelled of outdoors and something distinctly male.

"Need help?" he asked as he leaned over her shoulder.

Her breathing quickened. "I've got this. How about you make the patties?" Preferably somewhere far away, like Texas.

He took the meat out of the fridge and made the patties standing next to her, while she concentrated on not cutting off her finger. Hard to do since she was acutely aware of him and his big body nestled beside her.

Her kitchen was small, which meant not much maneuverability with two people in it. His elbow bumped her arm, her hip nudged his, their shoulders touched. While it didn't seem to bother him, it bugged the hell out of her, and not in an annoying way, either. Body contact with men was off-limits, yet she found herself inching a little closer, despite her self-mandate to stay as far away from Luke as possible.

Even with potatoes frying in oil and bacon sizzling in the other pan, she could still smell him.

And he seemed utterly oblivious of her.

After piling the patties on the plate she'd provided, he asked, "How about a spatula or something to flip these?"

"Sure." She dug out the one she used for the grill and handed it over to him.

"How do you like your burger?"

"Well done."

He grinned. "Me, too. I'll be back soon."

"I'll be here cutting up condiments for the burgers and finishing up these fries. Also, if you aren't tired of baseball, there's a game on."

"See? We make a great team. I'm game . . . for the game."

She laughed, then slumped against the counter after he closed the slider.

He was funny, gorgeous, he smelled good, and he was great with animals.

And he had an awesome body, a killer smile, and hands she wanted all over her.

One hell of a time for her libido to wake up and decide it wanted men again. Especially since she and Luke had decided they could be buddies. Which put her firmly in the He's Not Having Sex With You category.

She pulled the fries out of the oil and grated cheese, crumbled up the bacon she'd fried, then finished up making the cheese fries. By the time Luke came back in with the cooked burgers, she'd set up trays in the living room, the game was on, and she had lettuce, onions, and tomato set out on the counter, along with buns and all the stuff he could possibly want to spread on his burger.

"This is a feast," he said, as he set the platter of burgers down on the counter. "You didn't have to go to all this trouble."

She smiled at him. "This was no trouble at all. You're obviously very easy to please."

"Hey, I would have stopped for take-out on my way home, so, to me, this is a very big deal. Thanks, Emma."

"You're welcome." She didn't entertain. In fact, Luke was the first person she'd had over besides her mom. In South Carolina, she'd never had anyone over to her apartment.

Again, she had no idea what had gotten into her.

She fed the dogs in the kitchen, then they settled into watching the game and eating their burgers.

"Perfect," she said as she took her first bite.

"You don't get your man card unless you know how to

cook a burger," Luke said, sliding a French fry into his mouth. "And these fries are awesome."

"Thanks. I never have anyone to fix them for, and they're my favorites, so you actually did me a favor."

"So what you're saying is that you had an ulterior motive in inviting me for dinner."

She waggled her brows. "Maybe."

He shoved in another, chewed, then cast a smile her way. "I can accept that I was used to satisfy your lust for bacon cheese fries. I'm glad I was here to help you out. You just let me know whenever the urge strikes. I'll help you satisfy your cravings."

She took a deep breath. Yeah, she had a list of services she'd like him to perform for her. "I'll definitely keep that in mind."

His gaze met hers, and suddenly, she didn't believe either of them were thinking about fries anymore.

SOMEWHERE IN BETWEEN the ballpark that day and dinner that night, something major had changed in the atmosphere between Luke and Emma. He'd picked up some seriously hot signals from her, both at the park and over dinner. And yeah, maybe he'd inadvertently thrown out a come-on with that line about satisfying her cravings, but he'd actually been talking about food.

Until she'd shot him a hungry look that had nothing to do with French fries, and everything to do with sex.

He thought they'd been on the same wavelength. He'd had a great time with her. She was easy to be with. She was fun, had a great sense of humor, and for a woman, wasn't demanding at all, something he found refreshing.

And she'd even cooked him dinner instead of making him dress up and take her out somewhere. Not much more he could ask for in a woman. Sure, he wouldn't mind taking her to bed—after all, she was hot, but he'd resigned himself to the fact that Emma was off-limits in that department.

Until she started throwing out those sex signs. He knew he wasn't misreading them, either. A guy had to be dead to miss that signal. He wasn't dead, and neither was his dick.

He focused on finishing his food, likely better than thinking about how soft her hair looked, or the way she licked her lips every time she took a bite of her burger. Because if his thoughts kept leaning in that direction, it would only get him in trouble, especially since she kept looking at him in ways that were definitely not "Hey, let's be best buddies" kind of ways.

And Emma seemed to notice he was looking back.

"I think I'll go clean up in the kitchen." She pushed back her chair and hightailed it out of the dining room. Now she was uncomfortable. He grabbed his plate and followed her into the kitchen. He leaned in to rinse his plate under the running water, catching a whiff of the sweet scent in her hair.

Vanilla, maybe?

She turned to glance at him, and there was that deer-in-the-headlights look again.

She snatched the plate away from him. "I've got that. Why don't you—"

He waited, deciding she should figure out what she wanted. He quirked an eyebrow at her. "Why don't I what?"

"Uh . . . never mind."

Instead, he rolled up his sleeves, grabbed the pot she'd cooked the fries in. "Where do you want me to dump this oil?"

"I can do that."

"So can I, Emma."

"Trash can is fine."

He dumped the oil, then brought the pan over to the sink. She washed it, and he grabbed the towel hanging next to the sink to dry.

"You really don't have to help."

"You really can't stop me if I want to."

She took a deep breath, then handed him the clean pot, her slippery hands colliding with his. "Thanks."

Even being friends with a woman was complicated. They were better relegated to sex partners, and leaving it at that. He should have known this would never work out. He was way too attracted to Emma to be this close to her and not touch her, not want to kiss her.

And she seemed to be struggling with it, too, which made him wonder what the problem was—other than maybe she only had relationships, and she'd had a bad one, just like he had, so she'd like to steer clear of entanglements.

But it had been a long time since he'd had a fun day like he'd had today, and he'd like to see where it went with Emma. Not relationship-wise, but they had off-the-charts chemistry, and he sure wanted to explore that part of it.

So when she turned the water off and dried her hands, he made his move, stepping toward her as she turned around.

She moved into him at the same time he wrapped his arms around her.

Their lips met in a collision that rocked him hard in an instant. Her mouth opened and his tongue slid inside, and it was an explosion of fireworks. He pushed her against the counter with his body and her fingers tangled in his hair.

The room suddenly seemed devoid of oxygen, both of them gasping for breath as Luke deepened the kiss.

Yeah, it was just like he thought it would be—all hot and fiery passion. He let his hands roam her back, touching her the way he'd wanted to touch her since he'd first laid eyes on her, mapping every luscious curve while she tightened her hold on his hair, every whimper escaping her throat making him painfully harder.

And when he caressed her ribs and coasted his hand over the curve of her hip, she moaned against his mouth. He kissed his way along her jaw and down the column of her throat, listening to the hard and fast sound of her breathing.

He turned her around and pulled her against him, lifting her T-shirt out of her jeans so he could palm the soft skin of her stomach.

"Tell me yes," he said. "Or tell me no. You decide."

She flipped around to face him, twining her arms around his neck. He felt the hard thump of her fast heartbeat against his chest. "Yes. Now stop talking."

He took her mouth again, that same frenzied need making him dizzy. He grabbed her butt and lifted her and she wrapped her legs around him.

"Bedroom," he said.

She pointed, and that's all the direction he needed. He found her bedroom, the only open door down the hall. He put her down next to the bed and pulled his shirt off. She was already out of her tennis shoes and unzipping her jeans.

He liked a woman of action. And as she shimmied out of her jeans, he really enjoyed the revealing of skin and the fact she seemed to be in as much of a hurry as he was to get clothes off.

He shucked his sneakers and jeans, then pushed her down on the bed, coming down on top of her.

Oh yeah. Now this was good, especially her legs twining with his.

She gasped as their bodies connected.

"Did I mention I'm a big fan of pink underwear?" he asked.

She reached up to brush her fingers through his hair. "No. I don't believe that topic came up during the baseball game today."

"Huh." He lifted up and ran his fingers over the swell of her breasts where the cups of her bra met flesh. "I'm surprised. It was on my mind."

He watched as her breasts rose and fell as she breathed. "It was?"

"Sure. I was sitting there, watching the game and imagining what color underwear you had on."

She frowned. "You were not."

He laughed, rolled over and dragged her on top of him, then pulled her ponytail holder out, letting her hair fall over her shoulders. "Emma, all guys think about women. And sex. Almost all the time."

"You were thinking about baseball."

He gripped her hips and arched against her, letting her feel how hard he was. "I'm not thinking about baseball now."

"Neither am I."

She sat up and unhooked her bra, letting it fall from her shoulders to reveal the most perfect breasts he'd ever seen. He pulled her down to him, taking a nipple into his mouth.

She was soft, but her nipple hardened into a tight bud when he sucked on it. And the sounds she made drove him crazy.

"Luke. Oh, Luke, that's so good." She surged against him, and he almost lost it.

It didn't take more than a few minutes of licking her nipples to realize that Emma was very vocal.

He liked that, and wanted a lot more of it.

He flipped her onto her back and kissed her ribs, moving his way over her stomach. She smelled good, her skin was soft, and when he reached her panties, she arched upward, offering herself to him.

She might have been reluctant at first, but now that they'd decided to do this, she was more than eager. Luke liked a sex partner who wasn't shy or hesitant, and Emma fit him perfectly. When he grasped her panties, she wriggled out of them, seemingly in a hurry to have him touch her.

Yeah, he was in a hurry, too. He pressed a kiss to her hipbone and spread her legs, shouldering his body between them to kiss her inner thighs.

He looked up to find her watching him, a combination of curiosity and hungry desire on her face. And when he bent his head to take a long swipe of her sex, she made those sounds again—a long moan followed by a whimper.

"Yes, right there," she said, her head falling back against the pillow at the same time her hips arched up as she let him have access.

He tasted her, using his tongue and his lips to explore her. She was like heaven here, soft and warm and everything he'd expected. All he wanted to do was drive her right over the edge.

Emma gripped the sheets and dug her heels into the

mattress, trying hard not to come so fast. But it had been a long time and, oh, God, Luke had a magical tongue. She knew as soon as he'd grabbed her, kissed her, and pushed her against the kitchen counter that this was going to be a slamming hot experience.

And now, as she hovered ever so close to a climax, she knew that she'd been right. He was a force to be reckoned with, and she was veering out of control. She came with a wild cry, bucking against him as wave after wave of orgasm crashed over her with dizzying effects, leaving her shattered.

She barely had time to recover when Luke loomed over her, taking her mouth in a kiss that left her breathless. Her body still quivered with the aftereffects of her mind-blowing orgasm, and the way he touched her, the way his body moved over hers, had her right there all over again.

The man was relentless in all the right ways.

A thought suddenly occurred to her, and she grabbed his arms. "Please tell me you have a condom."

He gave her a devilishly sexy smile. "I have a condom."

She quirked an eyebrow. "For those random, side-of-the-road hookups?"

"No, in case I arrest a hot perp."

"Seriously?"

He cocked his head to the side. "No. Not seriously." He reached for his pants and grabbed a condom out of his pocket.

"Surely that wasn't for me."

"It wasn't. But I like to be prepared."

She swept her fingers across his jaw. "Thanks for that. Now let's get you inside me."

He took a deep breath. "Happy to oblige, ma'am."

He put the condom on, spread her legs and slid inside her, his gaze fixed on hers as he entered her, slow and easy.

Emma wasn't prepared for this intimacy, would have much preferred he slam it home and screw the living daylights out of her, all fast and furiouslike. These slow and gentle movements, the way he glided in and out of her while holding his gaze to hers was about to undo her. It was . . .

intimate. Emotional. And not just faceless, random sex, which was what she'd been all in for when he'd kissed her with such passion in the kitchen.

Now it was slow. Stirring. And it made her feel things more than just the physical. Though the physical part was pretty damned good. Luke knew how to move his body in such a way that when he levered his hips against her, she was already on the verge again, her breath catching every time he thrust. Add the emotional aspect to the passion, and it was overwhelming.

In both good ways and bad.

But when he bent and kissed her, she was lost, reaching for him and holding tight as control fled. Now it was need that took hold, Luke caressing her body with his hands as he moved faster within her, taking his movements deeper until she whimpered against his lips and tightened against him.

He lifted up and looked at her, and she shattered, coming with a moan, her body quivering around his. She watched him as he went with her, and it was a magical thing to see a man lose control like that. She clung to him as they both went over, and didn't let go until long moments later after they both caught their breath.

Emma stroked Luke's sweat-soaked back, reveling in the bliss of afterglow.

She hadn't expected this. But she refused to regret it.

And when Luke looked down at her and smiled, it was obvious he didn't, either.

But now it was over, and it was going to have to be a one-time thing.

"I have a lot to do tomorrow," she said.

"Which is your cue for getting me the hell out of your house?"

"I didn't say that, but it's my only day off, and I catch up on paperwork. And I have to clean my house. I'm usually up really early. You probably like to sleep in."

He rolled out of bed and stood, giving her a magnificent view of his very fine ass and spectacular body.

"No problem." He grabbed his clothes and got dressed while she put on a pair of shorts and a tank top so she could see him to the door.

"I hope you're not offended," she said when he called for Boomer and headed to the front door.

"I'm not. I wouldn't have stayed anyway. It's not really my thing."

"We're on the same page, then."

He turned to her and smiled. "We are. Thanks for dinner and . . . after dinner."

"You're welcome."

"I'll see you later, Emma."

She leaned against the doorframe and watched him walk to his car. He waved good-bye as he drove away. She shut and locked the door, let the dogs out one last time, then brushed her teeth, washed her face, and climbed into bed.

The after-sex euphoria had faded, which was disappointing, but she was just being practical. Neither she nor Luke wanted a relationship. She was just being smart, to not get involved with him emotionally.

Smart didn't feel very comforting as she lay in her now-cold bed.

Alone.

Chapter 8

EMMA WAS NERVOUS and excited about Adoption Day at the Hope Small Animal Hospital. But thanks to the local animal shelter, they had eighteen animals—a group of dogs and cats—available for adoption today.

They'd had the sign running for over a week on the outside marquee, and her mother had helped her by advertising it in the local paper and on the town website and social media pages. It was up on the clinic's website, too. She could only hope people would show up. If they could get even a few of these animals adopted out today, she'd call it a win.

Jane came by early with her boyfriend, Will, along with Jane's kids, Ryan and Tabitha, two of the cutest kids Emma had ever met. Tabitha was so excited she was bouncing on the heels of her purple tennis shoes. Ryan tried to play it cool, but his eyes widened at all the animals on display.

"I'm so glad you're here," Emma said to Jane as the kids looked at the animals with Will.

"Are you kidding?" Jane said. "It's all the kids—and Will—have talked about for the past week."

"Mom. You have to come see this dog," Ryan said, taking her hand and dragging her away.

Jane gave her a look and a grin and wandered off.

After that, the clinic started to fill up as people wandered in, some with kids, some without.

"This is looking good," Leanne said.

"I hope so."

When Luke came in with Boomer, Emma's stomach twisted in a mix of delight and trepidation.

It had been a week since they'd slept together. She hadn't exactly expected him to come by today, had figured they'd had one night of awesome sex, and she probably wasn't going to see him again.

It had been the right thing to do. Luke was a complication she didn't need in her life. Not right now.

Maybe not ever.

And he'd seemed willing enough to walk away at her suggestion.

But she'd missed him during the week. And she hadn't wanted to miss him. Several times she'd thought about picking up the phone to call him, or to send him a text. Which would have been a very, very bad thing. Because seeing him now caused every nerve ending in her body to ping to life, and every memory from that night she'd spent with him rushed forth, causing her face to heat.

But she was so glad he'd shown up and had brought Boomer today. He was in uniform, too, which made all the kids excited.

And he was smiling at her, which made her stomach tumble.

Guess he wasn't out of her system entirely just yet.

"Morning, Emma."

"Morning. I'm so glad you came today."

"I said I would. So here we are."

"Are you on duty?"

"I did a late shift, covering for someone. So I thought the kids might get a kick out of the K9-cop thing."

"I'm sure they will. Thanks so much for coming today."

He grinned and her knees weakened. "Wouldn't miss it. I heard there'd be donuts."

"Funny. There are, plus coffee."

"I could use the coffee."

She lost sight of Luke as the shelter manager came over to talk to her. Then she got busy examining a calico that had just been adopted, which sent her heart soaring, because after that, there seemed to be one animal after another that ended up having a clinic file started because they'd been adopted.

Things were going so well.

Her mother stopped in and came to the back when she was examining a sheltie/poodle mix. And her mom had the biggest grin on her face.

"Picking up some new clients today?"

She hugged her mother. "I don't always tell you thank-you like I should, but thank you. And not just because I'm ending up with new clients today, but animals have been adopted."

Her mother looked around. "It seems like a successful event. You should do it twice a year."

"That's a good idea." She squeezed her mom's hand. "Stick around for a bit?"

"Of course."

After her mother disappeared, things seemed to quiet down.

"We've got six new files," Rachel said with a wide smile. "That's so awesome."

The one thing she loved most about Rachel and Leanne was that they didn't just work at the clinic because it was a job. They had a love of animals as big and as fierce as Emma had.

"It is awesome."

"There's a black-and-white kitten I have my eye on," Leanne said. "But I don't know what Oscar would think about me bringing another cat home."

Emma leaned against the desk. "He probably wouldn't like it one bit. But he'd adjust, and he might enjoy the company during the day while you're at work."

"That's what I'm thinking. Plus, she's a female, so there'd be no fighting for territory. I'm going to give her another nuzzle and see if she needs to go home with me."

Emma looked at Rachel.

"She's a goner," Rachel said. "That kitten's going home with her today."

Ten minutes later, Leanne caught up with Emma. "I've already told Patrice that the black-and-white kitten is mine. I had Rachel set up a chart for her. I'm going to call her Olivia."

"Oscar and Olivia? So cute, Leanne."

"I know, right? From the minute I saw her, I knew she was mine."

Emma patted Leanne's shoulder. "We're doomed sometimes. Same thing happened to me with Annie. I don't know why I bothered posting signs."

Leanne laughed and then moved on.

"Dr. Emma. Look what we got." It was Tabitha, Jane's daughter, with the cutest golden retriever/lab mix puppy.

Emma crouched down and pulled the puppy into her arms. "Well, isn't he the cutest thing." She looked up at Jane, who stood next to Tabitha. "He's the one?"

Will came up alongside Jane. "He's the one."

"His name is gonna be Archie. We all agreed," Ryan said.

"All right, then. Let's go do Archie's exam and get him updated on his shots. I'll have Rachel start a file for him."

By the end of the day, they'd adopted out thirteen of the eighteen animals, and Patrice, the shelter manager, had received interest on the remaining five. In addition, several people stopped in and made appointments to spay or neuter their pets, since Emma's mother had also suggested Emma advertise that anyone who stopped in that day to become a new client would receive a discount on spaying and neutering services, or twenty percent off on a first appointment.

It had been a spectacular day.

"Thank you, Emma. I can't tell you how well this went," Patrice said. "Just making the community aware of the importance of adopting a shelter dog instead of buying purebred animals will go a long way to improving community relations. I have high hopes the other five animals we had here today will be adopted."

"I hope so, Patrice. And I hope we make this a regular function. I'd like to do it again in the fall."

Patrice smiled. "Definitely. When I get back to the office on Monday, I'll give you a call, and we'll put it on the calendar."

By the time they helped pack up Patrice's cages and the rest of the animals, Emma was wiped out. She headed back inside to find Luke in conversation with her mother.

Uh-oh.

"Mom," she said. "Do you know Officer McCormack?"

"I do now. I make it my business to know our fine police force. I hear you treated Boomer for a sprained leg not too long ago."

"Yes. He's doing fine now, though. And Luke—Officer McCormack—was nice enough to bring Boomer by today. He was a big hit with all the kids."

Her mother crossed her arms and grinned. "Yes, he was. It was so nice of you to do that."

"No problem," Luke said. "Emma's done a great community service by offering the shelter dogs for adoption. Which I heard was your idea, Mrs. Burnett."

"Really." Emma's mother looked from her to Luke. "So the two of you must be having regular chat sessions, then. Or are you dating?"

Emma coughed. Luke smiled. "We went to the Double-A ball game a week or so ago. It was Bring Your Dog to the Ballpark Day."

"Oh. That's so interesting."

"Well," Emma said, leading her mom by the elbow. "We have a lot of cleanup to do here, and it's already been a long day. I can't thank you enough for this idea, Mom. It was brilliant."

"Uh huh. In other words, you'd like me to leave."

"Of course not. You can stay. There's plenty of mopping and cleaning up to do."

Her mother grabbed her purse and dug out her keys. "No thanks. I just think up the ideas. You execute, then clean up after."

Emma walked her to the door, then kissed her cheek. "I love you, Mom."

Her mother kissed her back. "I love you, too, Emma." She turned and waved to Rachel and Leanne. "Luke, you have Emma bring you by the house for Sunday dinner."

Luke smiled. "I'd love to."

"Great. Next Sunday, then. Emma, make it happen."

Emma just stared. Luke shrugged. "Okay. Next Sunday, then."

"Mom," Emma said, stepping outside with her. "Luke and I are not dating."

"Sure looked to me like there's some chemistry between the two of you."

"I don't want to talk about this here."

"Fine. I'll call you later."

She did not want to have this conversation with her mother now. Or ever. "We're not dating. There's no chemistry."

Her mom laid her hand on her arm. "Don't let *him* win by shutting yourself down forever, Emma. Luke's a very nice man. Go out. Have some fun. Start living again."

Her mother had emphasized *him*, and she knew who her mom had been referring to.

Vaughn. Her huge past mistake. She took a deep breath. "I'll think about it."

"Good. And I will talk to you later. Now go clean up, and then have a glass of wine and relax. You did good today. And don't forget Sunday dinner. With Luke."

"Bye, Mom." Emma watched her mother leave, then went back inside. Rachel and Leanne had disappeared, no doubt to the back to start the cleanup. Only Luke was out front with Boomer.

He was leaning against the counter, still looking sharp and fresh and oh-so-sexy in his uniform. His hand was wrapped around Boomer's leash, and her gaze tracked there. She liked his hands. They were big, strong, and masculine.

Powerful hands. A man's hands. She still remembered how they felt gliding across her skin. She suddenly flushed hot, inhaled a very deep breath, and pushed those thoughts to the back of her mind.

"You're mom is awesome," Luke said.

"Yeah, she is. So are you. Thanks so much for being here today. I'm sure you were exhausted after working last night."

He shrugged. "It's no big deal. I wanted to be here."

"I'll walk you out."

Watching Emma in her element had been fun for Luke. He'd mostly stood by and had fun with the kids, who loved Boomer. And Boomer, as always, was great with all the kids.

It made him want to have a few of his own so Boomer would have kids to play with all the time.

But he wasn't ready for that, and he didn't know when— or if—he'd ever be ready.

Although watching Emma with all the kids today had been a revelation. Not only did she love animals, she also had a natural rapport with children, something his ex-wife had never had. The few times they'd been around kids, Becca had acted like children had some kind of communicable disease. She hadn't wanted anything to do with them. He should have noticed it early on, but he'd been so lovestruck by her, he'd been blinded to many of the issues that should have been lightbulb moments for him.

"I'm sorry about that whole invitation thing to my parents' house for dinner," she said. "You don't have to come."

"It's okay. I like your mom. And I'd love to come for dinner. Unless you don't want me there."

She cocked a brow. "Seriously?"

"Hey, I'm a single guy. Home-cooked meals are a treat."

She shook her head. "You don't know my mom. She'll grill you. About us. I mean, I know there's really no 'us,' but you know what I mean. She thinks there's something going on between us."

He laughed. "I understand. And I can take it."

"Don't say I didn't warn you. Sunday dinner it is, then. I'll call you with the details."

He walked out, actually happy about the dinner. He hadn't been lying about the home-cooked-meal thing, but he was surprised to find he wanted to be with Emma, to hang out with her family.

And it was just dinner. It didn't mean they were a couple. He could compartmentalize Emma as a friend.

With benefits.

Or not.

Or something.

Hell if he knew what they were. And if he didn't think about it, he didn't have to name it, right?

Chapter 9

EMMA WAS RIDICULOUSLY nervous about having Luke over for dinner at her parents' house. The last time she'd done this, she'd been a teenager. The boy had been Henry Mayer, a gawky, rail-thin type more interested in science and video games than Emma. She hadn't realized it at the time, of course. But she'd had a serious crush on Henry's blond hair, dark glasses, and serious eyes. They'd been lab partners in chemistry, had gone to see old movies at the discount theater together, and had a shared love of Mel Brooks films. Henry could be so funny when you got him alone.

He was a terrible kisser, but Emma had overlooked that for his other fine qualities. Ah, young love.

Her father had been sorely disappointed in Henry's lack of enthusiasm about baseball. Her mother had talked his ear off, and poor, shy Henry couldn't wait to get the hell out of there.

She expected much the same from Luke. She fully expected it to be a short evening, with Luke coming up with some excuse to flee.

She'd arrived an hour early to help her mother with dinner,

which, of course, was totally unnecessary because her mother was an advance planner.

"Tonight your father is grilling steaks. I'm making asparagus and potatoes au gratin and a new salad recipe I've been dying to try out. Oh, and I made two pies for dessert."

"Of course you did. And when did you find time for that?"

"Silly girl. I have Saturdays off to grocery shop and cook."

"Mom, I can only hope to have your energy level when I'm your age."

Her mother smiled. "I'm going to take that as a compliment."

"Please do. Now, is there anything I can do to help?"

"You can open the wine."

"That part I can handle."

"So how are things with you and the hot cop?"

She knew it was going to come up—the grilling before Luke arrived. "He's fine. I actually haven't seen him this week. We've both been very busy."

"Which means you *have* been seeing him. That's great, Emma."

Crap. Her mother was so crafty. She was going to have to get better at wording her answers. "We've hung out. I told you, we're friends."

Her mom paused and leaned against the counter. "Emma. I'm hardly old and blind, and I'm very adept at reading chemistry when I see it. You and Luke have loads of it."

"I think you'd like me to be in a relationship."

"You're right. I would. You deserve to be happy."

Emma had no response to that, and fortunately, the doorbell rang. She went to answer it and smiled at Luke, who looked amazing in a navy blue button-down shirt and dress jeans.

"Wow, you look nice."

"So do you. I like you in a dress."

She felt ridiculously complimented, especially by the way he looked at her. "Thank you. Come on in."

"Are you sure it's okay that I brought Boomer?"

"My mother would be disappointed if you hadn't. They

have a huge yard and a dog, Pokey. And Daisy and Annie are out back with Pokey. Come on."

He'd brought flowers. And wine. God, the man was such a gentleman.

"Oh, Luke, how are you?" Her mom had come into the living room.

"Mrs. Burnett. I'm great, thanks. These are for you."

Her mom took the flowers and wine, then kissed Luke on the cheek. "Thank you so much for these. Aren't you just the sweetest man? And call me Georgia, please."

"Okay, Georgia."

"Emmett is out back with the dogs. Emma, show him the way while I put these flowers in a vase."

She led him out back, where her dad was sitting in a chair on the shady porch while the dogs all frolicked in the over-sized yard.

He stood when Luke came out with Boomer.

"Hi, Luke."

"Mr. Burnett."

"You can call me Emmett. It's nice to have you here for dinner today. I don't get male conversation at the dinner table all that often. Even when Emma comes over, it's all girl talk, all the time."

"Hey, Dad. I talk sports."

"That's true, sweetie. You do. I taught you well."

Emma turned to Luke. "Can I get you something to drink? There's beer, wine, or iced tea."

"An iced tea sounds great."

"I'll have one, too, honey."

"Sure. I'll be right back."

She went inside to fix the drinks. "How's it going out there?"

"Just fine, Mom. Dad and Luke are deciding on what tuxes they're going to wear for our wedding."

"Very funny. Tell your dad I'm ready for him to start grilling the steaks. We'll be ready to eat in about thirty minutes."

She grabbed the iced teas. "Will do."

She stepped outside with the tea.

"Dad, Mom's ready for you to start grilling the steaks."

"Okay." He went inside.

"I like your dad," Luke said.

"Thanks. Me, too."

"This is a nice place. Have they lived here long?"

"My whole life. They remodeled several years ago. Dad said he'd buy mom a new house if she wanted something different, but she said this is home and always will be."

"Yeah, I know what's that like. There's just something about home."

She looked out over the backyard where she and Molly used to play as kids. There used to be a sandbox and a swing set, which were now long gone, but it was still the same place it had always been. "Yes. There's nothing like knowing you have a place to call home, even if you don't live there anymore."

Her dad came out with the steaks.

"Can I help you with that, Emmett?"

"Nah. I got it. So as I was saying earlier about Kansas City . . ."

Apparently, her father and Luke had been deeply embroiled in a baseball discussion. Her father was a Kansas City fan, and Luke a St. Louis fan, so their discussion was on topic about last season's playoffs.

Emma took a seat and listened to the passion both of them displayed about the sport, her gaze occasionally flitting to the dogs. Boomer and Daisy were wrestling over a stick they'd found. Annie ran circles around them, and Pokey had found a nice quiet spot under one of the tall trees, observing the action.

She loved watching the dogs. Boomer and Daisy got along well. There was no aggression from either of them. It was a natural, fun sort of play. She was glad. And Annie had a great time barking and wagging her tail, trying to get in on the action. Even Pokey eventually got up to join in, which Emma was happy about, since he needed the exercise.

"What do you think, Emma?" her father asked.

She shifted her focus to her dad. "What do I think about what?"

"We were talking about football."

"You were? I thought it was baseball."

"Subject change," Luke offered with a smile.

"Oh. I missed that. Sorry. I was watching the dogs play. Pokey's looking like he's lost a little weight, Dad. That's good."

"I've been taking him for walks like you told me, too. Every night after dinner."

"Thank you. It's good for him."

Her mom came to the door. "Dinner's ready. How about those steaks?"

Her dad nodded. "These are done, too."

"Perfect. Y'all come in."

They went in and washed up for dinner. Her mother set an elegant dining room, centered by the flowers Luke had brought, and of course all the wonderful food. Emma's stomach had been growling, smelling the steaks cooking, and she couldn't wait to dive in.

And so far, Luke was still there and hadn't gone running out the front door.

A promising sign.

LUKE WAS STARVING. The steaks smelled great, and he really liked Emma's dad. He was a sports nut, so they had a lot in common. And Emmett hadn't grilled him about Emma, thankfully. Luke figured that as Emma's dad he might want to know what his intentions were, but so far . . . nothing.

"So, Luke, how's police work going?" Emma's mom asked.

"Good. I stay busy, which I like. It's not high crime, but there's enough going on that it's interesting, even for a small town like Hope."

"I'm sure you're busy with those drug thefts. Like the one at Emma's place," her dad said.

Luke nodded. "Yes, sir. And we're working diligently on catching the person who did that."

"Scared the life out of me when that happened," Georgia said. "Especially since Emma was there at the time."

"But I'm fine, Mom. And Luke said they probably would have never hit the vet clinic if they'd known someone was there. I just happened to be parked across the street."

"That's true," Luke said. "Someone looking to burglarize, especially after drugs, isn't going to want potential witnesses. If Emma's car had been in the parking lot, they wouldn't have bothered. It was just an unfortunate set of circumstances."

"Luke got there in a hurry, thankfully."

Luke looked at her. "And, fortunately, you did all the right things, so you were safe."

"Thanks."

"Sooner or later, they'll screw up, and we'll catch them."

"Hopefully sooner, rather than later," Emmett said, then went back to eating his steak. "The last thing we need in Hope is someone out stealing drugs from businesses. Who knows what they'll do next."

"It makes me feel a little less safe," Georgia said. "Even though he isn't breaking into homes."

Luke nodded. "I know. And we'll catch him. That's a promise."

Georgia squeezed his hand. "I know you will. We're confident in you."

"Well," Emma said. "Enough about that. I have exciting news. I got to assist the birth of a litter of the sweetest golden retrievers yesterday."

Her mom's eyes widened. "Oh, I love goldens. How many?"

Emma was obviously going for a change in subject. Luke grinned at her.

She smiled back before turning her attention to her mom. "Eight of them. Just the cutest little things."

"Oh, Emmett. Wouldn't it be great to have a golden retriever again?"

"No. Pokey is enough for now."

"The owner is going to sell some of the puppies," Emma offered.

Her father glared at her. "You are not helping, Em."

Emma shrugged, then smiled. "Think of all the exercise Pokey would get with a pup running after him."

"So you think it's a good idea?"

"I think Pokey likes it when Daisy and Annie are here. He doesn't object to other dogs. And yes, he's older and set in his ways, but a companion is a good thing."

"Dammit," Emmett said, scooping potatoes onto his fork. "I already know I'm going to lose this argument."

Georgia looked over at Emma and smiled.

Yeah, Luke didn't think Emmett was going to win that one, either.

After dinner, they all cleared dishes into the kitchen. Emmett and Luke rinsed and loaded stuff into the dishwasher while Emma and her mom put the leftovers away. With four people in the kitchen, cleanup was done in no time. Then everyone headed out back to hang out with the dogs.

Luke listened in while Emma chatted with her mom about some of her mom's work-related stuff. Georgia was a very accomplished businesswoman. He could see where Emma had picked up her drive and ambition.

"Next week we're launching a marketing campaign for the chamber of commerce," Georgia said. "We designed a new website for them, because, oh, Lord, theirs was antiquated. It's a wonder anyone even knew where Hope was or what services were offered in this town before."

"I'm excited to see it, Mom. I know it's going to be awesome."

"All the businesses in town will be highlighted. Including yours, Emma. And information on all of Hope's municipal agencies, too, including the police station."

"That's great, Georgia," Luke said. "It's an update that's been desperately needed for a while now."

"Thanks. I'm pretty thrilled about it. It's taken us about

two years to get it off the ground. A long process, but worth it."

"I'm very proud of you, honey," Emmett said. "I know how hard you've worked on this one."

Georgia cast Emmett a glowing smile. "Thank you, Emmett. And thank you for building me an office. It's my sanctuary here at home. You're my hero."

Luke loved the way they supported each other. And the way they looked at each other. Even after all these years together, they were still in love.

It was so unlike what he had grown up with.

That's what he wanted. Someday.

He looked over at Emma, who was watching her parents with a goofy smile on her face. She shifted her glance over at him, and something elemental sizzled between them.

Yeah.

When it got dark, Luke stood. "I should be going. Thank you both for having me over today."

"We're so glad you came, Luke," Georgia said. "You're welcome anytime."

Emmett shook his hand. "What Georgia said. And Kansas City is still the better team."

Luke laughed. "Well, we'll see about that during the course of the baseball season. I enjoyed myself today. Thanks."

He called Boomer, who came to his side right away.

"I'll walk you out," Emma said.

They headed out to the driveway. This was the first chance he'd had to be alone with her the whole day.

She looked pretty in her black-and-white sundress, and he'd wanted to touch her. And kiss her. But she'd kept her distance.

He understood that. She hadn't wanted to give her parents the impression there was anything between them.

"Thanks for having me over."

"You can thank my mom for that. She can be a little relentless. I hope it wasn't too painful for you."

The wind had picked up, blowing Emma's hair this way

and that. He swept it away from her face. "Emma. You have really nice parents. It's obvious they care a lot about you."

She smiled. "Thanks. And yes, they do. I probably worry too much. I just didn't want you to feel . . . obligated."

"I never do what I don't want to do, so stop worrying about me."

"Okay. I will."

Dammit. He knew he shouldn't do it, but the words spilled from his mouth before he could stop them.

"How about a run by the lake with the dogs after work tomorrow?"

The reward was the bright smile she gave him. "Sure. I'd love to."

"Great. I'll give you a call."

"Thanks again for coming today."

"No problem."

He walked out to his truck, and she headed to the door.

He wondered what the hell he'd been thinking, inviting her to go out with him again. They'd gone out. They'd had sex. Monumental, mind-blowing sex.

Now he'd come to her parents' for dinner.

He never saw a woman over and over again. It went against his code. And he sure as hell didn't go to a woman's parents' house for dinner.

Then again, he wasn't really even dating Emma. They were friends, and that was all. The sex thing had been impromptu. Letting off some steam.

So maybe they could just go back to the friends thing. Like running with the dogs after work.

As he climbed into his truck, he glanced up at the front door of her parents' house. Emma was still there, watching him.

She waved, and as he backed out of the driveway, he waved back.

His gut told him Emma was way more than a friend.

And he couldn't wait to see her again.

Chapter 10

FORTUNATELY, EMMA HAD a particularly busy day, including performing a double ACL repair on a very overweight rottweiler. The surgery had been complicated, but successful. Leanne was currently overseeing the recovery of Delbert the rottweiler, while Emma spoke to the pet's owners, advising them that Delbert would need to go on a restricted diet, since the dog's obesity had been one of the contributing factors to his leg injuries.

Once that was done, she had a full patient load that took up the remainder of her day. She didn't even get a chance to stop for her planned lunch with Jane and Chelsea at Bert's. Instead, she grabbed a protein bar and a glass of juice while she slipped out of one patient room and into another.

"Business is good," Rachel whispered as Emma breezed through the reception area late that afternoon. The waiting area was full, and several customers smiled and waved.

Her heart squeezed.

At the end of the workday she checked on Delbert, washed her hands and blew a stray hair out of her face, then met up with Rachel and Leanne in the back room. "It was good today, that's for sure."

"It'll be good every day, Dr. Emma," Leanne said. "Doc Weston was busy like this all the time, and word's getting around that you're here and you're an awesome doctor. Trust me, you'll be swamped."

She hoped so. She liked being busy. It kept her mind occupied and, she hoped, it would keep her bank account full.

She hung out with Rachel and Leanne for a few minutes, then looked at her phone.

"Crap. I have somewhere I need to be."

"Got a hot date, Doc?" Rachel asked, waggling her brows.

"Um, not really. I'm meeting Luke for a run in the park with the dogs."

"Officer Luke McCormack? That Luke?"

"Yes. That Luke."

Rachel took a big breath in, and let it out. "Now he is definitely hot."

"Agreed," Leanne grinned. "Tell us all about him."

"It's not a date, if that's what you're wondering. We're just friends. And you two can quit giving me that look."

Leanne looked at Rachel. "Look? What look?"

Rachel shrugged. "I have no idea. I think she's seeing things."

Rolling her eyes, Emma hollered for Annie and Daisy. Daisy came running. Annie, of course, didn't, so she had to search her out. She was chewing on one of the clinic towels.

"Annie," she said, shaking her head. She scooped Annie up and slid the pup into the crate.

"Would you two mind locking up?" she asked as she grabbed her purse.

"Not at all," Leanne said, "seeing as you have a hot date with the very sexy cop."

Emma rolled her eyes. "Not a date."

"Sure, Dr. Emma," Rachel said. "Keep on denying."

"Gossips." She headed out the door, then hurried home,

fed the dogs, and ran Annie outside. She changed into her capris and tank and slid on her running shoes. Since the sun was going down and there was a chill in the air, she grabbed a hoodie. Annie gave her a sad look.

"Yeah, you're not trained to run yet, missy, so off to the crate you go."

Annie went willingly into the crate, curled up on her towel and next to her toy, and seemed ready to go back to sleep. Since the puppy had run amok all day at the clinic, Emma knew she'd be ready to crash again. Besides, she was sure she wouldn't be gone more than an hour. Just a quick run with the dogs and she'd be back. Luke probably had other plans after their run.

A hot guy like him had to have women waiting to go out with him, right?

She shivered as she recalled his hands on her, the way his mouth had moved over her skin, the way she had felt when he'd moved inside her.

Yeah, he likely had other plans. With other women.

And didn't that just suck?

Shaking off thoughts she had no business thinking, she put Daisy in her truck and headed over to the lake. One of the things she loved the most about Hope was its nearby proximity to some awesome water. There was a bigger lake for boating in the next town over, but there was a smaller lake and a park in town. She found Luke's truck already parked in the lot when she got there, so she pulled up next to it.

Luke was sitting on one of the cement benches, Boomer calmly waiting beside him.

"Sorry I'm late," she said as Daisy bounded up to Boomer and greeted him with excited sniffs. "It was crazy busy at the clinic and I lost track of time."

"No problem. I haven't been here long. We had an accident up on Third just as I was ready to go off duty. I thought you'd be the one waiting for me."

She finally exhaled. "Sounds like we both had a stressful day."

He gave her a smile that sent skitters of awareness down her spine. "Then let's go run it off."

They warmed up, Luke leaning over the cement picnic table to stretch out his long, lean body. Emma couldn't help but drink in the sight of him in his gray sweats and T-shirt. The sweats hung loose on him, the shirt snugged tight against his muscled chest. His arms had some guns that had nothing to do with the hardware he usually had attached to his hip when he was in uniform. Even dressed casually like this, he took her breath away.

And she was going to need that breath for the run they were about to take.

"Ready?" he asked.

"Let's go." She needed this run to shake off her rampant thoughts about Luke and his hot body and all the things she'd like to do with it. One taste of him hadn't been enough. She was tense. It had been a rough day, and what was a better tension reliever than sex?

But she was absolutely not going to have sex with Luke again. So a run would have to do.

They took off down the trails at a relaxed pace, the dogs staying right with them. That night at her house, she'd been so easy, nearly throwing herself at him. But the sex had been so good, and she'd wanted it as much as he had.

And then she'd thrown him out of her house.

Some hostess she'd been. She was clearly conflicted. It was a wonder he wanted anything to do with her after that night.

But he had shown up at the adoption event at the clinic. And he'd come to her parents' house for dinner. He'd been friendly with her at both events. And he had asked her to run with him today, so maybe things between them were back to normal again.

She was going to have to be more careful. She wasn't practiced around men. She'd had exactly one long-term relationship in her life, a long time ago, and she sure hadn't been in charge of herself in that one. She'd given up complete control of her life, her education, her sense of self . . .

This wasn't helping reduce her tension, and she'd vowed never to think about *him* ever again. It was much better to sink back a little and focus on Luke's fine form as he ran a few feet ahead of her. He was in prime physical shape, his long legs eating up the trail as he jogged with ease. Boomer stayed in perfect stride alongside him. It was easy to see why Luke and his dog were such great partners.

Daisy, of course, did the same, running devotedly right beside her, but Emma's focus was on Luke's very fine ass. So, of course Emma missed the curve in the road and the uneven pavement, her toe got stuck, and she took a very unflattering dive, skidding across the road. She threw her hands out to protect herself, feeling the stinging burn as her skin rubbed along the asphalt.

"Emma. Are you all right?" Luke was right there, crouching down next to her.

So was Daisy, licking her face in sympathy.

"Ow," was all she could manage, trying to blink back the tears as the initial shock wore off and the pain intensified.

"What happened?"

"I tripped over . . . something." She started to push up, but he placed a firm hand on her shoulder.

"Stay there and let me check you over."

"I'm fine, really." Except for her entire body trembling from shock and the *oh my God* excruciating pain.

"You're not fine. You're bleeding." He looked down at her knees, which were raw and bloody.

"That's not . . . too bad."

He lifted his gaze to hers, and she knew as well as he did that, while the fall was definitely not life-threatening, she was a mess. Fortunately, she'd thrown her forearms down and not her hands, so while her jacket was torn up and she could feel some tenderness on her arms, she'd at least saved her hands. She used those at work and she needed them.

"How are your arms?"

"Throbbing. I don't think anything's broken."

"Let me look." He eased her jacket off and checked out both of her arms.

"See, I told you."

"You're right. You have a few scratches and your jacket is toast. You're going to be bruised."

"I've been bruised before. I'm pretty tough."

He swept her hair out of her face. "I'm sure you are, Doc. Now let's stand you up."

He slipped an arm around her and lifted her. Her knees were throbbing, the pain like sharp needles pricking her skin. She bit her lip and focused on taking a few steps.

"Feel okay?"

"I'm fine." It was agonizing.

He helped her walk to the nearest bench, then sat her down. "You stay here with Daisy. Boomer and I are gonna run up and get my truck."

She thought about arguing and toughing it out, but they'd run a fair distance and she didn't much feel like legging it out with her knees hurting so badly. Plus, blood was trickling down her shin. She nodded. "Okay. Thanks."

"I'll be fast. Don't move."

She laughed. "I'm hardly going to run away."

He smiled at her. "You're right. I'll be back in a hurry. Come on, Boom."

She watched as he hustled away at a fast clip. She settled back against the back of the bench and tried to focus on anything but the constant burning and throbbing of her knees.

Stupid. If she hadn't been looking at his butt, this wouldn't have happened. Nothing good ever came out of focusing on a man. Lesson learned—again.

It didn't take long for Luke to come back with his truck. He must have really run fast. He was sweating as he came around from the driver's side to help her stand.

"I'm not dying, you know. You didn't have to kill yourself running."

"It's good exercise." He swept his arm under her legs and lifted her.

"Luke. This isn't necessary."

"Yeah, well, I say it is. So indulge me. Come on, Daisy."

Daisy dutifully followed and climbed into the backseat

of the truck. He set Emma down on the passenger seat and helped put her seat belt on, then climbed in and headed out of the park.

"I don't think you need an ER visit since nothing's broken. You have a good first aid kit at your house?"

"Of course."

"Then we'll go there."

"What about my truck?"

He shot her a look. "I'm not letting you drive all banged up like that. I'll get your truck back to you."

She pursed her lips. "Fine . . . officer."

His lips curved as he headed out onto the main road and toward her place. She might not like it, but he was right. If she was alone, she could have made it, but she was shaky and in no shape to drive, especially if there was someone else to take her home.

He pulled into her driveway and held out his hand. "Can I have your keys?"

She handed him her house keys and he hustled the dogs out first, got them into the house, then came back for her.

"I already got Annie out of her carrier. All the dogs are out back."

"Thanks."

"Now let's get you taken care of."

She hobbled inside and he took her right into her kitchen. "Okay, where's the first aid kit?"

"My bathroom, under the sink. But you don't have to do this, Luke. I'm perfectly capable of performing my own first aid."

He was already heading down the hall toward the bedrooms, ignoring her. He came back a few minutes later with the kit in his hand, then crouched down in front of her. "This is a good refresher course for me. I need some clean cloths you don't mind getting bloody."

"Any of the ones in there." She pointed to the bottom drawer next to the sink and Luke pulled out a couple of clean cloths, ran them under hot water and squeezed out the liquid, then reached into the kit and put on the sterile gloves.

"I have to clean these wounds first. This is going to sting."

She nodded. "This isn't my first rodeo. I can handle it."

She sucked in a breath as he scraped away the bits of gravel and dirt that clung to the wounds. It hurt—really badly. She looked up at the ceiling, over his shoulder, at his shoulder, anything but at the bloody, ragged mess she knew were her knees.

"That looks better."

Emma took a peek. The wounds weren't as dirty now, just clean, raw, and still horrible.

"Yeah, they look great."

He laid his hand on her leg. "You tore them up pretty good."

"Well, I hate to do anything half-assed."

He laughed. "Now this part will really hurt."

"I love your bedside manner. So soothing."

"Hey, you're the one who was looking at the clouds or something and took a knee slide on the asphalt."

"Yeah. Or something." Like his most excellent behind. He lifted his gaze to hers. "What were you looking at?"

"I don't remember. Probably keeping an eye on the dogs."

He smiled at her, that devastating half-smile that curled her toes. For a moment she forgot all about the pain. Until he hit one of her knees with the hydrogen peroxide.

She hissed out a breath. "Shit. That hurts."

"Told you it would." He bent and blew over the wound, the gentle warmth not at all softening the blow of the peroxide. But the way he held her leg so gently—his fingers flexing around her calf as he finished cleaning out the wound—and applied antibiotic ointment was so incongruous with his big, tough exterior, it momentarily surprised her. And then he did the other knee, which hurt just as bad, but the aftermath was just as sweet.

The last man in her life hadn't been gentle with her, hadn't cared for her when she'd been hurt. She'd been left to take care of her own wounds. After all, it had been her own fault when she'd gotten injured. He'd made her apologize.

She shook her head, shaking loose thoughts of the past. "Everything going okay up there?"

She gazed down at Luke. "You're very good at this first aid thing."

"Thanks. Coming from a doctor, I take that as a high compliment."

She laughed. "My patients very rarely voice a complaint."

He leaned back on his heels. "Oh, but I'll bet you can tell when they're in pain."

"I can. I don't like it when they hurt. I don't like it when anyone is hurt."

He was gentle as he applied the bandage to her other knee. "I think you're a softy, Emma."

"I can be when it's called for. I think you're a bit of a softy, too, Luke."

He pressed a kiss to both of her bandaged knees. "I don't like to see anyone hurt."

She let her eyes drift closed for a fraction of a second. He was so different from any guy she'd ever let get close to her. When she opened her eyes, he was eye level with her.

"Are you all right?"

She shuddered as she inhaled. "Yup. Just fine."

He held out his hand. "Let's stand you up before you start to get stiff."

She grasped his hand, and he pulled her upright. Her knees hurt like hell, and she was going to be sore for days, but it could have been a lot worse. He walked her over to the kitchen sink, where they washed off her arms. Those weren't as bad because she'd been wearing her jacket. A few slight scrapes, and she wouldn't even need a bandage. Luke cleaned the wounds out and applied some antibacterial salve.

"You're kind of a mess," he said.

"That's kind of an understatement."

"How about I order us a pizza, and you go change out of those clothes and get into your pajamas?"

"You don't have to stay."

"I know I don't have to. I want to. Besides, I'm hungry."

Warmth curled around her. "Me, too."

She hobbled into the bedroom and took a look at herself in the mirror. Ugh. Her hair had half come out of her ponytail, and dirt smudged her face. She looked a wreck. She washed her face, combed her hair and pulled her shirt off, then sat on the bed and tried to peel off the tight workout capris, with very little luck because the bandages were in the way. She needed an extra set of hands to hold the elastic up while she moved her legs.

And it hurt.

"Crap."

"Emma?"

Her gaze shot up to the closed bedroom door. "Yeah?"

"You doing all right in there?"

She was in her bra and her capris. "Uh. Not really."

"Can I help?"

She'd already embarrassed herself enough for one night. But she really wanted to get out of these pants. Heaving a sigh, she said, "Come on in."

He opened the door, and to his credit, didn't ogle. His expression remained flat. "What can I do to help?"

"Get me out of these pants?"

Now he smiled. "It's every guy's dream to hear a woman say that, you know."

She laughed. "Yeah, well, not in the way you think. They're really tight and the bandages are in the way. I need more hands than what I have. I guess we should have taken the pants off first."

"Probably. But that would have rubbed the wounds. We could have cut them off of you."

"Hey. I like these workout pants."

"Then let's peel them off. That's the problem with you women wearing this tight workout gear. You should wear sweats, like me."

She rolled her eyes at him. "Whatever, fashionista."

"Okay, tell me what you need me to do."

"I'll roll them down. Just pull the bottoms apart enough that I can slide my legs out."

"Sure."

Now that he was there, she realized she'd have to shimmy out of the pants and shuck them off until they hung at her knees. But she wanted them off, and that was her first priority. Embarrassment wasn't going to be an issue, at least not until she got the pants off. She slid them down over her hips, hoping her underwear would stay in place.

And hey, at least she had underwear on.

"I'll stretch these enough for you to ease your legs out, okay?"

He was doing a really good job of just looking at her legs. "Yes."

She eased one leg out, then the other, then breathed a sigh of relief when he handed her the pants.

"That's done."

"Thanks, Luke."

"You're welcome." He grinned. "Always happy to see a hot woman in her underwear. It's like a bonus."

She laughed. "Get out of here."

He turned and shut the door behind him while she went up in flames.

She was a wreck. Bandaged, bloody, and dirty, and he still thought she was hot, huh? She was sure he was just being nice, considering both her knees were swollen and bandaged, and she had cuts and bruises all over. But as she hobbled back into the bathroom, she took a close look at her pink-and-beige lace panties. The pink sports bra wasn't all that unattractive, either. She was glad she had worn them because other than the bumps, bruises, scrapes, and totally wild hair, she didn't look too bad.

Not that she was trying to impress Luke with her half-naked body.

But still. Not too bad.

THAT HAD BEEN absolute torture. It had been bad enough when Emma had shown up in those skintight running pants that cupped her ass and showed off every one of her curves.

Curves he could still remember running his hands over not that long ago.

Luke had been glad she'd hung back and run behind him, because if he'd let her get ahead of him and he'd had to watch her while he ran, all the blood would have rushed from his brain to his dick, and he more than likely would have passed out or something.

And then he'd had to walk in on her half-undressed in her bedroom and fulfill her request to take her pants off, leaving her in that practically see-through underwear?

A guy could only take so much. He knew she was hurt and in pain, but his dick only saw soft, creamy flesh and a beautifully curved body, instead of a vulnerable woman in need of tender care. Everything in him that was a man wanted to take her in his arms and kiss away her hurt, then use his tongue on every part of her until she screamed in pleasure.

He'd already gotten her there once, knew what she was like when she came apart. He wanted to ease her pain, and what better way to do that than to give her pleasure?

Shit. And now he was staying for pizza. He must be some kind of glutton for punishment.

"That's better."

She came out limping, but dressed in loose sweatpants and a T-shirt.

And she still looked hot. Christ, he had it bad. It was time to suck it up and take it like a man. One fast pizza, tuck her in bed, and then he was outta there.

"I ordered the pizza. Come sit down."

She made her way to the sofa, which had reclining seats. He got her situated, pulled one of the throw blankets off the back, and propped her legs up to rest them.

"Comfortable?" he asked as he leaned over her to tuck the blanket in next to her hips, trying not to think about the soft curve of said hips he'd seen when she'd been wearing nothing but her underwear.

"If my knees weren't throbbing, I might fall asleep before the pizza got here."

"I'll make you something to drink and get you a couple Tylenol. Where do you keep them?"

"Kitchen cabinet next to the sink. And you don't need to do that."

"It's no problem, Emma. You need someone to take care of you tonight."

He went into the kitchen and poured her a soda, grabbed the pills, and drew in a couple of long breaths, reminding himself that he was there on a mercy mission. But damn, did she have to look so sexy with her hair spread out across the back of the sofa, her cheeks soft and pink, and her eyes so trusting?

If she only knew the nefarious thoughts going through his head, she'd toss him out on his ass.

He came back out with the drink and the Tylenol. "I also fixed some ice packs for your knees. It'll help to keep the swelling down."

She took the pills and swallowed them with her drink, then set the glass on the side table. "You think of everything. If you hadn't been here, I'd have driven myself home and likely crawled right into bed to drown my sorrows."

He pulled the blanket aside and gently laid the ice packs on top of her knees. "I don't know. Even though you're a vet, you're still a doctor. I think you know the importance of taking care of injuries right away."

"Maybe. Right now I just feel like a stupid girl."

He laughed. "You're not the first person to trip and fall, you know."

Her direct gaze gut-punched him. "I realize that. I still feel like a moron."

He replaced the blanket, then leaned over and got close. "Prettiest moron I've ever seen."

Her gaze caught and held his. He waited, knowing this was a really bad idea, but Emma did something to him. Maybe he was offering comfort, and maybe what he was doing was purely for his own selfish reasons.

Either way, she didn't look scared, or pissed off.

Just . . . curious. Maybe even a little inviting.

He drew in closer.

And then the doorbell rang.

Like a pin in a balloon, the moment burst. Emma blinked, then offered up a shaky breath.

"Pizza guy."

"Yeah." He pushed up and went to the front door, mentally cussing out the pizza guy for having really shitty timing.

They ate, though Emma only nibbled on a couple of pieces. It was obvious her accident was wearing on her as her lids started to droop down.

"You need to go to bed."

"I'm fine."

"You're tired, and rest is the best thing for you. Do you have to work tomorrow?"

She laughed. "When you're the single owner of a business, it's not like someone else can go in for you."

"Come on." He pushed the recliner to a sitting position and helped her stand.

She winced. He looped an arm around her waist and led her toward her bedroom.

"You're going to be sore tomorrow."

"I know. I'll make it."

"You could always reschedule your appointments and take the day off."

"I don't think so. People are counting on me, and I have a reputation I'm trying to build. I'll tough it out."

He pulled back her covers, and she climbed into bed. He grabbed her extra pillow so she could slide it under her legs, propping up her knees. When he pulled the blanket up, he laid his hand over hers and her gaze met his.

"Would you like me to stay here tonight? Make sure you're okay?"

"No. I'm fine, Luke, really. You've done more than enough already. But I appreciate it, more than you know."

"Okay." On impulse, he bent and brushed a kiss across her lips.

He pulled back, searched her face, her chocolate brown

eyes melting him, making him want to do a hell of a lot more than just kiss her.

And the way she looked up at him was an invitation.

But she was hurt, and vulnerable, and tonight was hands-off, no matter how much her eyes said yes.

He stood. "I'm going to go get your car so you'll have it for work tomorrow. I'll lock the front door on my way out."

She reached for his hand, her eyes partially closed. "Thank you, Luke. You're my hero."

He was nobody's hero. Especially not hers. Not with the kinds of thoughts he was having about her right now.

"Night, Emma."

Chapter 11

THE PAST FEW days had been brutal. Emma had come home, fed the dogs, and fallen into bed in a pained, exhausted stupor.

Her knees had finally started to form scabs, but they still ached, and being on her feet all day hadn't helped any, though it was probably good for her to keep moving. It was just at night when she got home and finally sat down that the stiffness settled in. And since she was sore and tender, she'd been missing her regular workouts, which made her tired and grumpy.

At least she hadn't had trouble sleeping. She was going to bed early and getting plenty of sleep, making it easy to get up in the morning.

Luke had called her the day after the accident to check on her. She'd been busy and hadn't had much time, but enough to thank him again for taking such good care of her and to tell him she was doing fine.

She didn't know what to make of him, so unused to a man who would look out for her the way he had.

Maybe most men were like that, and she'd just drawn the

short end of the stick on her first long-term relationship, making her reluctant to ever enter another. Perhaps she was missing out. Reluctant to talk about men and relationships with friends or, God forbid, her mother, who would either push her toward Luke or worry incessantly about her because of what she'd been through with Vaughn, she had no idea what a normal man/woman relationship was like. Was Luke a typical guy, or was he an anomaly?

She decided she might broach the topic at her girls' night out with Jane and Chelsea. They decided to forgo their typical dinner at Bert's and, at Chelsea's suggestion, were trying out one of the new all-you-can-eat buffets that had recently opened.

"I don't know," Jane said, as they pushed their trays around the different stations. "I had kind of set my mind on Bert's biscuits and gravy tonight."

Chelsea rolled her eyes and hip-checked Jane. "I don't know how the hell you stay so thin, given your atrocious diet."

"That's easy," Jane said with a smug smile. "Two kids, one in sports, one in dance, and a very active sex life."

"You suck, and you're only saying that because you know I currently have no sex life."

"And whose fault is that?" Emma asked as they reached their table and set down their trays. "Chelsea, you're gorgeous. I'd kill for red hair like yours. And your body? Please. I mean, I know I'm a heterosexual female, but geez. You're built."

Chelsea laughed. "Well, thanks. But it's like men are afraid of me. It's not like I'm throwing out don't-approach-me signals. I'm very, very available, if you know what I mean."

Jane picked up a carrot. "So you're saying you're advertising your wares like a slut, but no one's buying?"

Emma nearly choked on her iced tea. "Jane. I don't think that's what she meant at all."

But Chelsea just laughed. "Well, yeah, kind of like that. I mean, it's been a very long dry spell. Men just don't notice me." She shrugged.

Emma shook her head. "Men are blind sometimes. Or stupid."

"Definitely stupid if they aren't noticing you, Chelse."

"Y'all are good for my ego. We should go out more often."

"I would, but it might interfere with all that sex I'm having."

Chelsea narrowed her gaze at Jane. "I don't remember you being such a bitch. Why are we friends again?"

Emma laughed. Being with Jane and Chelsea was good for her. They made her laugh.

"Have you heard from Molly lately?" Jane asked her.

Emma nodded. "I talked to her yesterday."

"Still in . . . where is she now?"

"She's still in Little Rock. It hasn't been that long. She's usually good for about three to six months before she has to take off."

"How long has it been since she's been home?" Chelsea asked, using her chopsticks to slide noodles between her lips.

Emma blew out a breath. "I can't remember. Too long."

"Why does she stay away? Or is that too personal a question?"

"She has a hundred reasons. Or excuses. She left kind of abruptly after high school graduation, bailed on her college of choice, even though she had a scholarship. And she's never come back."

"I assume you've asked her why." Chelsea slid a wonton into the lively sweet red dipping sauce.

"I've repeatedly asked her why. She just says she changed her mind and decided she wanted an adventure instead of school. Which is fine, I mean people change their minds about education all the time. But never coming home? She's never produced what I consider a good reason. She always tells me that home is wherever she lands, and if she came back to Hope that might signal the end of her adventures, so she's afraid to do that. But I don't think that's it. I think there's a bad memory here."

"Something bad happened to her here?" Chelsea frowned.

Emma shrugged. "Not that I'm aware of. Or not that she ever told me, but Molly has always carried her emotions within. She wasn't one to share. For all I know, she got fired from a job and that scarred her enough to never want to come back."

Jane gave her a look of disbelief. "Oh, come on. That wouldn't keep her from coming home. Did she have a guy?"

Emma nodded. "Carter Richards. Molly and Carter were inseparable from the time they were kids. God, since they were twelve up until high school graduation. Until Molly left town."

"So they broke up when she left?"

"I guess. I was away at school during those last couple years, so I don't really know what went down with the two of them. As far as I knew, they were still together, still madly in love. They had planned to go to the same college. Carter went to college, but Molly didn't."

"So maybe it was something with the two of them. Some bad breakup," Jane suggested.

"I asked her about it, but she said her relationship with Carter had run its course, and he had nothing to do with her leaving town."

"Do you believe her?" Chelsea asked.

Emma shrugged. "With Molly, I don't know what to believe."

"What about seeing your mom and dad?" Jane asked. "Ten years is a long time to be away from home."

"They fly out to wherever she happens to live and visit her a couple times a year. And always try to convince her to come home. Or at least they used to. I think over the years they've stopped trying."

"That's just so odd," Chelsea said.

Emma scooped rice onto her fork. "Tell me about it."

Explaining her younger sister to people had never been an easy thing. She wished she and Molly had been tighter, that Molly felt comfortable enough to confide in her. When they were younger, they were so close, would tell each other everything. After Emma went away to college, she lost touch with Molly, which was Emma's fault. She'd gotten wrapped up in school.

In Vaughn. And he'd taken away everything, including her relationship with her sister. And with that distance, Molly stopped confiding in her.

She'd lost so much because of him. Because of her weaknesses. Which was why she was such a bad judge of relationships.

Of men.

She pushed her plate to the side.

"How are your knees, Emma?" Jane asked.

Happy to not talk about her sister anymore, or dwell on the past, she smiled and said, "Healing. Better. Thanks."

"Good thing you had the hot cop there to help you. Was he your knight in shining armor?" Chelsea teased.

"Actually, he was more than that. He drove me home, bandaged me up, and settled me on the sofa. Then he ordered pizza, and when I got tired, he tucked me into bed and left."

Chelsea arched a brow. "I'm surprised he didn't offer to sleep there."

Emma took a sip of her tea. "Actually, he did. On the couch, in case I needed anything."

"Aww, that was so sweet of him," Jane said.

"It was. Just so very nice of him." She stared down at her tea, wanting to ask the question but not wanting to appear naïve.

"Will's like that, too. He always does things that surprise me."

She lifted her gaze. "Does he? Like what?"

"Well, for example, the other day I got stuck with monitoring detention at school, so he picked up the kids and dropped Ryan off at baseball practice, then got Tabby ready for dance. Can you imagine Will doing Tabby's hair? But he did, and she looked adorable. He stayed through dance class, then picked up Ryan, and had dinner on the table when I came home."

Chelsea leaned back in the booth. "He's a regular Prince Charming, isn't he? Wherever did you find him?"

"At the gym," Jane said with a serene smile. "And you dated him. You know what he's like."

"I do know what he's like. But I didn't have kids, and he and I are better as friends. And hey, I go to the gym. Trust me, there aren't guys like him there."

"So you're saying men like Will—and I guess Luke. That's not typical guy behavior?"

Chelsea snorted at Emma's question. "Uh, no. Not all men are nice guys."

No one knew that better than Emma.

Jane squeezed her hand. "Hang on to Luke, Emma. Trust me when I tell you that great guys aren't a dime a dozen. When you find a good one, you don't want to let him go."

She had a lot of thinking to do.

Chapter 12

_____

IT HAD BEEN a few days since Luke had seen Emma. He'd pulled a couple of double shifts, and he wanted to give her some time to recover. On his breaks, he'd texted her a few times to check on her knees, and she'd texted him back that she was doing fine and healing up fast. He'd been relieved to hear that. He wished he'd had time to stop by and check on her, but damn work had gotten in his way.

Plus, he'd made that whole mental promise to himself that he wouldn't see her again. She was too hard on his—well, his everything. His libido, for one thing. He knew she wasn't looking for a relationship, and he sure as hell wasn't.

The problem was, he kept thinking about her. About that night they'd spent together. He wanted to be with her again. Which was a clear sign that he shouldn't see her again. Another night together could only spell trouble.

Since this was his day off, he decided to spend it working on his truck, which needed way more maintenance than his screwed-up love life. After a punishing workout at the gym in the morning, he went home, took a shower, and headed to his friend Carter Richards's flagship auto-repair shop, the first of the many he'd opened in his growing chain.

He didn't expect to see Carter coming out of his office as he entered the shop.

"Surprised to see you here. I thought you'd be at one of your other shops in Tulsa."

Carter gave him a grin. "I had some . . . personnel issues to deal with here today."

"Fired someone, huh?"

"Yeah. And now I want some coffee. You up for it, or do you need to leave?"

"I have time. I was dropping the truck off for some diagnostic work anyway."

"Good. I have a craving for cinnamon rolls from Bert's."

"Let's go. You'll have to drive."

They pushed through the front door, and Carter led him to his car.

Luke arched a brow, then trailed his fingers down the clean edges of the classic '67 Mustang Shelby. "Really?"

"Hey, I've always wanted one. Now I can afford it."

Luke shook his head and climbed into the car. It smelled as sweet as it looked, and Luke was envious. "You've done well."

"Thanks. I'm having fun with the car. Beats having a wife."

"Ouch."

"Hey, at least you got smart and got rid of her."

Luke buckled his seat belt. "If you remember, she dumped me."

"She was a social-climbing bitch. That's all I remember about Becca."

Luke laughed, but then Carter turned the key and the Shelby rumbled to life.

"This one talks back," Luke said.

Carter grinned. "No, she doesn't. She purrs, like every woman should."

Luke shook his head, but couldn't help admiring the lines

of the Shelby. What he wouldn't give to own something like this. On a cop's salary, though, it wasn't likely to happen.

"You could have one," Carter said, as if he'd just read Luke's mind.

"Not a chance."

"Just buy a junker and restore it. I worked a lot of weekends on this one. She wasn't perfect when I got her, but she's an original, and she's beautiful."

He swept his hand across the sleek leather seats. "Maybe. Someday."

"What else do you have to do on your off days?"

What else, indeed?

Carter parked in front of Bert's, and they went inside and grabbed a seat. Luke ordered coffee and, with not more than a second's hesitation, one of those cinnamon rolls that Carter was craving.

It didn't take them long to dive into the food, which they did pretty quietly. Even though Luke had already eaten breakfast, there was no use denying himself a roll. Freshly baked, thick, and slathered with icing. When he was full, he pushed the evidence of his gluttony to the side.

"It's going to cost me a lot of running time to burn those calories."

"Worth it, though," Carter said, taking a sip of coffee.

"Yeah, you're right. So who was the guy you had to fire?"

"One of the dudes in the body shop. His skills just weren't up to par."

"Bodywork is important. You can't afford to keep someone on who isn't good."

"Tell me about it. I've gone through three guys in the body shop here in Hope in the past year. I don't know why I can't get a good body guy."

"Maybe you can fill in until you find someone," Luke teased.

"Yeah, you're a laugh riot."

"As I recall, it used to be your specialty. That and rebuilding engines."

"Sure, in high school. Now I have enough to do just running the stores."

"You don't miss getting your hands dirty under the hood of a car?"

Carter grinned. "Who says I don't get my hands dirty anymore?"

"That manicure and the lack of grease under your nails."

"Manicure my ass. You're such a dick, McCormack. I could strip down an engine before you've even dragged your lazy ass out of bed in the morning."

Unfazed, Luke sipped his coffee. "So you say, rich boy. But I still say your hands are too clean to be doing the grunt work."

Carter signaled for the waitress, who presented him with the check. "Let's go take a look at your truck."

Two hours later, Luke and Carter were filthy, staring under the hood of Luke's truck.

"It's a fuel injector problem," Carter explained. "They all seem to be injecting fuel, but not firing properly on all cylinders. I think a couple of them are clogged. You're getting fuel to all your cylinders, but the number three and number five are running lean, like they're not getting as much fuel as the rest of them."

Carter's formerly white shirt was now covered in grease, and he seemed unconcerned about it. He grabbed a rag and wiped his hands.

Luke nodded. "I thought that might be the issue, but I didn't have the diagnostics at home."

"It doesn't appear to be a problem with getting fire to the injector. The injector is either getting clogged up, or it's just plain toast. We'll run some cleaner through it and see if that takes care of it, but I seriously doubt it will. My suggestion is to replace these. That should solve your problem."

"Sounds good. Try the cleaner, but if that doesn't work, replace them."

Carter signaled for one of his mechanics, stating instructions. The guy nodded and walked away.

"Satisfied now that I know what the hell I'm doing?" Carter asked as they both headed to the sink.

"Hell, you always knew what you were doing. I just enjoy giving you shit."

Carter cocked a grin. "It was fun getting into an engine again. Thanks."

"My pleasure. Do I get a discount since I helped with the diagnostics?"

"No. You have to pay extra because the diagnostics came from the owner."

"Now who's the dick?"

Carter laughed. They headed up to his office to get a soda. Luke sat in the chair and crossed his feet at the ankle.

"So now that you know how I spend my days, tell me about your job. How's the cop business?"

Luke shrugged. "Keeping me busy enough that I'm not bored."

"Good enough. Hope's not really a high-crime kind of town. You still crave the excitement of a big-city police force?"

"Kind of. But I like protecting my hometown. So I'm torn."

"Understood. How's the love life?"

Luke snorted. "Don't have one. And I like it that way."

"Word on the street is that you're seeing Emma Burnett."

"I'd like to know where this 'word on the street' shit is coming from."

Carter smiled. "Oh, you know how it is in a small town. I get my tidbits of gossip here and there. And how is Emma?"

"Gorgeous. Hot. Skittish."

"Not exactly your type. You much prefer them sexy, available, and not interested in commitment."

"Well, she is sexy."

"One out of three isn't very good odds."

The one annoying thing about Carter was his persistence, no matter the topic. "I'm also not dating her."

"But you want to."

"I don't *want* to date anyone. We're friends."

Carter snorted. "Luke, you're not friends with any woman."

"That's not true. I'm friends with a lot of women."

"Sure you are. After you screw their brains out, they stay friendly with you. Not sure how you manage that, but you do. So is that the way it is with you and Emma? You got her into bed, and now you two are . . . friends?"

"No."

"No, to which part? The getting-her-into-bed, or the you-two-are-friends part?"

Luke didn't answer the question.

"Huh. Interesting."

"You've got this all wrong. We really are friends. It's just . . . complicated."

"Definitely not your kind of woman. Or . . . exactly the kind of woman you need."

"This coming from a man who hasn't had a serious relationship since Emma's little sister Molly in high school."

A shadow crossed Carter's face. "That was a long time ago. Molly and I were kids."

"And I still remember how broken up you were when Molly left. You cared about her."

"As much as an eighteen-year-old boy could care about someone. I told you. We were kids. It was young love. And it was over a long time ago."

There was something in his voice, in the way Carter didn't make direct eye contact with him that told Luke it had been way more than just young love between him and Molly. As a cop, Luke knew how to read body language. And when someone couldn't look you in the eye when they were talking, that usually meant they were lying. Maybe Carter was still mixed-up over how he felt when Molly had run off. They might have been young, but it didn't make it hurt any less. And maybe time didn't heal everything.

Luke and Carter went way back to elementary school. They'd shared a lot of secrets and had been through a lot of shit together. They'd always been honest with each other, but if there were truths being withheld, how Luke felt about Emma was probably one of them.

Hell, even he didn't know what was going on in his own head about Emma. How could he explain it to his best friend?

Luke stood. "I'm going to head out and let you get some work done."

"Do you need a ride somewhere?"

"Nah. I need to walk off that cinnamon roll. I'll hang around town for a bit and run some errands."

Carter nodded. "We'll give you a call when your truck is ready."

He shook Carter's hand. "Thanks for figuring out the problem."

Carter grinned as they walked to the front door. "My mechanics could have done that. They're good at their jobs."

"Yeah, it's just your bodywork guys who suck."

"Smart-ass. I'll talk to you later."

It wasn't often that Luke had a chance to take a stroll around Hope's main part of town. And he really did need to walk off all the calories he and Carter had taken in at Bert's. The police station was two blocks away, so he made his way over there and stopped in to see what was going on. The captain on duty gave him a hard time for coming in on his day off. He laughed, but visited for about a half hour, then took off.

Emma's clinic was another block down the highway. He decided to stop by, surprised when he saw Logan's truck in the parking lot.

He went inside. Rachel spotted him as soon as he walked through the door.

"Officer Luke. How are you doing?"

"Fine, Rachel. How about you?"

"Great. You don't have Boomer with you."

"Off duty today. I was in town doing a few things, so I thought I'd come by. I see my brother is here."

"He is. With Whip. The poor dog got some wire stuck in him, so Dr. Emma's taking it out. You can go on back. They're in room three."

"Okay, thanks."

He headed left and down the hall, knocked on the door, and opened it. Logan was sitting in there alone.

"What are you doing here?" Logan asked.

"I saw your truck when I was walking by."

Logan arched a brow. "Walking?"

"My truck has fuel-injector issues, so it's over at Carter's garage."

"That sucks."

Luke stepped in and closed the door. "Rachel said Whip got snagged in some wire?"

"Yeah," Logan said. "We were replacing some fence on the south property, and Whip had come along. While we were puttin' up the new row, he got tangled in the old fence we'd taken down. I tried to get him untangled, but he got scared and fought me. Some of the discarded pieces got wedged too deep in his skin for me to pull out, so I brought him in here for the doc to take care of him."

"And how's that going?"

"Fine, I guess. Doc has Whip in the surgery room now. She said it's not too bad. He ground some loose pieces fairly deep, but they needed to anesthetize him because he wasn't too damn happy about having that wire pulled out."

"I imagine he wasn't."

Luke took a seat on the bench next to Logan.

"So . . . fuel injectors, huh?"

"Yeah." He told Logan about his morning with Carter.

Logan laughed. "Got him to get his hands dirty, anyway. That was a win."

"True. I don't imagine Carter has much opportunity to work on cars like he used to."

"No, now that he's busy owning all those shops, he has to take care of business. I'll bet he enjoyed getting under the hood today."

"Speaking of taking care of business, how come you brought Whip out here yourself? You could have sent one of the hands or had Martha bring him."

"What? And miss checking out Dr. Emma, the woman who has your balls in a knot?"

Luke rolled his eyes. "She's not doing anything to my balls."

"Yeah, that's why they're in a knot."

Logan laughed at his own joke. Luke didn't find it amusing.

Fortunately, Emma walked in then, sparing him from more of Logan's awful humor. She looked pretty today with her hair pulled back in a ponytail and her blue scrubs on.

Her brows rose when she saw Luke.

"Oh. Hi, Luke. I didn't know you were here."

"I saw Logan's truck, so I wandered in to see what was up."

"I see. Day off?"

"Yup."

She gave him a sweet smile. "How nice for you."

She turned her attention back to Logan. "Whip's fine. All the wire is out. He has a few spots that needed stitches, so you'll have to watch those. I assume you can take those out yourself."

"Not a problem, Doc."

"All right. I'm going to send you home with some antibiotics and pain meds, though I doubt he'll need the pain medication, but just in case. Keep him quiet for a couple days and keep the stitched areas clean."

Logan stood. "I know the drill, Doc. Thanks."

"No problem. He's a really cute dog."

"Yeah, we kind of like him. So do the other dogs."

She walked out with him to the reception area. "Do you have a veterinarian for your other dogs? Are they all up on their shots? Have they had a checkup recently?"

Luke loved the way Emma was concerned about Logan's dogs. From the smirk on his face, so was his brother.

"Dr. Burnett, are you hitting me up to become one of your clients?"

She gave him a grin. "Well, to be honest, I was concerned

about your animals. But, yes, I'd love your business. I realize we're not close to your ranch."

"You're close enough. And I like the way you treated Whip. I'll have Martha, our housekeeper and general keeper of the animals, bring the others by next week for a checkup."

Luke crossed his arms. "Won't Martha love that?"

Logan gave him a look. "Not so much."

Logan turned to Emma. "I think it's been a year or two since they had shots. I don't know where the hell their records are. We have six ranch dogs."

Emma's brows raised. "Six? Maybe it would be easier if I came out to the ranch and took care of things?"

"That would be great." Logan turned to Luke. "Why don't you have Luke bring you out on Sunday? Martha makes a great pot roast on Sundays. You can eat with us."

"Oh, that's not necessary. I can always come by after work one night."

"No reason for you to make one of your long days even longer. Come hang out with us. You can see the horses and the cattle, get a tour of the place, and see where Luke grew up."

Emma looked at Luke. "Now that might be fun. I'd love to. Thank you for the invitation."

"No problem."

Leanne brought out an awake but slow-moving Whip. "Here's your boy."

Logan took the leash. "Hey, fella. Have a good nap?"

Whip leaned groggily against Logan's side.

Emma gave the chart to Rachel. "Well, it's back to work for me, guys. Nice seeing you, Luke. I guess you'll call me about Sunday?"

"I guess I will." He gave Emma a smile. She blushed and said good-bye to Logan.

"You set that up," Luke said to Logan after Emma disappeared.

"Set what up?" Logan asked as he took out his checkbook to pay the bill.

"Me and Emma coming to the ranch on Sunday."

"Believe it or not, Luke, everything isn't about you. I thought maybe you'd want to show Emma the ranch, and this way, Martha doesn't have to drag all the dogs in here, which you know she'd grumble about. It works out good for me, Martha loves having company—and she loves to see you, because you don't come for Sunday dinner all that often. See what a great plan that is?" He slapped his brother on the back.

"I guess." Though Luke was still convinced Logan had manipulated him.

Logan tucked the checkbook in his pocket and grasped the leash. "See you Sunday, brother."

"Yeah. Sunday."

Logan walked out, leaving Luke leaning against the front counter.

"So, you and Dr. Emma have a date at the ranch on Sunday, huh?" Rachel asked.

"Not a date. I'm just bringing her to the ranch so she can treat my brother's dogs."

"Sure you are," Rachel said, busying herself at the computer. While smiling.

Shit.

Chapter 13

AS THEY PULLED through the massive and oh-so-impressive scrolled gates of the L&M Ranch, Emma shifted in her seat to face Luke.

He'd been mostly silent on the way over there, and Emma was certain he was bringing her reluctantly. His brother had kind of wrangled him into accompanying her, and really, she could have come on her own. Still, he had agreed, when he could have said no. So, did he want to come with her, or was he just being a gentleman?

She had no idea. His expression gave away nothing, so Emma focused her attention on the massive sprawl of land in front of them.

"You grew up here?"

"Yeah."

She all but plastered her nose to the window, miles of tall, honey-colored grass waving in the wind as they drove down the gravel road.

"All of this is yours."

"Mine and Logan's and our younger brother, Reid's, yes."

She tore her gaze away from the majestic panorama of trees and scrub and you-can-see-forever to look at him. "This is amazing."

His lips finally curved. "You think so?"

"Yes. Oh my God, Luke. I had no idea you owned this much land. Oh my God again, look at the horses." She rolled her windows down as they approached the property.

"You're kind of cracking me up here, Emma."

"Shut up. I'm a city girl."

They pulled up to the house. Excited, Emma punched the button on her seat belt and climbed out of the truck. Their dogs scampered out and were greeted by a pack of barking dogs of all shapes and sizes, Whip being one of them. Emma crouched down to meet and pet them all.

"Hey, Whip, how are you doing?" She smoothed her hands over his sides. He was healing up just fine, despite his exuberance. She knew he wouldn't be lying calmly on a bed of pillows in the house. Ranch dogs rarely sat still for a minute.

Logan had quite a pack of dogs. There was Whip, the border collie, an Australian shepherd mix, a beagle, a Labrador mix, a terrier mix, and a pit bull like Annie. And they were all friendly to Daisy and Annie. Boomer joined the fray, too. It was one enormous dog party.

"You're walking better," Luke said.

She lifted her gaze to his. "I've been sleeping a lot. Apparently falling down makes me sleepy."

"It was a rough injury."

"I'm feeling a lot better now, though. Thank you for asking. And again, thanks for that night."

"You're welcome. I'm sorry you got hurt."

She shrugged. "It was my own fault for not looking where I was going. I should know better. I'll be a lot more careful in the future."

"I'm just glad you weren't hurt worse. Are your knees healed?"

"Yes. Scabs and everything."

He laughed. "Scabs are good."

"I'm sorry. Probably not what you want to talk about."

"I'm not squeamish about scabs, Doc. You can't scare me away."

She studied him. "Apparently not. You're tougher than most men."

"I'd like to think so, but you can feel free to put me to the test if you'd like."

He was teasing her. And she blushed, so aware of him all the time it was embarrassing.

"I don't think that'll be necessary. I believe you."

Logan came outside.

"Hey, Doc. Glad you could make it."

She smiled at Logan. "Thanks again for inviting me."

"Logan," Luke said with a nod.

"Luke."

She watched the interplay between the brothers. They didn't hug, but both of them offered up curved lips. It was as if there was a secret language between them, where nothing needed to be said. She caught the sparkle in both their eyes.

Brothers. She and Molly used to be that way, too, where one look said it all. Her stomach tightened as she realized how much she missed her sister.

"You have a great pack of dogs, Logan," she said.

"Thanks. We couldn't run the ranch without them. Or at least they think so."

She laughed. "All dogs like to think they're important." She bent to pet Annie.

Luke's lips curved again. "Come on inside. The dogs will be fine out here."

"I'll be out by the truck," Logan said. "Go on in and make yourself at home. Luke, give Emma a tour of the place. Martha's in the kitchen."

She followed Luke up the steps of what was a beautiful two-story house, painted white with blue shutters. Pots with a myriad of colorful flowers hung on the porch, their blooms spilling over. She loved the rocking chairs and the porch swing and could already imagine sipping tea at sunset on that swing.

How could Luke ever leave something so idyllic?

Because it obviously hadn't been his idea of idyllic.

She stepped inside to polished wood floors and the smell of something amazing coming from the kitchen.

She turned to Luke. "Will you show me the house?"

"Sure. Downstairs is the kitchen and dining room. There's a living room off to the right . . ."

He led the way and she followed, in awe of the rustic charm of the place, the utter beauty of the natural wood floors, and oh, the pictures on the walls made her heart ache. Generations of family members must have been in these photos.

"Are these your . . . grandparents?" she asked as they paused in the hallway.

"Yeah. And that's my dad, with Logan, when he was little."

She grinned at the photo of Logan as a small boy of no more than five or six years old sitting astride a horse. The man holding on to him was tall and rugged, with dark hair and a very stern-looking face. "Your dad was very handsome."

"He was a hardworking man. He loved this ranch."

The one photo that caught her eye was in the living room—three young boys, so adorable, sitting outside on the front porch steps. One with his hair cut very short, wearing a Western shirt. That had to be Logan looking all mature and serious. Luke, the middle one, with a happy smile on his face, his hair a little longer and shaggy. And then the baby, Reid, freckles spread across his nose with gaps in his front teeth.

"How old were all of you in this photo?" she asked.

Luke studied the photo. "Logan was thirteen, I was eleven, and Reid was eight. And if I recall correctly, none of us wanted to sit still long enough for that photo to be taken."

She laughed. "I can imagine that. You were all probably like tornadoes. Hard to settle down."

"Yeah. Something like that."

He took her up the stairs. "Bedrooms up here. Four of

them. Mine was here." He opened the door, and there was a double bed with a quilt, a maple dresser with a mirror, and a beautiful window overlooking the land. She walked in and headed toward the window.

"I'll bet you did a lot of daydreaming while sitting on your bed looking out the window."

"I might have done some. Also threw some plastic military guys out that window when I played Army men with Logan and Reid. My army guys were always doing secret night missions, jumping out of airplanes."

"Which just happened to be your window."

"Of course. Got yelled at a few times for doing it, but hey, an Army guy's gotta do what an Army guy's gotta do."

"Of course. I always got in trouble for cutting my Barbie doll's hair. Parents. They just don't get it."

He grinned and showed her the rest of the bedrooms, all similar to Luke's, except the master, which was larger and had its own bathroom. Then they went back downstairs and headed into the kitchen.

"You must be Dr. Emma. I've heard so much about you. Welcome to our home." A tall, thin woman with short dark-brown hair swiped her hands on her apron. "I'm Martha. I run this house and try to keep Logan and the hands in line, though as you can imagine that's not easy."

Martha had a welcoming nature and an easy smile. "It's very nice to meet you, Martha. Something smells really good."

Martha grinned. "That's my pot roast. It's Logan's favorite—Luke's, too, though he hardly ever comes over for Sunday dinner anymore."

Luke kissed her on the cheek. "Howdy, Martha. How's Ben?"

"Ben is a pain in my butt, like always." Martha turned to her. "Ben is my husband. He works as the foreman on the ranch, so he and Logan go way back. He's been around since the boys' daddy was still alive. Come on in and sit down. Would you like some iced tea?"

Emma blinked. Wow. Martha could certainly talk, but

she was very nice, and the kitchen was clean and there were snacks set out on the oversized wood table.

"I'd love tea. Is there anything I can do to help you, Martha?"

"Of course not. You're company, so just sit and take a load off. Logan told me what a great job you did fixing up Whip. That darned dog is always getting into something. All the dogs try my patience on a good day, but I love them all like they're my kids. I hear you brought your two with you today?"

"Yes. Daisy and Annie."

"I'll have to go outside and greet them. I love when Luke comes and brings Boomer with him. I grew up on a farm, and there were always animals around. I don't know what I'd do if there wasn't a dog underfoot."

Emma laughed. "I know what that's like. We always had dogs when I was a kid."

"I think I'll head outside and see what Logan's up to," Luke said.

Martha waved her hand. "You go ahead. Dr. Emma and I will be fine in here."

While Emma sipped her tea, Martha did all the talking. Emma learned that Ben and Martha never had kids, so Martha became an animal lover, and she unofficially adopted Logan, Luke, and Reid as her own after their father died.

Interesting that Luke's mother was never mentioned. She wondered why, but knew it wasn't her place to ask Martha about that.

"Lord, listen to me go on and on. How's the new practice goin'? I used to bring the dogs into Doc Weston. He was a great vet."

"Yes, he was. I used to bring my dogs to see him, too. I was sad to hear he was retiring, but so happy when I worked out a deal with him to buy his practice."

"Let me tell you, without you taking over his practice, Hope would suffer."

"There is the other clinic."

"There is that, and those docs are fine, but there was

something about Doc Weston. He had a way with animals. I hear tell you've got that same magic."

Emma's heart swelled with pride. "Thank you. To be compared to Dr. Weston is a very high compliment. I think I have a lot of years of practice ahead of me to be as good as he was, but I hope to someday be thought of as highly as he was."

"Keep doing what you're doin', and I think you'll get there."

Emma stood. "Speaking of animals, how about we take a look at yours, and get them vaccinated. Do we have time before lunch?"

"Plenty of time. Let's head on out. We'll wrangle the boys into helping."

Once outside, Martha stopped and petted Boomer, then greeted Annie and Daisy. It was clear she was an animal lover, allowing the dogs to sniff and lick her.

Emma could always tell when someone was comfortable with animals, and Martha was quite obviously one of those people animals gravitated to. Animals could tell, too, when a human loved them, because as soon as Martha walked away, they followed her.

Luke and Logan were looking at Logan's truck, so Martha hollered for them and they came over.

"Let's get these animals worked on, and then we can eat."

"All right," Logan said. "We can do that in the barn. There's a worktable and a sink for you, Emma."

Logan called his dogs, who followed along, clearly all well trained.

Emma grabbed her bag from the truck. In the barn, she took the dogs one at a time, examining each, then giving them all their shots. When she was finished, she handed the rabies tags over to Logan.

"They're all healthy and in fine shape, Logan. You've got them on flea and heartworm meds?"

Logan nodded. "I get those at the animal-supply store."

"Good. I've started a chart on each of them, so we'll send reminders out to you when they're due for their boosters. And Whip's stitches look good."

"You can thank Martha for that. She's done a fine job of

making sure he's not running amok all day long. I think she's kept him in the house more than not the past few days."

Emma looked at Martha, who winked. "Whip enjoyed it, too. Slept on the sofa, and lorded it over the other dogs when he went outside."

Emma laughed. "He can go outside now, as long as you clean the stitched areas once a day."

"Good enough, Doc," Martha said.

"I appreciate you taking care of all this out here," Logan said. "Will you have your office send me a bill?"

"I'll have Rachel take care of it. And it's not a problem doing their exams and shots out here. Especially if I get to eat that great-smelling roast."

"Which should be just about ready. So why don't you both help Dr. Emma clean up her gear, get washed up, and then we can eat?"

"Sounds good," Luke said. He and Logan helped Emma pack up her supplies. They shooed the dogs out of the barn and headed back to the house.

By then Martha already had the table set, and an older man was in the kitchen.

"Dr. Emma, this is my husband, Ben."

Ben was tall and rugged-looking, with a shock of white curly hair. Emma shook his hand. "Nice to meet you, Ben."

"You, too, Dr. Emma."

"Please, both of you can just call me Emma."

"That'd make you like family around here," Martha said. "Which means we hope you'll come around more often."

"This is a great ranch. I'm hoping Luke will take me out after lunch so I can see more of it."

"I'm sure he'd love to do that," Logan said, giving Luke a smirk.

She wondered what that was about.

"Sure. I'd be happy to," Luke said, ignoring his brother.

The roast was tender, the potatoes and vegetables perfect.

"This is an incredible meal, Martha. Thank you so much," Emma said.

"You're welcome. And thank you for the compliment."

"So I got a phone call this week from some movie-production company," Logan said as they ate.

Luke paused. "Yeah? What did they want?"

"They're scouting locations for some film they wanna make, and they wanted to know if they could get a tour of the L&M. They think the locale is perfect for their movie."

"Huh," Luke said, leaning back in his seat. "Is there money in that?"

"Apparently a substantial amount. They pay you for use of the land for the time they're on it filming. They bring in their crew, stay in the trailers, bring in their own food. They tell me other than use of the land, they wouldn't inconvenience us any more than absolutely necessary."

Emma watched the interplay between the brothers. It was fascinating to see Luke's expression as Logan explained the whole movie deal. As part owner of the ranch, he had a business interest in whatever went on. She could tell this was something that would require some thought.

"Are you going to let them come in?" Luke asked.

Logan shrugged. "I figured it wouldn't hurt to let them have a tour, then if they're interested, they can make an offer and we can all talk about it. What do you think?"

"I think it sounds like a good idea. When do they want to come?"

"Next week. Do you want to be here for it?"

"Not necessary. You can handle it. Just let me know what they say."

"All right."

"It sounds fascinating," Emma said. "I saw a movie crew doing a scene in Savannah when I lived in South Carolina."

"Yeah? How was that?"

"A lot of cameras and booms and extras, and it was a whole lot of wow, at least from my perspective. But it was on one of the city streets, so that's probably why it seemed so jam-packed to me. I imagine if they want to film on some of your acreage, it would be more widespread. Maybe you wouldn't even notice them."

Logan shrugged and picked up a roll. "No idea. We'll see what they have to say."

"I think it sounds exciting," Martha said. "I wonder if we'd get Johnny Depp."

"Why? Do you think you can get Johnny Depp to come over for Sunday pot roast?" Ben asked, glaring at his wife.

Martha lifted her chin. "He just might. I make pretty darn good pot roast."

Logan and Luke exchanged smirks. Emma looked down at her plate.

After that, the subject of the potential movie on the ranch died, and the guys resumed normal ranch talk. Emma focused on the delicious food, especially Martha's chocolate cream pie she'd had for dessert. By the time the meal was over, Emma felt as if she needed to walk the entire ranch acreage to rid herself of all the calories she'd consumed.

"I don't know how you all stay so slender after a meal like that," she said, helping clear the plates from the table.

"Fortunately, ranch work burns a lot of calories," Ben said with a wink. "Otherwise we'd all be fat because my wife cooks great meals like that all the time."

Emma laid her hand on Ben's arm. "You are one lucky man, Ben."

He grinned. "Believe me, I know."

"Okay, now y'all are gonna make me blush. Luke, take Emma out and give her a look at the ranch while I clean up in here."

"Oh, please let me help you with the dishes, Martha," Emma said.

"Nope," she said, shooing them out with a wave of her hands. "You already did your work for the day with the dogs. This is my work, and I get paid for it. Go enjoy this warm weather."

Emma sent a pleading look to Luke, who shrugged. "You heard her. Let's go take a ride."

"All right."

"I'm going to go check on the cows in pasture three,"

Logan said, grabbing his cowboy hat from the hook at the front door. "I'll meet y'all back here later."

Obviously, she wasn't going to get to help Martha clean up the dishes, so she followed Luke out to his truck and climbed in. "Will the dogs be all right?"

"They'll be fine. Ben's going out to the barn. They'll follow him out there. Once with the pack, none of them will wander off, and Ben will keep an eye on them. Trust me."

"Okay."

Luke took off down a gravel road with a fence on each side. No one was working today, but there were pens and gates.

"You work cattle here?"

"Well, Logan and his crew do, but yeah. They bring the cattle in from the other pastures and separate the herd, do inoculations, and whatever else needs to be taken care of."

She stared out the window as they passed by some of the grazing cattle. Mothers and their young stayed close together.

"They're beautiful."

He laughed. "You wouldn't say that if you had to get close to one."

"Please. I did my large-animal rotation in vet school. I've had my hand in every cattle orifice there is. And I know how bad they smell. Doesn't mean they aren't pretty."

"You think they're pretty."

She turned her gaze on him. "Yes."

"You are one strange woman, Emma Burnett."

Now it was her turn to laugh. "Shut up."

He made a turn, taking her deeper into the ranch property. "This is where the wild horses roam."

She saw them, hundreds of horses grazing across a hilly meadow.

He pulled the truck over so she could climb out. She leaned against the fence post and he came to stand beside her.

"Oh, wow. They're gorgeous."

"Now that I don't disagree with. I always loved the horses. Of course we leave them alone other than providing feed for them in the winter, but I always wanted to get in there and ride with them."

Their markings and colors were beautiful, from solid black to paints and chestnuts. "I don't blame you."

Suddenly, she felt his hands around her waist. "Go on, climb on up. We'll sit for a while, and you can watch."

While he steadied her, she climbed on top of the wood fence and took a seat. He hopped up and took a spot next to her.

"Logan, Reid, and I would come up here when we were kids and just watch the horses run. In the winter, we'd drive the feed trucks and drop feed for them. Though they're wild, they'd come close enough when you were dropping feed that you could almost touch them. But they're skittish, and we didn't want to scare them, so we'd back away and go about our business. They sure are nice to watch, though."

Emma was transfixed. She loved horses, and these were breathtaking. The horses grazed happily in the meadow, so still for the longest time as they ate. Then, suddenly, the herd took off and ran wild over the hill, disappearing from sight, their hooves thunderous in the quiet afternoon.

"Amazing."

Luke hopped off the fence, then grasped Emma around the waist and helped her down. She noticed his hands lingered for a few seconds on her waist. And her gaze lingered on his. He looked like he might want to kiss her.

She waited, but then he let her go.

She pushed back the disappointment, trying her best to be logical about this.

They had both decided that one time was going to be the only time, so she had no idea why she was upset when he didn't kiss her.

This was what she wanted, right? They were friends again, and nothing mucked up a good friendship more than sex.

They climbed back in the truck and Luke pointed out various working areas of the ranch.

"It's sizeable," she said. "A lot for Logan to handle."

"I guess it was Logan's lot to get stuck with the ranch, though he doesn't see it that way. This is his life, what he says he was born to do. He loves living out here."

"I can see why. It's a beautiful way of life. Tough, of course, but it would be amazing to live out here."

"So you're saying I was crazy to give it up."

Her gaze shot to his. "Of course not. This just wasn't your calling, what you were meant to do. I spent a lot of time on ranches and farms when I was in vet school. You're either born to love it or not. And if you're forced into that life without it being under your skin—a part of you—then you'll grow to resent it."

He nodded. "That's pretty much what Logan said to me when I told him I couldn't live here anymore."

"So he wasn't mad at you."

"No. It takes a lot to get him riled up. He's usually a pretty mellow guy."

"I don't know. He looks fierce to me."

Luke made the turn to head back to the house. "Oh, I didn't say he couldn't get mad, and once there, he's got one hell of a temper. But it takes a lot to light his fuse."

She liked that he stood up for his brother. She watched the scenery roll by. "It's a really big ranch, Luke. Amazing that your brother handles it all."

"He manages, and he's got a good crew."

"Do any of them live on the ranch?"

"Ben does, and a few of the guys have rented some property on the ranch. A couple live along neighboring land. We'll hire a few extra hands during busy parts of the season. Our cousins will come help out then, too."

She cocked a brow. "Just how many McCormacks are there?"

He laughed. "Just me and Logan and our youngest brother, Reid, but he lives in Boston. And we have a few cousins sprinkled around here and there."

"Yeah, you mentioned Reid earlier when we were looking at photos. I don't know much about him."

"He hightailed it out of here after high school, scholarship to Yale in hand. We don't see him much."

"Yale? Nice. What does he do?"

"He's an architect. Ranching wasn't ever his thing. He was always the brainy one."

She leaned back in the seat. "Oh, and I suppose you and your brother were the dumb country boys?"

"Not exactly, but Reid—now he was smart. Always the studious type. Logan and I used to make fun of him because he always had a book in his face. Logan would be plastered to our dad's side, learning everything there was to know about ranching."

"And you?" she asked. "What were you doing?"

"Down at the pond, fishing, trying to stay out of trouble and get out of doing any work."

"I can't imagine you got by with that."

"Uh, no. My dad had a sixth sense about his sons. He always knew where we were."

She laughed. "I can picture that. Though usually it's the mothers who have their thumbs on top of their kids."

Luke's smile disappeared. "Yeah, she wasn't much on keeping tabs on us. She was usually busy in the city, shopping with her friends or going to her exercise classes."

Emma sensed the bitterness in that statement. "You didn't get along with your mother?"

He didn't answer for a few minutes. "She wasn't much into having kids."

"Yet she had three of them."

His lips curved. "Yeah, she complained a lot about how hard she had to work at exercise class to keep her figure, and how having us boys had messed it up."

Ouch. What mother would blame her kids for that? "She blamed you for the way her body looked?"

"Sort of. She still had a great body, always watched what she ate and worked out all the time. It was like an obsession with her. I think having me and my brothers freaked her out."

"You would think if having children bothered her as far as her body image, she would have stopped after Logan." When he shot her a look, she touched his arm. "Though I'm glad she didn't, of course."

His lips curved. "Yeah, me, too. Anyway, she wasn't the best mother. She did the barest minimum, and then after my dad died, she remarried almost right away and hightailed it off the ranch and out of Oklahoma."

"You can't be serious."

"Dead serious. She always hated this ranch, hated being tied to it and couldn't wait to get away from it."

And from her sons? Something he hadn't mentioned but surely felt. She squeezed his arm. "I'm sorry, Luke."

He shrugged. "Don't be sorry for me. She isn't missed around here. My dad was the one who was always there for us. He's the one who's missed."

"I'm sure he is. It seems like he was a great guy."

"Yeah. He was. He was always hands-on with us. Taught us about ranching, but the important things, too, like focusing on our education, how to act like a man, how to be polite, how to treat a woman."

His father could have been so bitter, saddled with a woman who hadn't wanted to be with him. And yet he'd obviously raised respectful sons. Luke was warm and affectionate, and had been there for her when she needed him. And they weren't even dating.

"I'm sorry I never got the chance to meet your dad."

He smiled at her. "He would have liked you. Mainly because you like his ranch."

She laughed. "I do like his ranch. I like your brother, too."

"Eh. He's prickly. He's just on his best behavior today because, one, he's trying to impress you, and two, Martha would kick his butt if he was rude."

"I might like to see you two brothers go at it."

"The real fun is when Reid comes to visit."

"You don't pick on him, do you?"

He pulled up in front of the house. "Not more than a lot."

When she gave him a look, he said, "Come on. Tell me you don't pick on your little sister?"

She unbuckled her seat belt. "I see her so rarely that when I do, I'm so thrilled that I spend all my time worshipping her."

He arched a brow. "I find that hard to believe. It's the

nature of siblings to argue. When was the last time you saw your little sister?"

She had to think about it for a minute as she climbed out of the truck and met Luke around the front of it. "Probably a year and a half ago. I was still living in South Carolina and she came to visit me. Molly is . . . interesting."

"Now there's a word."

She shoved at him. "Hey, it's a compliment. It means she's quirky."

"Sure it does. Is that like fixing a guy up on a date with your best friend and telling him she has a great personality, when in reality it means she's a real dog?"

"No," she said with emphasis. "That's not at all what it means. Molly's gorgeous, smart, and fun."

He took a seat on the porch steps. "But?"

Emma sighed. "She has secrets."

"Who doesn't?"

"She left town after high school, and won't come back home. And no one really knows why."

They started walking down the dirt road. "Not even you?"

"Not me. Not my parents. No one."

"Do you think something bad happened in Hope to make her leave?"

She tilted her gaze up at him. "Maybe. I don't know. I've asked her time and time again why she won't come home, but she says she craves adventure and new places, and she's afraid if she comes back home she'll never leave again."

"But you don't believe her."

"Not really. Though she does move a lot. Every three to six months it's a new job in a new city."

"It might just be that simple, Emma. Some people are born wanderers, never setting down roots. They enjoy the thrill and adventure of new places and new experiences."

"Maybe you're right. I just worry about her."

He put an arm around her. "We always worry the most about the people we care about. Does she seem happy?"

Emma had to admit she liked Luke's arm around her shoulders. "She does."

"Then I wouldn't worry so much."

She stopped. "You make it seem so simple. In my head, Molly is so complex and mysterious."

He laughed. "Well, I remember her and Carter together. And that was a long time ago. And that ended kind of abruptly."

"It did. Which was also mysterious. Has he ever said anything to you about her, or about why the two of them broke up?"

Luke recalled the conversation he had had with Carter last week. "No. Carter hasn't said anything about Molly. I guess it was just a high school romance that ran its course."

"That's what Molly said, too."

"So maybe you're looking for some wild mystery that isn't there, and your sister just likes to travel."

"I guess you're right."

"And how are your parents?" he asked.

"They're great, as you know. My mom's a business-and-marketing genius."

"Yeah, she did a really nice job on your adoption day at the clinic."

Emma sighed and stared off into the distance. "Yes. She's just full of wonderful ideas like that."

"You sound like you're not happy with her."

"Actually, she's an amazing woman. Two degrees, owns a company, and still manages to have date nights with my father."

"She sounds like she juggles a lot."

"She does. But she handles it all well. She always has."

"And you feel like you don't measure up."

She tilted her head back to look up at him. "I didn't say that."

His lips curved. "You didn't have to. I always thought my dad was the most incredible human being on the planet. I felt he could run this ranch single-handedly and live on no sleep. It wasn't true, of course, but it had always seemed that way to me. I'm sure your mother is human, even though to you she seems like she has superpowers."

"She's just so energetic and full of amazing ideas. And she always has time for me, will sit down and talk to me about whatever's on my mind."

"And that's a bad thing?"

"I guess not. Sometimes I just don't think I'll ever have it together like she does."

He laid his hand on her shoulder. "Just be thankful you have a mother who loves you, cares about you, and is there for you when you need her."

She saw it from his perspective. He'd had a mother who was more concerned about her own needs, who didn't care at all about her children. And here Emma was, complaining because she had an overcaring, overachieving mother. That when she came right down to admitting it, she was jealous of.

"You're absolutely right. My mother is amazing. And she also asked me to bring you over for dinner again sometime."

He laughed. "I'd love to come for dinner again."

"Sure. Until she comes up with a marketing or advertising plan for the Hope Police Department."

When he gave her a look, she said, "Oh, she'd do it, too. There isn't anyplace in this town that my mom doesn't think can't be improved."

He laughed. "I consider myself warned. But I know I can always talk sports with your dad."

Emma laughed. "Yes. My father, my crazy, sports-loving father, yet also the very quiet, very stable CPA. The total opposite of my mother. He's like the calming force to her tornadic personality."

"And you adore him."

She let out a soft laugh. "I do. And I don't want you to get the wrong impression of my mother. She might be a little overzealous, but she's a wonderful person."

"I never got a wrong impression. I've been to your house, remember? I think she's fantastic."

She smiled at him. "Thanks. It was really wonderful to have you over for dinner with them. I'll definitely ask you again."

"That would be fun."

She let that settle, wondered what it would be like to have Luke over to her parents' house for dinner on a regular basis. What did it mean that she even considered how nice that would be? Did she want a relationship with Luke? Why was she so confused? And what was Luke thinking? He thought coming over to her parents' house for dinner again would be fun? What did *that* mean?

And why did she have to psychoanalyze everything? Why couldn't she just leave it alone?

After all, they'd had a nice day here on the ranch. Though he could have brought along a buddy of his with the same result. He'd shown her the house and the ranch, and they'd eaten. It hadn't been exactly romantic, had it?

"Thanks for showing me around."

"My pleasure, ma'am," he said with a wink.

She loved hearing him talk, the slight Southern twang in his voice reminding her how much she'd missed all those years living away from Hope. Though she had lived in the South while she'd been away, it just hadn't been the same as being in her hometown.

"I suppose we should head back, get out of Logan and everyone's way."

He looked at her. "Does it look like we're in anyone's way?"

She glanced around. No one was in the vicinity. She didn't even know where the dogs were at the moment. "I guess not."

"Or maybe you just don't want to be alone with me."

She tilted her head. "We're not exactly alone, Luke. Martha and Ben are inside, I'm sure, and your brother is . . . somewhere nearby."

"Maybe. But you didn't answer my question."

That familiar tingling returned, that feeling she got whenever Luke was near. "I don't think you asked one."

"Sure I did. The part about you not wanting to be alone with me."

"That was a statement, not a question."

"Now you're just arguing semantics. So, are you afraid to be alone with me?"

"No." Though that wasn't exactly the truth. And they weren't alone right now. That she knew of.

"Good. Then you won't mind if I kiss you."

Her eyes widened. "What? Here?"

"Shhh. It won't hurt. I promise."

He leaned toward her, and her heart started jamming what felt like a thousand beats a second. When he slipped his hand around the back of her neck to draw her close, she licked her lips, drawing his gaze to her mouth. She couldn't catch a breath as his lips hovered just a fraction of an inch from hers. She didn't know at that moment whether she was dying for Luke to kiss her, or whether she wanted to leap from the steps and get as far away from him as possible.

And when their lips touched, she felt the crackle of chemistry, even stronger than the first time. The way he deliberately took his time coaxing her mouth open, not caring that they sat on the front porch where anyone could walk outside at any moment.

Which she soon forgot when he slid his tongue in her mouth and pressed his lips harder against hers. She clutched his shirt and moaned against his mouth, wanting oh, so much more. Her nipples hardened and every female part of her body screamed *Yes, yes, oh, hell yes.*

She rose against him, and he drew her tight against him, his hand inching ever closer to her butt. She felt him, hard, as he held her tight in his embrace.

She'd missed this. She wanted him. Right here. Right now.

"Hey, there you two are. Oh. Well, shit."

Logan's appearance through the front door of the house jerked her out of the languorous stupor. She backed away from Luke in a hurry, brushing imaginary dust off her jeans. Luke, on the other hand, just gave her a regretful smile before turning to glare at his brother.

"Hi," she said, her face heating in embarrassment.

"As usual, Logan, you have lousy timing," Luke said.

"So I noticed a second too late. Sorry."

"It's no problem. We were just . . . uh . . . talking," Emma said, mentally trying to cool down her flaming face.

"Looked to me like there wasn't any talking going on."

Just then Ben came out from the barn, all the dogs trailing after him. Grateful for the distraction, she pivoted and headed toward them. When Daisy saw her, the dog took off at a fast run, with Annie doing her best to keep up. Boomer sauntered over like he was in no hurry.

"Hey, kids. Did you have fun today?" She busied herself petting all the dogs while Luke climbed the steps to have a word with his brother. She tried not to think about that kiss. And how much her body still throbbed as a result.

"They had a good time in the barn," Ben said to her. "They even chased a few chickens out back."

She laughed. "Good to know they weren't napping the whole time."

"I don't think much napping went on. They were all too busy playing. I know our dogs will likely pass out the rest of the day."

"I'm sure mine will, too. Thank you for keeping watch over them."

"It was no problem."

Luke came down the steps. "We should probably head out."

She stood, not yet able to meet his gaze. "Okay, sure."

They went inside, and she thanked Martha for lunch again. Then they said their good-byes.

"I'll see you again soon," Logan said, shaking her hand.

"You come around for Sunday dinner anytime," Martha said, pulling her in for a hug.

They wrangled the dogs into the truck, then climbed in, and she waved good-bye.

Emma was silent the whole trip back to her place, not knowing how to work through the awkwardness that had settled in between them since that kiss. Luke must have been having the same problem because he was as mute as she was.

He'd started it, and by the time he pulled into her driveway, she had no idea how to get past it and back to the fun friendship they'd settled into.

But was that what she wanted?

Yes. Of course it was what she wanted. She hadn't wanted him to kiss her.

Had she?

Lord, could she be more conflicted? As an adult, couldn't she make up her damn mind about what she wanted in life? Or from a man?

She had the life part down. She had her career trajectory in motion.

The man part? Not so much.

"Okay, here we are."

She lifted her head to see he'd opened her truck door. The dogs were eager to get out, so she supposed she should stop pondering and get away from temptation.

She slid out of the truck and the dogs followed. She tracked her gaze back to Luke.

"Thanks for today."

His attention stayed on her. "Anytime."

Even in the dark, she noticed the tilt of his head, the way he looked at her. The chemistry between them was unmistakable, and utterly dangerous.

"I have to get to work early tomorrow, so I should go in."

His lips curved, as if he knew she was trying desperately for a polite way to disengage herself from his presence.

"Sure."

She walked to the front door, unlocked it, and the dogs went in. She flipped on the light, then turned back to him.

Before she could say good night, he'd pulled her against him, his mouth on hers in another of those mind-melting, blistering hot kisses that made her forget all her logical, reasonable convictions. She fell against him and kissed him back, her arms winding around him.

But as soon as things got started, he pulled back.

"I've got to get up early tomorrow, too."

She blinked, still trying to reassemble her brain cells. "Uh, okay."

"Emma?"

"Yeah?"

"This isn't over between you and me. We need to talk . . . or something."

Yeah. Or something. "Okay."

"'Night." He got in his truck and backed out of her driveway.

Exhaling, she closed the front door and locked it, then leaned against it.

Whoa. What had just happened? Her body knew what to do, what it wanted her to do. It acted on its own. It wanted to be kissed, to lean into him, breathe in that sexy male scent of him. There was a part of her that eagerly wanted to explore him, with her hands, and her mouth.

And as soon as he'd pulled her against him and kissed her, her body went with its natural reaction to go for it. If Luke hadn't stopped, he'd be in her bedroom right now and she'd be tearing his clothes off with her teeth so she could get at all the good parts of him.

Which was pretty much all of him.

She shuddered as the mental images bombarded her. He'd looked good today in his jeans, boots, and tight T-shirt.

He'd look even better out of them.

Yeah, she'd definitely like to run her hands over his tight, muscled body, to get him hot and bothered and make him sweat, and then he, in turn, could make her sweat.

And thoughts like that didn't fall in line with her "no men" plan.

With a frustrated sigh, she pushed off the door to go see to the dogs. Dogs were a woman's best friend. Dogs weren't complicated. They would never hurt her, or break her heart.

The trouble was, that whole "no men" plan?

It was crumbling as fast as her resolve to stay away from Luke.

Chapter 14

OUT ON PATROL, Luke's mind wandered, especially when he pulled up along a stretch of Highway 66 to lay a speed trap.

It had been a slow day, and he and Boomer had been riding around for the majority of it. Except for the stop he had to make at the Davidson's house—something he had to do at least once a week. Paul was ninety-two and convinced that his eighty-nine-year-old wife, Maureen, was trying to kill him. Since Maureen was confined to a wheelchair and on oxygen, it was highly unlikely she'd been coming after him with a butcher knife. Paul and Maureen's daughter, Athena, who lived with them, always apologized and said it was the medication, coupled with her father's growing dementia. And it typically seemed to happen whenever Athena ran to the store or hopped into the shower. Paul would get hold of a phone and dial 9-1-1.

By the time Luke arrived, Paul had no idea what Luke was doing there. But it was his job to check it out, and he figured Athena enjoyed the company. Sometimes, if Paul was lucid, Luke would stay and visit with him for a few minutes, and Paul would recount his experiences in the South Pacific during World War II.

Other than that, nothing eventful happened that day, so he and Boomer sat back in the shade under an overpass and pulled over a few cars going well past the speeding limit. He wasn't one of those asshole cops who was going to ding someone if they went five or six miles over. But if they hit more than ten miles over the limit, they were getting a ticket.

In the hour he'd sat there, he'd only had to hand out two tickets. Not bad, though he'd registered some hotshot pulling twenty miles over the limit. That one was going to cost him. And the guy had been a belligerent dickhead on top of that, claiming he was late for a meeting.

Too bad. Luke explained it didn't much matter what he was late for, since twenty miles over the speed limit was still illegal. The guy said he was the son of a local congressman, which didn't bother Luke any. He could be the son of the president. He was still getting a ticket. So when Luke handed him the form to sign, he smiled at him.

Mr. Stanley A. Lexington III hadn't appreciated that much. In fact, Luke was certain he'd heard a whispered *fuck you* as he'd walked away from Stanley's Cadillac.

Luke grinned.

Sometimes it was good to be a cop.

"How's it going back there, Boom?" Luke asked.

Boomer snored.

"Some partner you are."

Boomer responded with a snort, then rolled over on his back, feet stuck up in the air.

"Yeah, I'd like a nap, too. Or maybe a beer. Neither one is gonna happen right now."

He cracked a smile when Will Griffin pulled alongside him in his highway patrol cruiser. Luke rolled down the window.

"Infringing on my territory?" Will asked, resting his forearm on the side of the car.

"I think there are plenty of douchebags on this stretch of highway—you can afford to share the wealth."

Will grinned. "You're right about that. How's it going?"

"Interesting day. You?"

"Wreck over on 75 North this morning. People in a hurry or on their cell phones don't pay much attention to road-construction signs. Someone plowed right through a construction barrier and went airborne."

Luke grimaced. "Anyone hurt?"

"Minor injuries, fortunately. The mess was in the cleanup and the rerouting of traffic. And the report I had to spend two hours writing."

"Fun."

"Yeah. Not really."

Luke pulled his attention away as a car sped past. He caught the brake lights in his rearview mirror, then checked radar. Seven miles over. Close, but since Will was there, he'd give the guy a pass.

"Gonna go after him?"

"Not this time."

"I'm sure he's sweating bullets and checking his mirror."

"Good. Let's just hope he slows down."

"He will. For a mile or two, until he's sure you're not throwing lights and showing up on his bumper or that you don't have a partner who's going to pick him up the next mile over the rise."

Luke let out a laugh. "Yeah. That's always fun."

"Especially if you're the one who gets to write the ticket. I never get tired of that deer-in-the-headlights look. Just when they thought they were out of the woods . . ."

"You're a little sadistic, Griffin."

Will shrugged. "Gotta have some fun in this job, ya know."

"How are Jane and the kids?"

A genuine smile lit up Will's face. "Good. Really good. We see each other almost every day—my stupid work schedule permitting. I'm coaching Ryan's baseball team, and Jane's busy with Tabby's dance classes. And we're housebreaking the new puppy, which isn't as much fun."

Luke laughed. "No, it never is. But I'm sure he'll get through it. And so will you."

"Yeah. And the kids like taking him for walks, so he's getting plenty of exercise. They really love him."

Luke liked seeing Will happy. "So, you've basically become a father to her kids."

"I love those kids. And their mom."

"Any marriage plans?"

"We're still taking it slow, and I don't want to push her, since Jane needs to believe I'm always going to be there for her."

"Because of that asshole ex of hers who ran out on her and the kids."

"Yeah. But we're talking about it. Actually, we talk about it a lot. I want to marry her and become a father to her kids. A legal father."

"Is that even possible, given the fact no one can locate her ex?"

"It's possible. We're talking to an attorney who can get us a court date to have his parental rights permanently removed due to abandonment. But again, no rush on that. I don't want to push Jane into anything she's not ready for. It'll all happen at some point. The most important thing is for her and me to get hitched so I can move in with her and the kids. We don't feel it's setting a good example for the kids for us to live together until we're married, so we're waiting. Which is hard."

"I imagine it is." He liked seeing Will happy and settled. Maybe it hadn't worked out for Luke, but Jane was awesome, and he could definitely tell she was the right woman for his best friend. "I'm glad things are going well for you."

"Me, too. How about you and Emma Burnett?"

Luke cocked a brow. "What about me and Emma?"

"Heard she was out at the ranch last weekend."

"What the hell. Is my personal business published on Facebook or something?"

"Uh, not that I'm aware of. But maybe. I haven't checked Hope's town Facebook page yet."

"Funny. How did you know Emma was at the ranch?"

"Jane told me."

"Oh."

Will shot him a wry grin. "Touchy, aren't we?"

"Maybe a little. Everyone just seems to assume Emma and I are dating."

"And you're not."

"No."

"But you'd like to be."

He paused. "Maybe. We're taking things slow. Or maybe I'm taking things slow. I don't know what the hell she's doing."

"Yeah, I understand that whole slow thing. But you know, a woman who's worth it is worth going slow for."

That was working for Will, but Luke wasn't searching for the same happily-ever-after his best friend had found. He'd been down that road once before and had been whacked over the head with the reality stick. "I'm not looking for a relationship, you know."

Will laughed. "Yeah, neither was I. Look at me now."

After Will took off, Luke leaned back in his seat and watched the differing speed numbers tick off on his radar while trying not to think about Emma.

For someone who only had the intention of taking her on that one date, he'd sure been seeing—and thinking about her—a lot lately. He'd even gone to her parents' house for dinner. What the hell was that about?

It had to be the whole physical-chemistry thing, and the fact he hadn't been with another woman in a while. Maybe if he just went out with someone else, Emma would fade into the background.

Though he thought about her silky hair and that sexy smile and her body, and the way her lips curved when she smiled. And that laugh of hers that hit him like a vibration straight to his balls. Not to mention what it felt like to kiss her. And make love to her.

Yeah, no way Emma was going to fade into the background. She was on his mind all the time and it didn't look like she was going anywhere.

He thought about the other women he knew, and he knew a lot of them.

There wasn't a single one he thought about calling. Except Emma.

Not good.

His radar beeped and he caught sight of a truck blasting down the highway. A quick glance at his radar showed the truck doing a good fifteen miles over the speed limit. He hit the lights and sirens and pulled out, hitting the gas hard.

Oblivious to Luke coming up behind him, the truck kept speeding, barreling through what were fortunately green lights.

Someone was in a damn hurry.

He pulled up behind the truck, which looked vaguely familiar, and finally the driver grabbed a clue, slowed down, and pulled over. That's when recognition set in and Luke's lips curved into a smile. He got out, grabbing his ticket clipboard, and sauntered over to the driver's side of the vehicle.

Emma rolled down her window, though she didn't look sheepish or embarrassed. She looked damned annoyed.

"Luke."

"Emma. Seventy-five in a sixty."

"I know. I have a heifer with birth complications, and I need to get there in a hurry."

He leaned against the windowsill. "If I had a dollar for every time I heard that one."

That at least got her to tilt her lips up a little. "I'm seriously sorry. I know I shouldn't have been speeding, but if I don't get there in a hurry, she's going to die."

He nodded, picking up on her distress. "Whose farm?"

"The Millers over on Route 45."

He knew the Millers, had gone to school with their son, Jeremy. They lived just outside city limits.

Since he was getting off duty shortly anyway, he asked, "Do you know where it is?"

She waved a piece of paper at him. "I have directions."

"It's kind of complicated. I'll show you. Follow me."

"Great. Thanks."

He headed back to his cruiser and led her the few miles

out of town, right past the water tower and down the dirt road that led to the Miller's farm. They pulled up in front of Fred and Abigail Miller's place. Abigail was there waiting for them, worry etched across her face.

"Thanks for coming, Dr. Emma. Hi, Luke."

"Mrs. Miller."

"Abigail, please. I'm just so glad you're here."

She started moving away, so he followed behind Abigail and Emma, who were talking and walking at a brisk pace to the barn.

When they got there, one of the heifers was in obvious pain—indicated by the sounds she made. Fred was there with her. Emma put on her gloves and knelt down beside the cow.

"Looks like a uterine prolapse," Emma said. "When did she calf?"

"A couple of hours ago. There's been some bleeding. More so than would be usual," Fred said.

Emma nodded, taking out tools. "We'll need to turn her over. First I need to clean the uterus, then figure out where this bleeding is coming from." She looked up at both Luke and Fred. "I'm going to need both of you to help, unless you need to leave?"

That she asked of Luke. "I'm off duty in thirty minutes. Unless I get a call, I can stay."

It took a few hours for Emma to repair the tear in the cow's uterus and fix it back in place. Cattle weren't the easiest animals to hold, especially when you couldn't knock them out. It required Luke and Fred to keep her in place. By the time she was finished, they were all covered in gunk that Luke didn't even want to think about. He'd likely just toss this uniform.

Emma gave the cow antibiotics and vitamins, then checked out the calf.

"Mom and calf are going to be fine," Emma said, removing her large-animal gloves. She went to the barn sink to wash up.

So did Luke.

Both Abigail and Fred shook Emma's hand.

"Thank you," Fred said. "We really didn't want to lose this one."

"Well, it doesn't look like you're going to, but call me if anything changes. Keep an eye on her tonight, though I'm sure she's tired and she'll rest."

They walked out to the house. "Thanks, Dr. Emma. You, too, Luke. We appreciate you lending a helping hand," Abigail said. "Since both the other clinic docs were unavailable, we didn't know what to do."

"It's no problem. Call me anytime."

Fred and Abigail went back to the barn. Luke turned to her with a satisfied grin.

She was obviously as pleased as he was with how well everything had turned out. "Thanks for staying. You were a big help." Emma looked like she wanted to hug him, but they were both a mess, covered in mud and other animal grime.

"It's no problem."

She put her supplies back in her truck, then turned to him and offered a smile. "I promise to drive the speed limit all the way home, officer."

"Yeah, about that. I know you get called out on emergencies sometimes, but if it hadn't been me today, you might have been facing one hell of a speeding ticket."

Her smile faded. "You're right. In the future I'll be more mindful of that. I was only thinking about the cow."

He tipped her nose with his fingertip. "Think about your safety first."

"Oooh, I get all tingly when you talk cop stuff and the law."

He stepped closer. "Don't tease me, Emma. I have handcuffs."

Her eyes went dark. "Yeah? And you know what to do with them?"

In an instant, he'd jerked her against him. "If we weren't standing in front of the Miller's house right now, both of us covered in cow—whatever—I'd show you exactly what I could do with handcuffs."

She swallowed. "Right. And I smell really bad, so don't you think I should take a shower first?"

He laughed. "You're right about that. We both need a shower."

"And I owe you at least dinner for helping me out. And for not giving me a ticket."

"I'll take you up on that."

"Meet me at my place in about an hour?"

"Sure." He let go of her and climbed back in his cruiser. She followed behind him until they got on the main high-way, where he noticed she drove the speed limit. He smiled at that. She turned off on the road leading to her house, and he went home and took a quick shower. After dumping his uniform in the trash, he changed into jeans and a T-shirt, then grabbed Boomer and headed out to Emma's place.

On the way, he stopped at the liquor store for a bottle of wine.

She met him at the door wearing jeans and a button-down shirt. Her hair was still damp.

"Oh. Wine? You didn't have to do that."

"I figured after the whole cow crisis, you might need it."

"You might be right about that. Come on in." She let him inside, and he followed her into the kitchen.

"Something smells good."

"Yeah, about that. It's Italian food from the restaurant down the road. Sorry. No home-cooked meal for you to-night."

"Any food tonight sounds good to me, even takeout."

"I'm so glad you think so, since my plan tonight was going to be something microwaved from the freezer. This is a much better option."

She handed him the corkscrew while she pulled plates from the cabinet. He opened the wine, then helped her set the table.

"Come on, Boomer," she said. "You can run out back with the other dogs."

"Thanks for inviting me over. Though I'm not sure if it

was gratitude, or if you're interested in my prowess with handcuffs."

She laughed as they sat at the table. "Well, I guess we'll see, won't we?"

The food was good, and Luke was starving. The wine was decent, too, and he was glad he'd picked up the bottle. Emma seemed relaxed, especially after the first glass.

"Rough day?" he asked.

"Busy day. Though they all seem to be busy lately."

"That's a good thing, right?"

"Yes, it is. I'm not complaining at all. Though I hadn't expected the cow thing. That's not really my area of expertise, since my focus is on small animals. But I was happy to be able to help out."

"There are large-animal vets in the area."

She took a sip of wine and nodded. "True, but they're not always available. And I can deal with it in an emergency."

"Kind of like a cop delivering a baby? Not exactly what we're trained for, but if it comes up . . ."

She lifted her gaze to his. "Have you ever had to do that?"

"What? Deliver a baby?"

"Yes."

He shook his head. "It hasn't come up. Yet."

She laughed. "I'm guessing you hope it doesn't."

"No. I'm hoping every set of expectant parents on my stretch of road gets to the hospital to have their babies."

"It's a good wish. But as we know, emergencies happen and sometimes events occur that you can't foresee."

"That's true."

She took another long swallow of wine, her gaze distant as she spoke. "Sometimes, life doesn't turn out as you plan it at all."

Somehow, he got the idea she was talking about more than just cattle emergencies and babies being born in the car.

"Emma?"

She jerked her attention back on him. "Yes?"

"Is there something on your mind?"

"No. Not at all. Why do you ask?"

"Because I don't think you were referring to cattle or babies."

"Oh. Sure I was."

"You know, you really haven't told me about your past. Or the guy who left you heartbroken and wary of relationships."

"Did I say there was a guy?"

"You mentioned it in passing."

"Oh. Well. Not much to tell."

"Yeah, you keep saying that, but I think there's a lot more to the story. And sometimes it helps to talk. I told you about Rebecca and the disaster that was my first marriage."

"You did, didn't you?"

"So . . ."

Emma took a deep breath, and another long swallow of wine. He could tell she was pondering whether or not to tell him something. Obviously it was a big thing to her, so he waited patiently.

"It's an ugly story, Luke. And it makes me look bad."

He reached for her hand and gave it a squeeze. "I find that hard to believe. But it obviously bothers you. I think you should tell me about it."

She nodded. "I met Vaughn my freshman year of college. He was one of my professors. I was enamored of him. He was so smart, and sharp and funny, and oh, I had such a crush on him. It was like our eyes met in the classroom, and that was it for me. He encouraged it, would meet with me in his office to go over my papers and my lab notes. One thing led to another, and we got involved in this very heavy relationship, which of course could have cost him his job.

"The fact that he didn't seem to care made it all the more thrilling for me. We were madly in love—or at least I was. He helped me with all my classes. He'd help me study, and I was doing so well in school. Of course I couldn't move in with him, because the school couldn't know about our relationship. I think the clandestine nature of it was what made it so exciting."

She paused, took another couple of sips, staring at the

glass, not looking at him. Luke knew she was reliving that time, and maybe she needed to in order to get it all out. He didn't want to say anything, because he realized this was important for her. He also realized she probably didn't talk about this time in her life very often.

"By my senior year, I was convinced that after graduation we'd move in together. I could be seen with him as a graduate student because he wouldn't be involved with me once I started vet school. I applied and got into vet school. I was so thrilled.

"That's when everything started to change, when his hold on me turned from encouraging to dominating. He told me he wanted me to live with him, but as a vet student I'd be immersed in my studies and we'd never see each other anymore, that I wouldn't be able to help him with his school projects anymore. It would be like we were strangers, so we should probably end it.

"I was crushed. For four years we'd been everything to each other—or at least he'd been everything to me. And he was ready to walk away from it all because I would have to focus on my studies?"

Luke frowned. "He forced you to choose between him and vet school."

"I didn't realize it at the time. I was so in love with him, I'd have done anything for him. But yes, that's exactly what he did."

"And you chose him."

She looked down at the wine. "I chose him. I dropped out of vet school and I moved in with him. And then I became his research assistant, helping him with his papers and his research. I'd do his laundry and clean his house, and whatever else he wanted me to do for him, whenever he wanted me to do it. He monitored where I was every moment of the day. If I was going to the grocery store, I had to call him before I left, and call when I got back. It got to the point where I was a prisoner in his home. I had no friends. I had lost them all years before because he wanted all my focus on him. He even cut my family off. So when he was teaching, I had to either be working on his papers or staying at the house."

Luke's stomach tightened. He knew where this was going, had seen it time and time again in women who were controlled and abused. "And if you didn't?"

She shook her head. "Then I was punished. If I really loved him, I would do it right."

He reached out and smoothed his hand over her hair. "I'm sorry he treated you that way, Emma."

"I don't deserve your sorrow. I was an intelligent young girl with career goals, and I allowed him to manipulate me into giving it all up to become nothing more than his slave." She lifted tear-filled eyes to his. "How could I have let that happen?"

His heart ached for her. "You're not the first woman that has happened to. Blame him, not yourself. Men like that have a way of making you fall in love with them, of making these promises for the future, and then once they have you hooked and seduced, they pull the rug right out from under you."

"I could have walked away at any time. Why didn't I?"

"Because you were afraid of him, of what he might do if he followed you and found you. He threatened you, didn't he?"

She nodded. "All the time. He threatened me; he threatened my family. He even said he monitored my sister's movements, knew where Molly was, and if I left him he'd hurt her."

Sonofabitch. This guy was evil. "How did you get away?"

"I was so lonely. He was at school all the time, or at evening functions. I was always alone at the house. He never let me go anywhere. I finally had had enough of living that way. I used to be fun and outgoing. I had once had so many friends, a plan for my future, and he'd stripped it all away from me. I decided I couldn't do it anymore, so when he had a business trip, I decided to seize my opportunity to leave. He hated travel because it took him away from me, where he couldn't monitor me. But after a few years, he was confident he had me so under control that he could go out of town and I'd meekly stay there. But this time, he had a three-day trip. I packed up everything, took money I had stockpiled, took the car, and hightailed it out of there. Then I went home to my parents and told them everything. They helped me get a restraining order against him."

"Did he get fired?"

Her lips curved slightly. "Yes. After I recovered enough of my backbone, I went to the university and told them what had happened between us during the entire four years I was an undergraduate, and after, including the restraining order. I saved all the e-mails we had written to each other when I was an undergraduate, up to and including the notes he wrote ordering me to do this or that, and I used those against him.

"He lost his job. He was furious with me, but with the restraining order, he couldn't come near me, or he'd be arrested. The last time I heard, he was living in Texas."

He took her hand. "Why didn't you tell me about him—about all this—sooner?"

She gave him a look. "Come on, Luke. Would you have wanted anyone you care about to know about such an epic failure in your life like this?"

"Emma. I care about you. I don't expect you to be perfect, or for your past to have been perfect. But if we're going to have a . . . relationship, we have to be up front with each other about everything, including the ugly parts."

"Yeah, well, this is really ugly and doesn't paint me in a positive light."

"Hey, I told you about my past."

She gave him a look. "Luke, it's not the same thing at all. You had a marriage that didn't work out, that wasn't your fault."

"It wasn't all Rebecca's fault. I didn't do my part, either."

"But you weren't a manipulating douchebag like Vaughn. And you weren't a coward like me."

He set down his wineglass and pulled her onto his lap.

"Stop. You realize this Vaughn guy is to blame for what happened to you, right?"

"I do now. I didn't at first. I put all the blame on myself. It took a while and some counseling to realize what he'd done to me. It's still hard to let go of the shame, though."

"Look at where you are now, what you've accomplished. Do you know how many women never get away from men like him? You got out. You should be proud of yourself."

He saw the tears shimmer in her eyes and realized how hard she was working not to let them fall.

She took a deep breath. "Well, thanks for that. I worked hard to fight my way back. And that's why my career is having a late start."

"But you have a career. And you got your education. So I guess Vaughn can just suck it."

She laughed. "I guess he can."

She took his hand. "Thank you. For understanding."

Chapter 15

AFTER HIS CONVERSATION with Emma, Luke decided she needed some time and distance to think about what they talked about. Hell, even he needed some time to think, because he knew if they got together again, he'd have to make a commitment to do more than just take her to bed.

Because what she was all twisted up about wasn't just sex. She had a past to get over, and it had been an ugly, painful one that had hurt her and had turned her off relationships and men. Hell, that she could even be around guys after what she'd been through was a testament to her strength and courage.

Just the things they'd done together was a big step for her. She'd been open and fun and, God, she was so sexy. But she was also reluctant.

Yeah, so was he. But he still wanted more. And that meant moving forward with Emma—like into a relationship. And Luke wasn't sure he was ready for that step, or if he'd ever be that ready. But it was becoming achingly clear he wasn't going to be able to get her out of his system until he found out where this was going.

Emma seemed as gun-shy about a relationship as he was,

so maybe this could turn out to be a good thing. They could enjoy spending time together without either of them needing or wanting a serious commitment.

She might just be perfect for him.

The only bad thing about that was he had the potential to hurt her, and that was the last thing he wanted to do. Someone had already hurt her enough. Which meant he'd have to tread lightly.

Off duty, he approached the clinic and decided to drop by. Rachel and Leanne were both up front and greeted him.

"Where's Boomer?" Rachel asked.

"Sacked out in the backseat of the cruiser."

"Awww. Rough day?"

"He saw a little action."

"I heard there've been more drug-related break-ins. The pharmacy on Fifth got hit this week?"

"Yeah."

"But you haven't caught them yet?" Leanne asked.

"Not yet. But we're still investigating leads. We'll find them."

"I hope so."

"Brutus is ready for boarding," Rachel said, handing Leanne a chart.

"Okay, thanks. See you, Officer Luke."

"Bye, Leanne."

Leanne took off with the only other patient who had been in the waiting room, leaving him alone.

"Light schedule today, huh?" he asked Rachel.

"Yeah. Long weekend coming up, so I think people are getting a head start. We have a lot of pets coming in to be boarded, but not so much in the way of patients."

One of the exam-room doors opened, and Luke heard Emma's voice.

"She'll be fine once she has a full day on this medication, Mrs. Schechter. Don't worry about a thing."

"Thank you, Dr. Burnett. I was so concerned."

"It's not a serious illness. The antibiotics will start helping right away. Flounder will be good as new in a day or so."

Emma walked out with an older woman carrying a white cat.

"Rachel will take care of you. And if Flounder isn't showing signs of improvement in a couple days, you call and let us know."

"I'll do that. Thank you again."

Emma smiled, then looked up and saw him. "Oh, Luke. Hi."

He hadn't seen her in a few days, not since that night they'd talked at her house. He'd left her after that, since she'd seemed wrung out after her big confession. Staying with her—pressing things between them—had seemed inappropriate. So he'd kissed her good-bye so she could get some rest. He'd called her to check in the next day, and she told him she'd felt better after some sleep.

He'd missed her, and her smile.

"Hi, Emma. I was in the area and thought I'd stop by, see how you're doing."

She shoved her hands in the pockets of her lab coat. "I'm doing . . . great. How are you?"

"Good. Do you have a few minutes?"

"Oh . . . Uh. I don't know. Do I?" She looked over at Rachel.

"You're done for the day, Dr. Emma. No more appointments."

Emma frowned. "Really?"

"Really. So you and Officer Luke can have all the time you need." Rachel shot Luke a grin.

"I need to check on this morning's surgery patient."

"Leanne just checked on Elsworth. He's still sleeping. BP is normal and she removed his IV. His owners are coming to pick him up within the hour. It's in his chart if you want to take a look."

"Thanks, Rachel."

She turned her attention on Luke again.

"If you're busy—"

"No. Come to my office. I need something to drink anyway."

He followed her back, winking at Rachel, who winked back and smiled.

She grabbed two sodas from the refrigerator in the break room, then led him into her office. Daisy and Annie came up to him, obviously excited to see him.

"Hey, girls. I've missed you." He petted them, and they licked his hand.

"They're happy to see you."

"I'm happy to see them, too. Boomer misses his friends. It's been a few days."

"Yes. It has. Where is Boomer?"

"In the cruiser. Napping."

"Oh. Busy day?"

"Yeah. He's taking a break."

She leaned against her desk, and he tried not to notice her lab coat was open and her scrubs stretched tight against her breasts.

He cleared his throat.

"So, what brings you here, officer?"

He liked when she talked to him in that slightly teasing, low-throated way. It was sexy.

"I just wanted to check on you. And to ask what your plans were for this weekend."

Her eyes widened. "Uh . . . this weekend?"

"It's a holiday weekend. The weather is supposed to be warm. I thought we'd go to the lake. With the dogs."

"The lake. With the dogs."

"Should I write this down?"

"Why would you write it down?"

"Because for some reason you feel the need to repeat what I say back to me."

"Oh. Sorry. You want to take me to the lake with you?"

"Yeah. I have a cabin there. And a boat."

"You have a boat?"

"You don't like boats? Or maybe water?"

"I love boats. And water."

"Good. Let's just go to the cabin over the weekend with the dogs and have some fun."

"Okay. Let's do that."

He'd expected more reluctance, that he'd have to cajole her into it. "Great. I'll pick you up at your house after you get off work tomorrow. Be packed and ready to go."

"Should I shop for food or something?"

"We'll do that when we get up there. There's a store nearby."

"All right."

"I should go so you can finish up your workday." He pushed off the wall, then reached for the door handle in her office.

"Luke?"

He paused, turned his head to look at her. "Yeah?"

"Thanks for inviting me. I'm looking forward to this weekend."

Her voice was soft, like a caress over his skin.

He came toward her and grabbed her lab coat, tugging her toward him for a kiss. It was long, lingering, and made him want to stay for more. But he had work to do, and so did she.

"Me, too, Emma."

Chapter 16

EMMA DWELLED ON her weekend with Luke all during the workday. After she'd spilled her guts about her past with Vaughn, she figured he'd run like hell and not look back.

Most men would.

She should have known Luke wasn't most men.

Most of her issues with the past were in her own head. It was high time she shoved the past into the closet, into the dark remnants of history where it belonged. She deserved to live again, to have some fun. And who better to have fun with than Luke, someone she trusted, someone she knew wouldn't hurt her?

Luke wasn't looking for anything long term, wouldn't put shackles of ownership on her and make demands of her. He was a fun guy, certainly hot, and more important, he wasn't out for a relationship. He was a fling kind of man. And when it was over, she could breathe a sigh of relief, put a checkmark on her "things to do to start living her life again," and move on.

With that in mind, Emma was thrilled at the prospect of having a weekend alone with Luke. She'd been working nonstop since she started up the practice, and it was exhilarating to think she had three whole days off. She'd worked out a deal with the veterinary clinic north of town. They were taking emergency calls for this holiday weekend. She'd be on call for the next holiday.

She finished packing, put dog food in a container for both Daisy and Annie, packed up their bowls and toys, and laid it all by the front door, which gave her just enough time to dash into the bathroom to look in the mirror one last time.

Hair in a high ponytail. Capris, tennis shoes, and a T-shirt. All very casual. It wasn't like she was trying to impress Luke.

Much.

Daisy barked, so that meant Luke was in her driveway. She opened the front door and saw Luke's truck, with one really cool ski boat trailered behind it.

The dogs ran to him, already so familiar with him that they sat and stayed when he gave them the command.

"Nice boat," she said.

"Thanks. I'm looking forward to taking it out in the water."

"I'm looking forward to being out on the water."

He grinned. "Annie's coming along with her training." He looked over his shoulder to watch her sitting next to Daisy.

"We've been working diligently on it. I didn't want her running amok at the lake, and I really didn't like the idea of boarding her this weekend. We practiced 'stay' a lot last night."

He smiled. "We'll keep watch over her. I think she'll stick close to Boomer and Daisy."

"She trails after Daisy like she's her big sister. I don't anticipate any problems."

He reached down for her bags. "Is this everything?"

"Yes." She grabbed the bag she'd loaded with the dogs' stuff and locked the door behind her. Daisy hopped up into the backseat of Luke's truck, and Emma scooped up Annie and deposited her next to Daisy.

"Hi, Boomer," Emma said, giving Boomer a scratch behind the ears. "Ready for a big weekend at the lake?"

Boomer licked her hand.

"Boomer loves the lake. Surprisingly, he actually likes the water."

"That's good. Not a lot of dogs take to water. It reminds them too much of having a bath."

"He also likes baths."

"Clearly an exceptional animal."

Luke gave Boomer a rub. "He thinks so."

The ride up to Grand Lake took less than an hour. Boomer and Daisy spent their time looking out the window, while Annie curled up on the seat and went to sleep. Emma had gotten to work before the sun came up, so she found herself drifting on and off, her head resting against the passenger-side window.

She startled at Luke's nudge on her shoulder and the sound of his voice.

"Hey, we're here."

She shot up. "Oh, God. I slept."

"Yeah, you did."

She took off her seat belt. "I'm so sorry. I got up really early today, but geez, I was terrible company for you on the ride."

"It's okay, Emma. I don't need conversation. And you obviously needed a nap."

She slid out of the truck and grabbed her bags. She and the dogs followed Luke the short walk to the cabin.

"Wow," she said, trailing behind him.

He stopped, his boots kicking up dirt as he swiveled to face her. "You like the place?"

What wasn't there to like? A two-story log-cabin style, it had pristine windows and a back deck upstairs she already knew would provide a stunning view of the lake. Trees so tall they shaded the hot afternoon sun surrounded them. It was isolated, which only added to its allure.

"The location is prime. Right on the lake. And one spectacular view."

"Yeah, my dad owned it. Now it belongs to my brothers and me. Logan's always busy on the ranch, though, so he rarely comes up here since he says there's plenty of fish in the lake on the ranch, and of course, Reid lives out of state, so he's never here."

He unlocked and opened the front door, holding it open for her. As she brushed by, she inhaled the fresh, outdoor scent of him, making her want to lean in closer.

Inside was all wood floors, and nicely furnished, with a great kitchen. The place smelled of recent polish. "Did you come up here recently to clean?"

"No, but we have people to take care of it routinely, so the place doesn't get musty."

People. Must be nice to have "people."

They let the dogs out back, and there were no neighbors, so the dogs could run free. They walked for a bit while the dogs stretched their legs.

"I don't know how you don't come here every weekend," she said as they walked a worn path parallel to the lake. The dogs stayed nearby. "It's beautiful and so peaceful."

"Yeah, it is nice. I come out here from time to time. I came here a lot after my divorce, to get away and work on things in my head."

"Some alone time is never a bad thing. Especially after going through a breakup."

"Back then it wasn't. Now coming here alone just makes me feel . . . I don't know."

She lifted her gaze to his. "More alone?"

His lips curved. "Maybe."

"But you like your bachelor lifestyle."

"I do. Doesn't mean I always like being alone."

Interesting. She'd enjoyed her freedom so much since she'd escaped from her relationship with Vaughn. She'd felt like a prisoner for so long, she'd vowed back then she'd never be tied to a man again.

But that had been a very long time ago. School and work had kept her so busy she'd never felt anything was missing in her life.

Until very recently.

"How was work today?" Luke asked.

"Easy. We took in a few dogs and a cat for boarding. I

had one emergency, a dog that had gotten into a fight and needed some stitches. Otherwise, very routine."

"Easy days are good. Seems like you're settling in."

"It does. I've been very lucky so far. Folks have been friendly and have been referring their friends and family, so my business is increasing."

"Hope's a friendly kind of town, you know. If you do right by people, they have no problem recommending you to others. They like to see good people succeed."

"You sound like a politician now."

He laughed. "Believe me, I'm not. I just know how it works in Hope, since I've spent my whole life here, other than a few years away for college."

"Any thoughts about living somewhere else?"

"I've thought about it, especially if the chance to work in a bigger city police force ever comes around."

"So you see what you're doing now as a stopover point, something temporary?"

Luke studied the earnest expression on Emma's face. He'd never considered the question, at least not in depth. He'd always thought of his job with the Hope police force as something he was doing right now, never giving much thought to whether it was something he wanted to do for the rest of his life. Sure, he'd often thought about working for a larger police force in a bigger city, but working for Hope satisfied him.

Did it satisfy enough, long term?

"Honestly, I don't know."

Her gaze held his. "Are you happy? With your job, I mean?"

"Yeah."

"Then maybe you don't need to look for that spot over the rainbow, to borrow from Dorothy in the *Wizard of Oz*. A lot of people are so miserable in their jobs their whole lives, and no matter where they go, they're never going to be happy. You are happy. Isn't that enough?"

The wind had started to pick up, grabbing a strand of her hair and whipping it across her cheek. He reached out and tucked it behind her ear. "Maybe it is."

She offered up a smile, and he wanted to pull her close, put his mouth on hers to see if she tasted as good as she looked.

She tempted him, made him want things he never thought he'd ever want again.

And that was the temptation of Emma.

Boomer barked, and Emma took a step back.

"Come here, Annie." She crouched down and the pup came running. She scooped her up in her arms.

"She's growing fast."

"I know," she said with a laugh. "Soon I won't be able to hold her. Which is why I'm doing it now. She may grow fast, but she'll be a baby for a while."

He grasped Annie under her chin and stared into her dark eyes. "She's a cutie."

"I wasn't intending on adopting another dog, not right now, anyway. I just started the new practice, and that's keeping me plenty busy."

"It's like having kids. I don't think there's ever a perfect time for that, either."

She laughed. "I guess not. Annie just showed up, and when no one adopted her, what was I supposed to do? Take her to the shelter? I was afraid no one would take her, and she'd bonded with Daisy, so she became part of the family."

"Admit it. You're a softy. Just hope you don't adopt every stray that shows up at your clinic."

"My house isn't big enough for that."

They continued walking. "You might have to get a bigger house."

"Or better resolve. I'm not one to let animals go unclaimed. If I hadn't been living in an apartment when I was working at the clinic in South Carolina, I'd likely have brought a few dogs and cats along with me when I came back home. Someone was always dropping off an animal they'd found."

"There are shelters for that."

"True. But people often take animals they find to their veterinarian because they figure the vet's office will feed them, give them their shots, and do a better job of finding a home for them. If we have the space, we'll give them a few days and put up a sign, hoping someone will adopt the animal. But if no one wants them, we have to take them to the shelter."

"Then hope for the best."

She nodded, her expression pained. "Yes."

They made it back to the house. The dogs bounded up the stairs, even Annie, though she was a little slower than the other two.

"I'll take you upstairs so you can stow your gear."

She grabbed her bag and followed him up the stairs.

"There are two bedrooms up here. One bathroom."

He was giving her the choice. He wouldn't push her. Even though they'd been together once, he would never assume.

"Which one's your room?" she asked.

"I usually stay in this one." He inclined his head to the right.

She pondered for a few seconds. "Okay if I stay with you?"

He felt the jolt of awareness all the way down to his balls and let her know by giving her a heated smile. "Very okay."

He led her into the bedroom where they dropped their bags and unpacked. After that, they went downstairs.

"You ready to head to the store and stock up for the weekend?"

"Sure. Do you want to make a list first?"

He leaned a hip against the counter and studied her." So you're a list maker, huh?"

She cocked a brow. "You say that like it's a bad thing."

"I'm more of a shop-by-the-seat-of-your-pants kind of guy."

"You forget important things that way." She went over and looked into the fridge, then grabbed the pad of paper and pen on the counter and started writing. "Like ketchup, mustard, and mayo. We'll also need hamburger and hot dogs."

She looked up at him. "I assume hamburger and hot dogs are okay? And how about some lunchmeat? What's your favorite?"

He laughed. "You're doing fine, and I'm not a picky eater. You throw it in front of me, and I'll eat it."

"Thank God. Me, too. Picky eaters annoy the crap out of me."

"Me, too."

"Chips. What kind of—oh, never mind. I'll just put the general items on the list. We'll figure out specifics when we get to the store."

"Beer."

She looked up at him, then smiled. "Definitely beer. And pop."

Luke drove them to a grocery store in Grove, even though it took a while to get there.

"We'll have a bigger selection this way. If we stayed in the lake area, all you're going to get is mostly convenience stores."

"This'll work fine." She grabbed a cart and her list, and in a very efficient manner went up and down the aisles, grabbing what they needed and moving on.

She was a fast shopper, didn't dawdle, and stayed on list. That is, until they got to the bakery, where she pondered the cupcakes.

"These look good. If I'd had more time, I'd have made some myself."

"You bake?"

She cast him a look. "Yes, I bake. When there's time. I love to cook."

"I'm going to keep that in mind and make you show me your skills."

"You're on."

They finished a lot faster than he thought they would. He'd been grocery shopping with women before. Becca used to dawdle, read labels, randomly pick up stuff that wasn't on her list. It would take hours to finish grocery shopping. It used to drive him crazy.

He and Emma were out of the store in twenty minutes.

As they finished loading the groceries in the truck, he turned to her. "I could kiss you right now."

Her eyes widened. "Why?"

"Because you made this so much more bearable than I thought it would be."

She laughed. "You have some shopping nightmares you'd like to share?"

"No. It's bad enough I endured them. The last thing I want to do is relive them."

"You poor baby. Traumatized in the produce aisle."

He grimaced, remembering how Becca would stare at tomatoes for what seemed like hours. To him, a tomato was a tomato. "You have no idea."

"I'm going to have to make you a drink tonight and probe this past horror out of you."

He walked over to his side of the truck. "You can try."

"Oh, but I am going to ask you to stop at the liquor store next. And I intend to buy whiskey."

As they climbed into the truck and he started it up, he looked over at her and grinned. "Whiskey, huh? I like the sound of that."

"Thought you might."

He stopped at the liquor store, and true to her word, Emma came out with a bottle of Jack Daniels.

"A woman after my heart."

"Hey, go get your own bottle. This one's mine."

"You wouldn't share?"

She stared down at the bottle. "Well, it is a pretty big bottle. So . . . maybe. It depends on whether I can pry any secrets out of you with whiskey."

He laughed as he pulled out onto the main road. "Darlin', I'm a big keeper of secrets. Not much for revealing any."

"Too bad. This is really good whiskey."

The more time he spent with Emma, the more he liked her.

Every time he was with her, he drew one step closer to her. And protecting his heart lost the battle a little more.

He didn't want a relationship, but damned if he didn't feel like he was smack in the middle of one with Emma. Out of control and going down for the count.

He wasn't sure if he was happy about that or not.

Chapter 17

BY THE TIME they got back from the store it was getting late, so they unpacked groceries, let the dogs out for a short run, then came back in and fixed sandwiches and chips for dinner.

Emma couldn't recall having a more relaxed night. Luke was fun, had a great sense of humor, and she no longer felt skittish or uncomfortable.

He knew all her secrets, hadn't run, hadn't judged her, and for some reason he liked being around her. He didn't tell her what to do, and he seemed to enjoy her independence.

This was a refreshing, new relation—

No . . . it was just a right-now kind of thing. But whatever it was, she intended to enjoy it.

"Do you like to water-ski?" Luke asked as they were cleaning up the dishes.

Emma paused, her hands shoved in the soapy water. "I don't know. I've never done it before."

"You grew up around all these lakes and you never water-skied?"

"I know. I lived such a sheltered life. I guess I was too busy hitting the books to have a social life."

He tilted his head down and gave her a look. "Somehow I find that hard to believe."

"Why?"

"You're too pretty not to have had a social life."

"I'll accept the compliment, thank you, but in high school my hair was frizzy, I had bad acne, and I wore braces until I was seventeen. It wasn't a pretty picture, and boys weren't interested."

"Obviously they were morons not to see through the hair, pimples, and braces to the beautiful young girl you were underneath."

She looked at him. "Do you always say just the right thing?"

He laughed. "No. Usually never."

"Well, you just did. Thank you."

"And tomorrow you water-ski. We'll head out early in the morning on the boat."

Water-skiing sounded exciting. Another new adventure.

"How about a look at the night view on the back deck upstairs?" Luke asked.

"Sure." She grabbed two glasses and the bottle of whiskey.

Luke gave her that mysterious but oh-so-sexy smile that sent her nerve endings skittering in all those questioning directions. This weekend, she decided she wasn't going to question anything. She'd just let things develop and see where they went.

The deck was located at the end of the hall, nice because it wasn't outside either of the bedrooms.

The sun had barely set, which meant a dusky glow still lingered over the lake. The wind had died down. Emma couldn't hear a thing except the sounds of nature. Tall trees blanketed her on all sides, their scents cool and fragrant.

She set the bottle and glasses down on the table between their two chairs and stared out over the water. No one was boating right now, so the lake was a mirror. She felt like she could walk right out and slide across it.

"This is beautiful. So serene, so quiet." She leaned her head against the back of the chair and closed her eyes, listening to the sounds of the crickets.

"Easy to lose your sense of time and place out here," Luke said, his voice lowering.

"Understandable. The real world is so far removed. All the stress is gone. No bills to pay, no work to do, nothing but utter relaxation. It's a fantasy."

She opened her eyes to find Luke's gaze fixed on the lake. For some reason, she liked that he wasn't looking at her.

"How about that whiskey?"

He turned to face her.

"What? You're not going to pry secrets out of me first?"

She opened the bottle, poured two shots. "I think if you want to divulge any secrets to me, you'll do that in your own time."

"I might just do that. Eventually."

She handed him a glass. "To a good weekend."

He lifted his glass and tipped it against hers. "I'll definitely drink to that."

He downed his shot, and she downed hers, too, the fiery liquid burning its way down her throat. "Whoa. That's good."

Luke laid his glass down. "You surprise the hell out of me, Emma."

"I do? In what way?"

"Sometimes you seem so quiet and shy. Almost as if you're afraid of me. Other times, you're like a saucy little flirt. I just can't figure you out."

She leaned back in the chair. "Good. I'd hate to be boring and predictable."

"You're definitely not either of those things." He poured another shot and handed it to her.

She took it and downed the shot, then placed the glass on the table.

"Like this."

She turned to him again. "Like what?"

"You. Doing whiskey shots. I would never have guessed you to be a whiskey drinker. More like the fine-wine type."

She laughed. "I don't know whether to be complimented or insulted. But I do like wine, too. Both out of the box and the kind you use a corkscrew to open."

"See? Again . . . unpredictable."

Her lips curved.

"You like being mysterious?" he asked.

"Not really. I just don't want to be . . ."

"Want to be what?" he asked when she didn't finish her sentence.

She shrugged. "I don't know. I'm just who I am, Luke. I don't try to be anything else." She got up and went to the balcony, looking out over the water, her emotions jumbled up inside.

She finally turned so she could face him. "We're all a product of our pasts. That's what shapes the choices we make, for good or bad."

"Is that how you ended up back in Hope? Your past?"

"Partly. I can't say it wasn't nice to be back with my family again. I liked working for the veterinary practice in South Carolina, but when the opportunity came up to buy Doc Weston's practice here, it seemed like kismet. I could be home again and near my family. I'd missed so much time with them because of Vaughn—because of the choices I'd made. I wanted to be home again."

"Home is good."

"Yes, it is. After all the mistakes I'd made, plus all the choices I'd had taken away from me, it felt good to make this decision."

"You made the right one this time."

She smiled at him. "Thank you, Luke." It felt good to be validated instead of criticized for a change. He was so . . . different. With him, she felt relaxed, like she could be herself for the first time in a very long time. She didn't have to try to live up to an image someone had created of her, or be afraid that every step she took or every word she said would be the wrong one.

It was quite the revelation. She had Luke to thank for it, too, because he'd given her the freedom to admit the mistakes she'd made, and hadn't judged her for them. He accepted her—past and all—and he still wanted to be with her.

He looked damn hot sitting there in the moonlight, his hair so dark and thick she itched to run her fingers through it, his mouth so tempting it physically hurt to know how it felt to brush her lips against his.

And he'd been great to her, really there when she'd needed him.

Like now, offering to listen. Luke was good for her, good for her ego. She needed that right now. Even more than that, she wanted it, wanted him.

There were so many things she wanted, so much she'd denied herself because of that stupid mistake she'd made so long ago.

If she'd had a normal life, she could have a wild weekend fling with Luke and walk away without looking back. She could be free and easy about her sex life without a second thought. Instead, she always second-guessed everything in her life because of the potential consequences. She was always afraid every choice she made would be the wrong one, that every man she chose would be the next one to hurt her as badly as Vaughn had.

But Luke hadn't hurt her. Not yet, anyway.

Yet every time she saw him, every minute she spent with him, she grew closer to him. And she knew that no matter how hard she tried to downplay her feelings, she knew just that—she had feelings for him.

And that meant he could hurt her. Which scared her more than just a little.

It scared her a lot.

Obviously this brave new Emma wasn't quite as brave as she thought.

Luke stood, came over to the balcony, and leaned against the railing, not getting too close but close enough that she picked up his scent. It made her want to take a deep breath so she wouldn't lose his unique flavor. He always smelled so good, and he never even wore cologne.

He tucked her hair behind her ear, and her skin prickled with goose bumps.

"I think deep inside you're still a little bit afraid."

She quirked a brow. "Of?"

"Men. Or maybe just me."

Her lips lifted, the two shots of whiskey making her feel braver than normal. She placed her palm on his chest, the thump, thump, thump of his heart making her own beat wilder and faster. "Are you trying to offer me some kind of therapy?"

He let out a short laugh. "I'd be the last person to offer to psychoanalyze anyone, Emma. If anyone's had one hell of a fucked-up life, it's me. But I know what it's like to be hurt by someone you care about. And if you want to talk about that, I want you to know you can trust me."

Her eyes burned with the tears that pricked them. She lifted her gaze to his, seeing the pain that lived in his eyes, too.

He understood. And she could talk to him, lay out her fears, but not now. Not tonight, when there was something else she wanted so much more. She dug her nails into his chest, heard the harsh intake of his breath, and knew right then that she was playing with fire.

She was more than ready to go up in flames, as long as he was with her.

"That's . . . really nice of you to offer, Luke. But I'm kind of talked out for a while. Wouldn't you rather kiss me?"

He inched closer, his body vibrating against hers as his hip brushed hers.

"You want me to kiss you. You sure about that?"

She nodded. "Very sure."

He reached up and swept his thumb across her bottom lip. "You're trembling, Emma. Are you cold?"

She shook her head. "No. I'm kind of hot."

He snaked an arm around her waist and tugged her

against him. His body was hard—all over. She grabbed hold of his shirt like a lifeline, as if she were afraid he'd disappear right in front of her eyes.

And when he slid his other hand across her neck, his breath warm against her cheek, their eyes met in this slow dance of heat and promise.

And still, he paused, his lips only inches from hers.

"Be careful what you ask for, Emma. You might get it."

"I really hope so, Luke."

His lips came down on hers, and this time there was no hesitation. She wound her arm around his neck as his mouth invaded hers.

It was always like this with Luke, this dizzying, crazy, make-her-knees-weak kind of kiss. And when his tongue slid inside to tangle with hers, she buckled, and Luke tightened his hold on her, but didn't break the kiss.

She caressed his shoulders and slid her fingers into his hair, tugging it until he groaned, which only made her nipples tingle. And when he backed her up against the wall of the deck and ground against her, letting her know that he was very much turned on and oh-so-ready to do something about it, her body responded by quivering and dampening in just the right place. If he had a condom on him, they could do it right there on the deck. She was primed for the kind of orgasm she hadn't had since the last time they were together.

And when he moved his hand from her hip to her waist, lifting her T-shirt, she was all in on this, breaking contact with him just long enough to pull her shirt over her head and toss it on the deck.

His gaze met hers, and he grinned, then pulled off his shirt.

"Wait," she said.

He frowned. "Is this too fast for you?"

"No. Definitely, no. I just need to look at you." She gave him a slight push so he'd take a step back.

She took in the sight of him. Well-sculpted shoulders, a wide expanse of chest, and oh, God, those abs. She was going to have to spend hours exploring his abs. With her tongue.

She took a deep breath, then sighed.

"Are you ogling me?" he asked.

"Maybe a little. Okay, yes. I've missed seeing you naked."

His lips curved. "You're killing me, Emma." He moved in and kissed her again, this time laying a very possessive hand on her breast. She gasped, especially when he deftly pulled one side of her bra down to brush a thumb over her nipple. If she came while he did that, it would be so embarrassing. Then again, she might not care, as long as she got a great orgasm out of it.

Except right now she was breathing so fast and so hard she was afraid she might hyperventilate. But the sensations he evoked when he touched her were almost more than she could bear.

His hand drifted down her rib cage, and when he reached her pants, he slipped his hand inside and cupped her sex.

She pulled her lips from his. "Oh, God, yes, please touch me there."

He met her gaze and moved his hand. "Like that?"

She grasped his wrist, too far gone and close to the edge to even care about how brazen she was being. "Yes. Just like that."

His erection was hard and thick as it rested against her hip.

"Have you come since the last time we were together, Emma?" he asked, slipping his fingers inside her panties.

She could barely form words, but she managed a strangled, "No."

His fingers were rough, and they felt so good against her skin as he took her right to the edge in a few expert strokes.

"Then let me take you there."

Taut with tension and teetering right on the edge of climax, she moved against his questing fingers, listening to the hard edge of his voice. And when he tucked his fingers inside her, she quivered and rocked against the heel of his hand as he moved it over her sensitized flesh.

"I know exactly what you need," Luke whispered, his voice a dark promise in her ear.

She was there, all she had to do was let go.

"You're so soft," he said. "So wet under my fingers. I can't wait to put my mouth on you and make you scream, Emma. And when I'm inside you . . ."

The sound of his voice, so direct, so coaxing, did her in. She came with a wild cry, digging her nails into his arm as she bucked against his hand. He took her mouth in a hot kiss that made her soar even higher, leaving her trembling in his arms and utterly satisfied, yet still wanting more from him.

He withdrew his hand and wrapped his arm around her, holding her close as he pressed soft kisses to her neck.

"That," she said as she rested her head on his shoulder, "was exactly what I needed."

"I could tell," he said against her neck. "That was one hell of an orgasm."

She laughed, loving that he kept it light. "That was just the first. I intend to have more than one."

He pulled back and looked at her. "I'm glad to hear that, since I'm hard as a rock right now."

She took his hand and led him inside the house. "I assume you brought condoms?"

"I told you, I'm always prepared."

She smiled. "I brought condoms, too."

Chapter 18

LUKE LAUGHED, AND dragged Emma into his room. "Again, Emma, you surprise me."

She flopped onto his bed. "Why, because I brought condoms?"

He kicked off his boots and climbed onto the bed next to her, pulling her into his arms. "Yeah."

"I like to be prepared, too."

"I'm glad, because I have a feeling there's going to be a lot of sex this weekend, and I don't want to have to go back to the store."

She rested her head on her hand. "Feel that supremely confident about your prowess, do you?"

He circled the swell of her breasts with his fingertips. "I made you come once already, didn't I?"

She drew in a sharp breath. "Yes, you did. How about we do that again? It's been a long time since we were last together."

"Challenge accepted." He pushed her onto her back and covered her with the top half of his body, kissing her so thoroughly that if she'd been standing, she'd have been left dizzy. She loved his mouth, the way he kissed her with slow, deliberate kisses, as if he had all the time in the world. This wasn't a man who gave her a brief kiss, then went for the action. He spent his time lingering at her lips, using his tongue to lick over hers, to draw her bottom lip into his mouth, to explore until she could barely breathe. And then he moved his lips over her jaw, down her neck and over her collarbone, eliciting chill bumps over her skin.

And when he rolled his tongue over the swell of her breasts at the edge of her bra, she wasn't sure she'd ever felt anything so teasingly sensual. She wanted to rip off her bra so he could get to her nipples, but again, Luke seemed to be in no hurry. He finally slid his hand down her back to release the clasp on her bra, drew the straps down her arms.

He stared down at her, using the tip of his finger to draw circles around her nipples.

"Pretty," he said, then bent and took one already erect bud into his mouth.

She breathed in, arching upward to give him more. She threaded her fingers into his hair to hold him in place as he licked and sucked her nipples and drove her crazy with the expertise of his mouth. She shuddered when he moved his tongue down her ribs and over her belly, anticipating his next move.

"Let's get these off," he said, tugging her capris down her legs, leaving her wearing only her panties.

And again, he took his time to caress and stare at her body.

"You're beautiful, Emma."

She reached for him, running her fingers over his torso. "And you have too many clothes on."

"I can fix that." He hopped off the bed, undid the zipper of his jeans and dropped them, along with his boxer briefs, revealing his magnificently sculpted body, and a very impressive erection.

"Uh, wow," she said, rolling over to her side.

He grinned. "You're good for my ego." He climbed back on the bed and rolled her onto her back. "But right now, let's worship your body. It sounds like you have some missed orgasms to make up for."

"I'd like to complain and say we should take care of you, but I'm all for you worshipping my body."

He laughed. "I like a woman who knows what she wants. And there's plenty of time for me later."

He was so . . . different from any man she'd ever known before. Night-and-day different from Vaughn, who'd always been about his pleasure first.

And that was the last time she was going to think about him tonight. Or ever. She'd much rather focus on Luke, who was gorgeous, built, and had already given her one amazing orgasm. How could she think about anyone else when Luke was drawing her panties down her legs, pulling her to the edge of the bed, and putting his mouth—

"There. Oh yes," she said, and then words were lost as Luke pleasured her with his expert lips and tongue until she was mindless, until all she could think about was climbing that mountain until she reached the peak and fell.

His tongue was a sweet balm to her tortured senses. And when she came, he was right there, holding her hand and taking her right over. She arched and cried out, her entire body vibrating as Luke held tight to her hips and made her his.

He kissed his way up her body. Her utterly motionless body. She was sure she was done for, but by the time he reached her mouth and planted a kiss on her that seared her, she was convinced he had magical powers. She twined her legs around his, aware of the ever-constant erection he'd had for a while now.

She reached for him, wrapping her fingers around his length and thickness. His body was warm, but here he was hot and pulsing. She stroked him, and he grasped her wrist.

"We don't want this to be over with in a hurry."

She smiled. "I think it's your turn."

"I could be gallant and give you some time to rest, but all I've thought about is being inside you, Emma."

Heat flared low in her belly. "I've thought a lot about that, too."

He palmed her stomach. "You have a beautiful body. A sweet mouth, a laugh that makes my balls tight, and a smile that makes me want to kiss you. I think about you all the time."

"Tell me what you think about." In the haze of this amazing afterglow, he made her feel brave enough to ask the question.

"How you challenge me. Your contradictions, how sweet you are, the way you love animals, and the way you move when you walk. And I've thought a lot about this." He leaned over her and took the tip of a nipple between his lips, rolling his tongue over it, then drawing it into his mouth to suck.

She shuddered out a breath at the exquisite sensation, her body tightening in reaction. She slid her fingers into his hair, unable to do anything but watch as he mastered her body. Giving up control was something she vowed she'd never do again, but she gladly gave over control to Luke because he demanded nothing. He only gave to her in a way that constantly surprised her. He seemed to draw pleasure from giving pleasure to her, which was something she wasn't used to.

She could get used to it in a hurry, though.

He lifted up, his gaze locked with hers. "And I've thought a lot about getting you naked so I could touch you." His fingers crept low, covering her sex, taking his time to coax a response from her that left her languid and needy and arching against him.

She lifted her gaze to his, hitching a breath as she saw the hunger in his eyes. "I really like your hands on me."

When he finally rolled over and grabbed a condom from his bedside drawer, she was more than eager to feel him inside her, to share that intimacy with him again.

He tore the wrapper open and applied the condom, then nudged her legs apart and slid inside her.

A moan escaped her lips, and he captured her mouth in a searing kiss that made her quiver, inside and out. And when he began to move within her, she clenched around him, the sensations overwhelming. Feeling as if she was falling, she flailed for something to hold on to. Luke grasped her hand and twined his fingers with hers, centering her.

"Emma." His voice was a gentle whisper in her ear.

She opened her eyes, and there he was, moving above her, his eyes dark and filled with the same hungry passion that wracked her body with a need she couldn't explain. She arched into that need and he fed her, levering his hips to hit that spot that brought her closer to the orgasm she was surprised she'd be able to reach after he'd already given her two explosive ones already.

Yet here she was, poised on the edge again, and as she tightened, he knew, and he smiled.

"That's it," he said, moving his body perfectly, as if he knew exactly what she needed.

He was exactly what she needed, and it scared the hell out of her.

She tensed, and he paused.

"What?" he asked, holding himself up on his hands. "Something wrong?"

This was ridiculous. It was only sex. Just fabulous, glorious sex, and nothing else.

She cupped the back of his neck and pulled him down to her again. "No. Everything's right."

She kissed him, wrapped her arms around him, and he moved against her, taking her right back to that spot where she forgot everything except that mindless pleasure he gave her. He grasped her hips and held her, rubbing his body against hers until she exploded. And then he went with her, groaning against her as he came. She held tight to him as he shuddered, then lay still, his breath warm against her neck.

They were both sweating, Luke's heart pounding against her chest. Or maybe that was her heart. She couldn't tell. She was wrecked, physically and emotionally, tied to Luke's body, wrapped around him, within him, in ways she hadn't expected.

He kissed the side of her neck, didn't seem to be in any

hurry to move, so she stroked his back, played with his hair and just . . . breathed.

When he finally rolled over, he left the bed. She watched him, enjoying the view of his great ass. He came back a minute later and climbed into bed with her, tucking her against his chest and wrapping his arms around her.

"Give me a few minutes' recovery time, then we're going to do this again."

She laughed. "You're on."

This was nice. And different.

She had to remind herself not to get attached to Luke. This was supposed to be fun and simple and just about sex and this weekend. They had agreed that neither of them was looking for a relationship.

But as she yawned and snuggled in close to him, she realized that she felt . . . safe with Luke. That's what was different about him. She never felt threatened or exposed when she was with him.

She felt safe.

And she hadn't felt safe with a man in a very long time.

Chapter 19

"COME ON, LAZY, time to get up and put your swimsuit on."

As the haze of Luke's voice reached her, Emma blinked against the harsh light that poured in through the open deck.

"It's morning already?" She rolled over on her stomach and pulled the pillow over her head.

"Yup. And we're burning daylight. Let's get moving."

"I need coffee."

"Already made. I'll meet you downstairs."

She groaned, but rolled out of bed. As she stood and stretched, she smiled at the unfamiliar soreness, remembering last night—the three times they'd made love last night. And each time, Luke had been a giving lover, making sure she was more than satisfied.

"Delicious," she whispered to herself. She went into the bathroom, brushed her teeth, and combed her hair. She found her swimsuit and threw on shorts and a tank top over it, forcing her eyes to focus as she made her way downstairs and into the kitchen. The smell of coffee was her savior.

Luke had already poured her a cup.

"You're my hero," she said as she took a sip of the dark brew.

"I'll bet you say that to all the guys who make you coffee in the morning."

"Yes, it's a regular revolving door of hot men brewing me coffee."

He leaned against the counter, and she drank her fill of him. He wore a pair of blue-and-white board shorts and no shirt, and that delicious thought continued. He looked hot and tan, his abs washboard tight and sexy, his hair still sleep-tousled. The last thing on her mind this morning was water-skiing. She wanted to drag him back upstairs and have her way with him about five or six more times until maybe she got tired of him.

"You keep looking at me like that, two things are gonna happen," he said, giving her a very hot look over the rim of his coffee cup.

"Yeah? What two things?"

"One, I'm gonna get hard, and two, we're never going to go water-skiing today."

Her lips curved. "And those are bad things?"

"Not necessarily, but there's plenty of time for those things later. Today I promised you I'd take you water-skiing."

With a sigh, she said, "I guess you're right." She looked around. "Where are the dogs?"

"Out back. I already fed them."

"Don't you sleep?"

"I got plenty of sleep."

"As I recall, we didn't sleep much last night." She'd drifted off, but he'd awakened her in the middle of the night, hard, and stroking her breasts. She'd gone willingly into his arms. Just the memory of the two of them making love in the dark had her body quickening, wanting more.

"You're giving me that look again," he said, arching a brow.

"Am I? You know, we could put off that whole water-skiing thing."

"Temptress. I'm going to go check the gear. You're dangerous to be around when you're sleepy and sexy."

She grinned and went out back, finding the dogs playing nearby. Annie was fighting Daisy for a stick, though it appeared to Emma that Daisy was merely humoring her. Boomer sat on the sidelines like a spectator, above it all. Annie would growl and Daisy would hold on, clearly stronger than the pup, at least for now. Eventually Daisy got bored and dropped the stick. Annie ran off victorious.

She brought the dogs inside and poured herself another cup of coffee.

"How about some breakfast?" Luke asked as he came back inside.

"Sounds great."

They put together eggs, bacon, and toast. Working with him in the kitchen was fun. Luke didn't sit there and expect her to do the cooking for him. Instead, he made the bacon and toast while she cooked the eggs. And since they worked next to each other, he'd lean over and kiss or touch her, giving her chills—and ideas.

They sat at the table and ate. It was very domestic, and quite romantic, as Luke poured juice and brought it over to her.

"Thank you."

"You're welcome."

He kept smiling at her, and staring at her, giving her looks that distinctly reminded her of how he'd gazed at her when he was inside her last night. Very direct, with not-so-subtle meaning. Which meant she'd get hot and flustered, and she had no idea why they were going water-skiing when right now they could be upstairs in bed together.

It wasn't that long of a weekend, after all.

But she understood he was trying to entertain her, no doubt afraid she'd get bored.

Though she didn't find sex with him boring at all.

Wow. Wasn't her mind on one thing and one thing only right now? Talk about the end of the sex drought.

After they ate, they cleared the dishes and she went upstairs to grab her beach bag and slide into her flip-flops.

"What about the dogs?" she asked after she came downstairs.

"There's a run over on the other side of the property. We can leave them outside for the day and not have to worry about them wandering off. Plenty of room in there, and since it's a nice day and not too hot, they can be outside rather than stuck inside the house."

Luke led her over to the dog run, an oversized fenced-in area even larger than she had imagined. It was well shaded, with a large bowl he filled with water.

She wouldn't have to worry about the dogs. They were well secured and had plenty of room to play. And Luke was right—she knew they'd much prefer to be outside than to be stuck in the house. This way, Annie wouldn't have to be crated.

"This will be perfect," she said.

Once the dogs were secured, she and Luke climbed into the truck and took off. It wasn't far to the ramp, so Luke gave her instructions on backing the truck down the ramp so he could get the boat in the water. They worked as a team, and before long he had the boat off the trailer. She pulled the truck and trailer forward, parked, then climbed onto the boat.

"Hey, nice job. You didn't even sink the truck," Luke said with a wink.

"Gee, thanks."

He backed the boat out and took it slow out of the shallows, then pushed the throttle. Emma held on as he sped past the lines of trees along the bank, wind slapping her ponytail across her back.

The breeze was wonderful, the sun already promising a very hot day as they cruised along the tops of the waves. She settled in and enjoyed the view of the lake as Luke throttled down and they moved along at an easy pace. She finally took a seat and looked out the side as other boaters breezed by, some of them waving as they passed.

She'd been working at a grueling pace for the past few

months, before and ever since the clinic opened. To be able to relax like this was a small bit of nirvana.

Luke finally pulled the boat to a stop in the middle of the lake.

"Ready to ski?"

She inched out of her seat. "I . . . guess so."

He smiled at her. "It's not that hard. I'll give you some instruction, and we'll have you up in no time."

He took her to the back of the boat and got out a life jacket and the skis.

"What about you?" she asked. "Won't you get to ski?"

"I'm fine. I've done it thousands of times. I really want you to do it today."

"I could drive the boat, and you can ski."

He cocked a brow. "Ever driven a boat?"

"No."

"Then get your skis on and get out in the water. I'm driving, you're skiing."

"Shouldn't there be three people on the boat?"

"What for?"

"One to drive, one to ski, and the other to watch the skier."

He gave her a look. "Emma. I'll have my eye on you the whole time."

"Then how will you be able to see where you're going?"

He laughed. "Trust me. I know what I'm doing here. Eyes in the back of my head, babe."

Dammit. She supposed she was out of excuses. Luke gave her a litany of instructions, told her how to squat down when he first got going until she felt herself balanced, to remember to hold on to the line, and to let go if she fell.

"I have all that."

"Then get in and have some fun."

She was dubious about the fun part, but she slid into the water and swam over to the skis, put them on, and grabbed the rope handle when Luke tossed it to her.

"Point the tips of your skis toward the back of the boat," he said. "And when you fall, raise your hand up so other boaters can see you. I'll keep an eye out for you and come around."

"Sure."

"Have fun." He grinned.

"Yeah. If I even get up."

"You're strong, Emma. And you're coordinated. You'll get up. Just remember what I told you."

"Okay." She was utterly terrified, and hoped she wouldn't embarrass him.

He started up the engine and went slow. The rope had slack, so she sat there for a few seconds, her heart pounding the entire time as she tried to remember everything Luke had told her. As soon as the rope started to pull, she tensed, ready to get up.

This was much faster than she anticipated. The rope pulled taut, and she promptly face-planted in the water.

That went well.

Luke came around right away, putting the boat back into position again.

"I didn't get up," she said as he threw the rope to her.

"You tilted forward, toward the rope. Don't worry about it. It's a natural instinct to do that. Just remember, lean back, away from the rope. And squat down a bit."

"I'll try to remember that next time."

Except she did the same thing the next time, smacking the water with her face and body.

"This is starting to hurt," she said to Luke, who grinned at her as he tossed her the rope.

"Your body or your ego?" he asked.

"Uh, both."

"Don't give up. Not everyone gets up on their first try."

"I suppose you did."

He didn't say anything to that, which obviously meant he had. And if he could get up, so could she. She was coordinated. She'd taken dance and gymnastics as a kid. She could do this.

With renewed determination, she pointed her skis,

grabbed the rope handle, and when it started to pull, she leaned way back and made sure to keep her knees bent.

She didn't face-plant that time, and she actually got up to a squatting position as Luke propelled the boat forward.

She was up! Exhilarated, she let out a squeal of joy, though it was short-lived because this skiing thing took a lot of concentration and a lot of muscle as the line tugged her forward. She was glad for all the Pilates and yoga classes Jane and Chelsea had forced her into taking over the past few months, because her core muscles were definitely getting a workout as she rode along the waves.

She made it about five minutes before losing it on a high wave. Luke came around.

"You did it."

"I did. Can I go again?"

"Of course."

Determined to stay up longer this time, she got up easier than the last time and stayed up. She spent about an hour skiing, though she'd fall and then have to restart. But each time, she learned something new about how to ride through a wake or adjust her body.

When she climbed back into the boat, her limbs felt like spaghetti, her arms and legs shaking from the effort.

Luke handed her a towel. "You did really good."

"Thanks. It was so much fun, but oh my God, what an effort. Definitely not as easy as it looks."

"Yeah, it takes some practice, but you handled it great."

"Now why don't you show me how to drive the boat so you can ski for a bit? Surely it's not rocket science."

Luke waffled a little, and she kept arguing because she knew he really wanted to get out there in the water. He finally caved.

"Okay. We're in the deep part of the lake, so if you head along the straights," he said pointing the way, "you shouldn't hit anything."

"You have such confidence in me. Just tell me where not to go, and I'll make sure to stay away from those places."

He dug out the lake map and showed her the shallows. She nodded and told him to get his life jacket on.

"I can ski for a long time. I'll just wave my hand when I'm done. If you feel like you don't want to drive the boat anymore, just slow it down and I'll drop. Then you can come alongside and pick me up."

She nodded, and he went in the water and got his ski on. Obviously he was an expert at this thing since he was going to do slalom, using only one ski for both feet.

When he gave her the signal, she pushed the throttle and slowly got up to speed, keeping her eye on him. When he was up, she kept her focus mainly on the water and the other boaters, occasionally looking back to be sure Luke was still up and behind.

He was right about staying up for a long time. He was a natural at water-skiing, and she enjoyed taking the occasional peek at him flying through the water, one hand on the rope, the other waving at her or other boaters as they rode past. When he finally let go of the rope and dropped ever so expertly into the water, she turned the boat around and came alongside him. He tossed his ski onto the boat and climbed back on board, shaking his wet hair at her.

She laughed. "Enjoy yourself?"

"Hell, yes. Thanks for driving."

"It was my pleasure. I liked handling the controls."

He pulled her into his arms and kissed her, his wet body doing nothing to cool down the raging heat his kiss had evoked within her.

"You like being in control, huh?"

She palmed his bare chest. "That wasn't at all what I meant."

"So you like giving up control?"

She pushed back. "And that wasn't what I implied, either."

He laughed and grabbed the towel, then started up the boat again and drove them to a shady spot where he dropped the anchor.

"How about some lunch?"

"That sounds perfect. Water-skiing makes me hungry."

They'd made sandwiches and she'd cut up fruit that morning, so they ate and drank in the shade while the boat bobbed in the water. The waves had started to pick up as clouds began to thicken.

"Rain might be moving in," Luke said as they both watched the sky.

"Should we head back?"

"Probably. We don't want to be caught out on the water in case there's lightning or a downpour."

They finished lunch, packed up all the gear, and Luke made his way back to the boat dock. Once again, Emma hopped out of the boat and backed the truck and trailer down the ramp, while Luke pulled the boat onto the trailer. Once secured, Luke climbed into the truck and drove them back to the cabin.

While Luke unpacked the truck and the boat, Emma went over to the run to release the dogs. By then the skies had darkened considerably and the wind was picking up, dirt and leaves blowing around on the ground. She was glad they'd made the decision to head back to the house.

She let the dogs inside. Luke was in the kitchen.

"Did you get everything unloaded?"

"Yeah. Looks like a good storm coming in."

She nodded as she met him in the kitchen and opened the cooler to unpack the sodas and leftover food. "Yeah, it does. Does anything outside need to be secured?"

"I'll handle it."

"Okay. I'm going to head up to take a shower."

"I'll do that myself after I finish outside."

Emma grabbed a quick shower and slipped into a cotton sundress, leaving her hair damp. Luke showed up just as she was finishing combing out her hair.

"Wow, you look gorgeous."

She laughed. "My hair's wet and I have no makeup on."

He kissed her shoulder. "I like you that way."

He was so . . . different from Vaughn, who'd preferred her dressed up, made-up, always perfect.

She took a deep breath. "I'll let you take your shower. I think I'm going to make us some iced tea."

"Sounds good. I'll be right down."

She brewed the tea, then poured it in the pitcher, adding ice. By the time she gathered up sugar and sliced lemons, Luke had reappeared in a pair of shorts and a sleeveless top, his hair still damp from his shower. He slipped his arms around her and pressed a kiss to her cheek.

"You smell good."

She took a deep breath. "So do you. I made sweet tea. I can brew a pot of unsweetened if you'd rather have that."

"Bite your tongue. All tea should have sugar in it."

She grinned and poured two glasses of tea.

Thunder had started rumbling outside. Emma glanced at the dogs, all three of them asleep in the living room, unaffected by the gathering storm.

"They must have had an eventful day," Emma said.

"Lots to bark at outside. Protecting the homestead, you know."

They took their glasses outside and sat on the front porch. It was still warm, but windy, the limbs of the trees stretching back and forth, the waves of the lake kicking up powerful crests as the skies darkened further.

"I've always loved storms," Emma said. "The sound of thunder, the crack of lightning, and the smell of rain. God, I love the smell of rain."

"It's a pain in the ass when I'm working, though. People don't know how to drive in it."

She looked at him. "And you have to deal with a lot of accidents."

"Yeah. But days like today, when I'm off work, I love the rain, too. Being here where it's quiet and all you have to deal with is nature, it's perfect. When we were kids, my brothers and I would build forts in our rooms during thunderstorms and pretend we were mighty knights defending the castle during a siege."

She laughed. "Obviously you all had good imaginations."

"We had to do something. Three rambunctious boys

forced inside due to weather? You can imagine the potential for destruction."

"You could have read books."

He cocked his head to the side and gave her a look. "Come on. I mean, books were fine later, when I was older. When we were young we wanted to be doing something, not reading about someone else doing something. Though my dad read to us. And would watch movies with us. That's where we got the warrior and castle ideas."

Again, not his mother. Sad. "I like that you envisioned yourselves as knights."

"We'd use broomsticks as our swords. I gave Logan a black eye during a particularly vicious sword fight one stormy afternoon."

She laughed. "Oops. Did you get in trouble?"

"Nah. My dad accepted that we were boys. It's not like we were fighting—just having some fun. And Logan laughed about it."

"You got lucky. I always got in trouble for fighting with Molly."

"I imagine your fights weren't physical like ours were."

"True enough. We mostly yelled at each other, then I'd get the blame for starting it because I was the older sister, when half the time it was Molly bugging me or taking one of my toys."

"Younger siblings can be a pain in the ass sometimes."

"Yes. I'd try to escape from her a lot. Fortunately, during stormy days she'd crawl onto my mother's lap. She was afraid of storms."

"And what would you do?"

"I'd sit on the porch like this, as long as I could anyway, until the rain would drive me inside. Then I would cuddle up alone in my room with my blanket and read."

"Oh, no. One of those bookish types."

She laughed. "Yes. I'd sink into one of my stories and get lost in it while the world outside thundered and crashed around me. But inside I was safe and warm, with a story to keep me entertained."

He reached over and slid a curl between his fingers. "Sounds pretty perfect to me. But you weren't afraid of storms."

"Never."

"Me, either. We'd have been out playing in them if my mother hadn't complained she'd have to do our laundry when we got muddy."

"Little boys are supposed to get muddy."

"That's what I thought, too. She wasn't much for anything that would cause extra work for her."

"I'm sorry."

He shrugged. "It's no big deal."

She slid her hand in his. "But it was, wasn't it, Luke?"

Her gaze met his and lightning arced across the sky, followed by a loud crash of thunder that drew their attention. The clouds burst, and rain came down in sheets so thick you couldn't see. The wind whipped around them, rain lashing the porch. They grabbed their glasses and dashed inside.

"Wow, that was rather abrupt," she said, shaking the water droplets off.

They went into the kitchen and dried off with a towel.

The rain came down hard for the first thirty minutes, then settled into a steady, light shower after that. Emma and Luke curled up on the couch in the living room to watch.

"Did you have fun water-skiing today?" he asked.

He'd picked up her legs and draped them over his lap, pulling her closer. Emma had to admit, she didn't mind this at all. She tilted her head back to look at him. "I had a great time. Thanks for taking me."

"Thanks for driving the boat so I could get in a little skiing."

"I enjoyed it."

"Oh, right. That whole control thing. We were going to discuss that."

She arched a brow. "No, I don't believe we were."

"Yeah. You said you liked being in control, and then I got hard thinking about you being on top."

She laughed. "I think this conversation played out entirely in your head."

"Did it? Huh. So about that control thing." He laid his glass on the table and pulled her on top of him. His hands splayed across her back, then started a slow trek south, stopping when he grabbed her butt.

Her body started up a fast rush of pleasure. She wriggled against him. "So not subtle, McCormack."

He quirked a wickedly sexy, bad-boy grin up at her. "I wasn't really going for subtle, Dr. Burnett."

She palmed his chest. His body was warm, a storm raged outside, and she couldn't think of anyplace she'd rather be than right where she was.

"No, you're definitely not being subtle." The hard proof of that rocked between her legs, igniting her passion. She surged against him, lost in his eyes, which, when he was laughing, were a light greenish blue, but when filled with passion, like now, turned dark as a churning sea.

"So, it's storming outside, Emma," he said, brushing her hair away from her face. His touch ignited her pulse rate as his hand lingered at the side of her neck. "Do you want to play indoors?"

"Swordplay?" she asked.

Luke laughed. "Yeah. Swordplay sounds good to me."

Luke watched the change of emotions on Emma's face, from playful to sexy to downright temptress as she bent and brushed her lips across his. His breath caught as she slipped her tongue between his lips.

She was just so damn sweet, a mix of innocence and sultry vixen that tightened his balls and turned him into a walking erection every time he was around her. She smelled good, her laugh drove him crazy, and she had a wicked sense of humor. Package that up in a body built for a man's hands and a mouth made to worship, and she was damned near perfect.

And as she moved that lush body of hers over his, she unraveled his senses. He let his fingers trek across her bare shoulders and over her back, feeling her breasts rise and fall against his chest as her breathing deepened.

"I like this dress," he said, smoothing his hands over the soft cotton that clung to her curves. "When you put it on after your shower, I wanted to take it off of you right away."

She sat up, looked at him, that sexy, fuck-me look in her eyes making his dick harden even more. "Is that right?"

"Yeah."

"I can take it off."

He tightened his hold on her hips. "No. Actually, I'd like you to keep it on."

Her eyes gleamed with wicked desire. "I can do that, too. I'll be right back."

She slid off of him and disappeared upstairs while he took several deep breaths. The rain had intensified again, sheets of it pelting against the windows. Lightning flashed just as thunder banged so loud it startled the dogs, who all lifted their heads, looked around for a few seconds, then went right back to sleep.

Emma came back downstairs with a condom packet in her hand.

He smiled. "Smart thinking. I'd hate to be interrupted."

She reached underneath her sundress and made quite the show out of shimmying out of her panties. While he never got a glimpse at the goods, he held his breath as the white cotton underwear slid down her legs.

"God, that's sexy, Emma," he said, when the underwear pooled at her feet and she stepped out of them, then strad-dled him again.

"I'm glad you think so, because I've never been much for stripping in front of a man."

He grasped her hips and grabbed a handful of her dress. "Good to know."

She reached down and laid her palm over his erection. "Now we need to get you inside me."

Heat flared throughout his body, his balls quivering in response. "Oh, I think we need more foreplay."

"Who's in charge here?"

He laughed. "You are."

"I know what I need. I've been watching you all day, with your tanned body on the boat and out on the water, your skin gleaming in the sun." She raised his shirt, sliding her hands underneath. "All I could think about was getting you naked and inside me. That's about all the foreplay I can stand, Luke."

He liked her way of thinking. And knowing she wore nothing under that dress had his hard-on raging.

"Then let's get to it." He leaned forward and pulled his shirt off, while she helped him by raising up enough so he could slide out of his shorts.

She reached for him, curling her fingers around his shaft. "Now this is what I need. You, naked, with me on top of you."

He reached for the condom packet, his fingers shaking as she stroked him. "You do too much of that and we'll be finished before we ever get started."

She leveled one hell of a naughty smile at him. "Oh, I bet you have a lot more willpower than you think."

He applied the condom and lifted her dress, her beautiful body exposed to him as she slid over him, onto him. She gasped and he swallowed, hard, as he entered her, filling her.

"Emma," he said, barely able to find his voice as she seated herself fully on him. He grasped her hips and stilled her, looking up at her. "Hang on a sec. I just need to feel you."

She stared down at him, her body quivering around him, beckoning him to thrust, to give her what they both needed. He drove into her. Emma tilted her head back, her eyes shuttering closed as she rode him.

In this, she was fully in control and he let her take the reins, content to just watch as her face flushed with arousal. He drew the straps of her dress down, exposing her breasts. He grasped them, brushing his thumbs over her erect nipples while she rocked against him, taking them both higher while thunder crashed overhead, rain pounded the shutters, and a storm raged equally within the two of them.

His breathing quickened as she hurried the pace, dragging her body against his, tightening against him. And when she opened her eyes and locked gazes with him, he knew she was close. He lifted his hips and thrust into her.

Her eyes widened and she bit down on her bottom lip, keeping that eye contact with him that enveloped him in a haze of need. He felt the tremors and grasped her hips, quickening the pace so he could give her what she needed.

Her lips parted and she cried out with her orgasm. He plunged deep, then shuddered as he came, holding tight to her as he rolled with the thundering climax that shattered them both.

She fell on top of him, her breathing fast, her hair a cascade of sweet softness over his chest. He stroked her back as the two of them recovered.

"Maifasaslp," she mumbled against his neck.

He smiled at her incoherent statement. "Huh?"

She lifted her head. "My foot's asleep."

He laughed. "Oh."

They disentangled, then went upstairs to clean up, though Emma kept laughing because her foot was, in fact, asleep, so she had to hobble up the stairs, giggling the whole way because she claimed her foot tingled.

Afterward, they came downstairs and fixed something to eat. By then the rain had stopped and the dogs were awake, so they all went outside. The air was crisp and clean, and the skies cleared.

Luke pulled Emma against him as the dogs frolicked nearby.

"Feel okay?" he asked.

She tilted her head up to smile at him. "Perfect."

Yeah, that's about how he felt, too.

Chapter 20

AFTER LAST NIGHT'S storm, the day had dawned dry and promised to be hot. They'd intended to get up early and head out for a hike, but Luke had kept Emma in bed all morning.

Not that she minded the staying-in-bed part, especially since they hadn't been sleeping. The man had many hidden talents.

But she finally got hungry, so they got up and fixed breakfast, then decided since it was getting hotter outside, if they were going to head out for a walk, it needed to be then. Fortunately, the ground was already drying, though Emma had brought along her hiking boots. And it was warm enough to wear shorts.

The lake was calm despite the previous night's turbulence. As they walked along a path that ran parallel to the lake, she saw a few sailboats in the distance. Boaters were already out cruising along the waves. She sighed in contentment and turned to Luke who walked beside her.

"You've spoiled me. I'm never going to want to go back to work."

Luke smiled. "Is that a bad thing?"

"It is when you spend mornings in bed having sex, and afternoons taking beautiful walks like this with the dogs. It's idyllic and a total fantasy. And tomorrow we have to go back to reality."

"Yeah, that whole working for a living to pay the bills really sucks."

She sighed. "I know. Why can't we be millionaires?"

Luke pulled a prickly branch out of her way so she could walk under it. "I'm not a millionaire because I keep forgetting to buy a lottery ticket every week."

"Well, there is that."

The dogs barked up ahead. They'd gotten out of sight, so Emma quickened her step to see what the ruckus was about. When she caught up to them, they were sniffing a few bushes, but nothing was there.

"Chasing rabbits again, guys?" she asked.

"Probably," Luke said, stopping beside her. "There are deer in this area, too. At least it's not a skunk."

Emma rolled her eyes. "Don't even suggest it. Someone brought in a dog that had gotten into it with a skunk a week or so before."

Luke stopped and stared at her. "Was the dog injured?"

"No. Just stinky. We had to give him a bath."

Luke made a face. "Ugh. You never forget that smell."

"Yeah. Stunk up the entire clinic. My eyes were watering, and I wasn't even nearby. I felt sorry for Leanne."

"It's in a dog's nature to want to do battle with a skunk. Doesn't make the dog very smart, though."

"And we're the ones who have to pay the price. I've bathed many a skunked-out dog. It's hideous work, and I don't care to ever repeat the task." She looked at her dogs. "Do you hear that, girls?"

Daisy looked up at her adoringly.

"Yeah, don't give me that look, Daisy. You're the worst at chasing after things you shouldn't."

Luke laughed. "Boomer does that, too."

"But he makes up for it by chasing after things he should—like the bad guys." She scratched Boomer's ears.

"That he does, and he does it well."

Luke took her hand. She looked down where their fingers were entwined and felt a decided tingle.

She was such a girl.

They trekked on, and Emma noticed she could walk beside Luke for long stretches without saying a word and not feel uncomfortable. She was rarely comfortable around guys, hadn't been for a long time. It was different with Luke, and she realized it had been since that first night he'd walked into her clinic with an injured Boomer.

She didn't know what that meant, especially since she doubted they'd be seeing each other after this weekend.

But at least it had been a wonderful weekend. She'd learned to water-ski, which had been so exciting. And the sex . . . well, it had certainly been passionate. Her body was sore and well used. Luke was a generous lover, and every time she thought about him, she wanted to get him naked. She supposed throwing him down in the woods would be fun, though would likely result in ticks, so not a good idea.

"You're quiet."

She lifted her gaze to his, always struck by his *GQ* good looks, especially now, with his dark, cop sunglasses and his hair a little mussed up. He hadn't shaved during the weekend, so his jaw was peppered with dark stubble. He looked dangerous, and sexy as hell.

"I was actually pondering having my way with you in the woods."

He stopped, tugging on her hand to halt her forward progress. "Is that right?"

"Yes. And then practicality took over, and I realized we'd likely both end up with ticks on parts of our body that should never have ticks on them."

He tilted his sunglasses down the bridge of his nose so she could see his eyes. "But just think how much fun the after-hike tick check would be."

She laughed. "Good point."

He took a step toward her, and she took one back. "So . . . do you want to tell me about this hiking sex fantasy?"

She took another step back and bumped into a tree. "Uh, I was just kidding, you know."

He braced a hand on the tree, laying the other on her hip. "I'm not."

He leaned in and brushed his lips across hers. Whenever he kissed her, common sense fled somewhere else, like maybe South America. She twined her arms around his neck, figuring she'd worry about ticks later. And as Luke reached around to cup a handful of her butt, she moaned.

"Are you sure we're alone?" she murmured, loving the way he rubbed his lips against hers.

"No. The dogs are watching us. Perverts."

She laughed, then peeked over his shoulder. The dogs were sniffing brush nearby. "They're not watching."

"Good to know. And yes, we're alone. There's no property within five miles of this area. Which is why I can do this."

He slid his hand under her T-shirt and cupped her breast, making her wish she wasn't wearing a bra. She arched against the warmth of his hand, needing to feel her skin against his, but not daring to take her shirt off, because despite what Luke said, she didn't trust that someone wouldn't come walking up on them. And she refused to be stark naked in the woods.

But when he pulled her bra cup down and teased her nipple, that whole naked thing began to appeal. She craved his touch, could never seem to get enough of being near him, of having his mouth and hands on her. And when he tugged at her shorts and panties, she willingly let him pull them off. She stepped out of them, grateful he balled them up and shoved them into the pockets of his cargoes instead of leaving them on the ground.

"I don't suppose you have a condom on you," she managed as he slid his fingers inside her to stroke her into a frenzy of wild need.

"Around you, I always have a condom. Tucked one into my pocket."

She laid her forehead against his. "Always prepared?"

"Better prepared than frustrated and hard."

She cupped him, rubbing his erection. "Oh, you're definitely hard." He made her damp, her body quivering with the need for an orgasm.

"And if I don't get inside you soon, I'm going to be frustrated."

She gave him a wicked smile. "Well, we can't have that, can we?"

She helped him unzip his pants, freeing him into her waiting hands. His gaze met hers as she stroked him, his body hot and hard and ready for her. While he opened the condom packet, she made a quick check of the dogs, who were still wandering nearby. Satisfied she didn't need to worry about them, she focused on Luke, who cupped her behind and shifted her legs apart, then entered her with a quick thrust that made her cry out, the sound magnified in the hush of the thick woods.

He took her mouth in a kiss that intensified the pleasure he gave her as he moved within her, each stroke taking her closer to the orgasm that had hovered ever since she'd begun to think about making love outside. And as he ground against her, using his body to roll over her most sensitive of places, she dug her nails into his shoulders.

He let out a guttural groan, the sound primal and oh-so-male. He lifted one of her legs and thrust deeper, his gaze meeting hers as he drove into her harder, faster, sensing how close she was to completely unraveling.

And when she came, she couldn't help the sounds she made.

"Christ, Emma," he said, taking her mouth in a blistering kiss that set her off again in an explosion as wave after wave of orgasm crashed through her. Luke powered into her, then shuddered with his climax, both of them hanging on to each other as they rode out the intensity of this fierce and passionate union.

When it was over, they clung to each other, sweating and breathing hard.

"I don't know about ticks," Luke said, "but I'm not sure if I'll be able to walk back to the house."

Emma laughed. "My legs are shaking."

He released her and handed her clothes to her, helping her with her balance as she climbed back into her underwear and shorts before fixing his own clothes.

They called the dogs and made the trek back to the house. They cleaned up and did a thorough tick check. Luke had been right—the tick check was fun, which meant another bout of lovemaking that made her catch her breath and left her panting.

After they ate, Luke suggested they take the boat out for one more ride. Emma was all over that. Luke let her do some of the driving, pointing out how to read the lake map and showing her areas to avoid. She knew how to drive over the wakes now, and by the time she'd captained the boat for about an hour, she had a pretty good feel for it.

They took turns water-skiing again, and this time Emma was a little better than yesterday, though not nearly as good as Luke, who chose the one-ski slalom again. She decided he was just showing off, though he had a right to. He was a very good skier, likely because he'd had years of experience.

After water-skiing, they stopped off at a small cove and anchored so they could swim a bit, playing in the water together, splashing each other and climbing up on the over-sized inner tube to soak in some sun. By the time the sun started sinking, they got back on the boat to head toward the dock.

"Ready to pack up and head back home?" Luke asked.

She looked over at the cabin. In a couple of short days, she'd grown to really like it. "Not really. But I guess we have no choice."

Luke cast a grin her way. "Yeah. Forgot to buy a lottery ticket again."

They gathered everything up and packed the truck, then did one more check of the cabin to be sure nothing was left behind. They'd swept the floors and washed the dishes, stripped the bed, which Luke assured her would be taken care of by the cleaning people who stopped by.

It was time to head out. They got the dogs settled in the backseat of the truck, and Luke pulled out.

Emma was relaxed but exhilarated. She decided that someday she was going to own a boat. She liked being out on the water, had enjoyed water-skiing and tubing. She might also buy a cabin like the one Luke's family owned. It would be a great place to bring her children.

Someday. When she had kids.

She didn't know when that was going to be, though. She was already over thirty and had a mountain of debt from college loans and buying the practice. When was she going to stop and have kids? When would she take time off to even have children? She was the single owner of her practice. It wasn't like someone else could take over for her while she took a few months off to have a baby.

She let out a sigh.

"You okay over there?" Luke asked.

She smiled at Luke. "I'm fine."

"Tired?"

"A little. It was a long weekend. But I had a great time. Thanks for bringing me to the cabin and to the lake."

"I had a great time, too."

She went quiet again and wished she hadn't pondered buying a cabin and a boat, which led her down the road to having kids.

She'd wasted so much time all those years ago, when she could have been in school, could have gotten her veterinary degree, could have gotten her entire life started so much sooner.

She'd made so many mistakes.

Love—or what she'd thought at the time was love—had made her do stupid things.

And it would be wise of her to remember that love wasn't her priority. It had been once, and it had cost her dearly. Falling in love again could be disastrous for her.

Of course, how was she going to have those kids she wanted if she didn't fall in love?

She rubbed her temple.

"You're quiet again," Luke said sometime later.

"Oh. Thinking."

"About?"

"Um . . . work stuff."

"No. No work stuff until tomorrow. Banish those thoughts. Think about warm sunshine and the lake. And hiking."

She looked over at him and he grinned at her. Her lips curved. "Okay. I'll definitely think about hiking."

By the time Luke pulled into her driveway, she had a full-blown headache, brought about, no doubt, by too much thinking. Much as she tried to push all those "what ifs" and "should haves" to the back of her mind, they kept pummeling her and wouldn't go away.

Luke helped carry her stuff into the house.

And now another question inserted itself into her already-too-cluttered mind.

What happened next? Now what was going to happen between the two of them?

"I had a fun weekend with you," she said as she walked with him to the door.

He pulled her against him and wrapped his arms around her. "Me, too."

The question hovered on her lips, but she refused to ask it. Instead, she brushed his hair off his forehead. "Get some sleep."

"You, too." He kissed her, and not a quick good-bye peck, but a bone-melting, deep kiss that curled her toes and woke up everything female within her. A kiss that made her want to ask him to come inside and crawl between the sheets with her so she could have him one more time before this idyllic weekend came to a final close.

Instead, he took a step back after the kiss and took a deep breath. "I really should get out of here, before I ask you to let me stay."

And she took a deep breath. "You really should go, before I ask you to stay."

He cocked a half-smile. "'Night, Emma."

"Good night, Luke."

He turned and headed back to his truck. Emma shut the door, the dogs sitting there, watching her.

"Come on, girls. I need some Tylenol and my bed. We'll worry about everything else tomorrow."

Chapter 21

LUKE WALKED THE Whitehall Pharmacy with a grimace.

The pharmacy had been burglarized late the previous night, the alarm dismantled, and the back door expertly jimmied.

It was the same MO as the other burglaries. They'd gone after the narcotics, and this time they'd scored a decent hit. According to Edgar Whitehall's inventory, there was more to this than just a junkie scoring drugs for the next high. They'd taken some heavy-duty narcotics, and a large quantity.

"It might be someone trying to score a fix, but I don't think so," Luke said to Pete Little, his captain, who'd shown up to review the scene. "This looks too well done. A junkie is going to do a smash-and-grab. Get in and get out in a hurry so he doesn't get caught. Like we saw over at Emma Burnett's place."

Pete nodded and wandered through the back of the pharmacy. "And you think that was mostly because Miss Burnett was on the scene at the time, not because they were in a hurry to snatch whatever drugs they could get their hands on and hightail it out of there?"

"Yes, sir. It's looking like this might be someone more sophisticated. No one getting high on the drugs he grabs would be this efficient. They wouldn't care about the alarm or the way they're bypassing the security systems. They'd just bash in a window or break down the door, grab whatever they could, and get out. You know the mind-set when they're toasted."

Luke walked the captain toward the video-surveillance equipment. "They even knew to disable video surveillance. Most of our local junkies wouldn't even be aware of that or would just wear a hoodie to hide their faces. This is someone who knows what he's doing."

His captain nodded. "So what are your thoughts?"

He liked his captain, liked that he wanted his officers to do the investigating. "I'm thinking this is maybe an after-market job. They snatch the drugs, then resell them rather than use them. With the quantities they're taking, it makes sense."

"It does. Have you checked out recent drug offenders on parole in the area?"

"We have. None of them have the smarts or the background to pull off something like what's been happening here. But we're still checking alibis for the nights in question."

"We've checked in with surrounding cities and counties," Pete said. "It's confined to Hope, so it's someone local."

"Or someone who wants us to think they're local," Luke said. "I wouldn't put it past an outsider to be targeting our area. A lot of people believe small towns are an easy target."

"You have a point, McCormack. Follow up on your leads and trust your instincts. This is becoming a pattern in our town, and I don't want it to continue. Let's find out who's doing this and put a stop to it."

"Yes, sir."

There were distinct advantages and disadvantages to

working for a small-town police force. The biggest advantage was the level of autonomy you got. Because you had a limited staff, you got to do a lot yourself. The biggest disadvantage was all the shit you had to do yourself because of the limited staff. Which meant Luke spent the next several days tracking down and interviewing parolees, checking out alibis, and working with other jurisdictions to see if they had anyone who might fit the MO of these crimes.

Which meant he'd worked a shit ton of double shifts. Not that he minded. He wanted to catch this asshole as much as everyone else on the force did. The last thing Hope needed was a new dealer out hawking the latest in narcotics outside the local middle schools. He'd work whatever hours needed to put this dickhead behind bars.

But working these hours meant he'd had absolutely zero time to see Emma. When he got off work, he managed a cold sandwich and a beer, and then he'd fall face-first into his bed, where it seemed as if only an hour later his alarm was ringing and he had to be back on the job again.

Of course, this was what he wanted, wasn't it? A fling with Emma, get her into his bed, then forget about her. Get her out of his system.

The problem was, after the long weekend they'd spent together, he couldn't stop thinking about her. Everything about her still lingered—the way she laughed, the way she smelled, the way she tasted, the way she moved when he was inside her.

And getting a hard-on when in his police car might just get him fired, especially if his captain or one of his fellow officers happened to come by while he was sitting in the parking lot of Bert's diner waiting for Anita to bring his to-go order out. He'd already missed lunch, and since he'd be working another double shift, he'd be damned if he'd miss dinner.

When Emma pulled in next to him, along with Jane and Chelsea, he didn't know whether to hide his face or get out and pull her into his arms so he could tell her how much he'd missed her.

She smiled and waved, started to go inside, but then paused, said something to Jane and Chelsea, then came over to his car. She leaned over, and he breathed her in.

Sweet. Like citrus fruit. He had a sudden urge to lick her neck.

"Hi, stranger," she said, smiling at him. She obviously wasn't pissed at him like she should be.

"Hi, yourself. You probably think I'm a giant douchebag."

She laughed. "Why? Did you do something wrong?"

"I haven't called you in a week. I'm sorry, Emma."

"I don't think you need to be sorry. I heard about the latest break-in at the Whitehall pharmacy. I've also heard you're all pulling double shifts. It's a wonder you're even allowed to sleep. I think I'm the last thing on your priority list right now."

She understood. She didn't hate him. "This is one time I'm glad for the Hope grapevine."

"Are you sure? Because they're also talking about the weekend you and I spent at the lake together."

"They are, huh? And what are *they* saying?"

"That I'll likely be pregnant before fall, it'll be a huge scandal, and there'll be a shotgun wedding."

He choked out a laugh. "Seriously?"

"I never joke about shotgun weddings. Luckily for you, my father doesn't own a shotgun."

"Wow. The rumor mill is really cranking it up, aren't they?"

"Well, they have to have something to talk about. Fortunately, the gossip about our torrid weekend together is neck and neck with the drug burglaries, so at least we're not the only thing people are gossiping about."

Anita came out, and just the sight of her and that brown paper bag made his stomach grumble.

Emma stepped aside.

"Here you go, Luke," Anita said.

"Thanks, Anita." He handed her the money.

"You're welcome. Any leads on the Prowling Pharmaceutical Pilferer?"

"The what?" Luke asked.

"Hey, that's what the local paper has dubbed him. Triple P, for short."

Luke rolled his eyes. "Uh, nothing to report today, Anita. Thanks for the burger."

Anita looked from Luke to Emma, smiled knowingly, and beat it out of there.

"Triple P?"

Emma laughed. "I heard that one." She laid her hand on his shoulder. "I'll let you eat. I'm having dinner with Jane and Chelsea."

"Okay."

She started to walk away. "Emma?"

She stopped. "Yes?"

"I miss you."

Her lips curved. She came back and leaned inside the window. "I hope this is legal." She grabbed his shirt to pull him closer, then kissed him—tenderly, sweetly, and so passionately she made his dick hard. Which made him forget how hungry he was—for anything but Emma, anyway. He cupped the back of her neck and held her there, wishing he was off work, wishing they weren't sitting in Bert's parking lot so he could do a lot more than just kiss her.

She broke the kiss and laid her hand on his chest. "I miss you, too, Luke. Be safe out there."

She waved at Boomer, then headed inside.

Luke mentally cursed three full sentences at whoever Triple P was because he sure as hell was putting a crimp in Luke's sex life.

Emma walked into Bert's, preoccupied with the kiss she'd just shared with Luke.

Until a round of applause broke out. She jerked her head up, and most of the patrons gave her a standing ovation, including Jane and Chelsea.

Blushing crimson, she found Jane and Chelsea, who of course had to have a booth at the window.

"That was some display of assaulting a police officer," Chelsea said, fanning herself with the plastic menu. "I was about to make a citizen's arrest."

"Forget the citizen's arrest," Jane said. "I was about to pour my glass of ice water over my head."

Emma rolled her eyes. "Oh shut up, both of you. It wasn't that much of a kiss."

Chelsea cocked a brow. "Who are you trying to kid? The entire diner is turned on."

"They are not." Emma chanced a look around. People either whispered to each other and looked at her while trying not to look at her, or they were just outright gaping.

"Oh, for heaven's sake. Haven't they seen two people kiss before?"

"Not like that, apparently," Jane said, stifling a laugh.

"This is ridiculous. I wasn't mauling him. I even left his clothes on."

"So what you're saying is you wanted to strip him down, straddle him, and have your way with him in his police cruiser, but you used restraint. Or was it that you used restraints on him? Do tell."

Emma glared at Chelsea. "You are not funny."

"To the contrary. I crack myself up all the time."

"She is pretty funny, Emma," Jane said, taking a sip of water. "And that really was one hot kiss. Surely you felt it from your end, because it sure looked hot from where we were sitting."

"Fine. It was hot. And I'm frustrated because we haven't seen each other in a week."

"So no hot sex for a whole week? My heart breaks for you," Chelsea deadpanned.

Emma pointed a finger at her. "You are not having hot sex, because you're too picky."

"And because there are no hot men left in Hope. You and Jane got the last of them."

Jane snorted. "Uh . . . no. Well, yes. I did get a hot one. And quite obviously from the flammable display in the parking lot, so did Emma. But I disagree that there are no hot men left. You're just not looking."

Chelsea shrugged. "You're right. I'm not looking. It's depressing out there." Chelsea turned her attention on

Emma. "And nice try deflecting. We were talking about you and hot cop."

"We were?"

"Yes, we were," Jane said. "So how was the holiday weekend at the cabin? I meant to call you, but . . . school and kids, you know."

"I know. And I was swamped after the holiday, too, so I haven't had a moment's free time, either. And the weekend was fine."

"Oh, no," Chelsea said. "You're going to have to do better than 'fine.'"

Emma looked around. The diner was crowded. It was Friday night, and therefore, chicken-fried-steak night. It was well-known that Bert made the best chicken-fried steak in the county, so people lined up to get served on Fridays.

She shook her head and leaned forward so no one else could hear. "I'm not spilling intimate details here."

"Gossip buzzkiller," Jane said with a pout. "Okay, here's what we'll do. Will's working the late shift, Ryan's spending the night at a friend's house, and Tabby's at my parents'. We'll grab some wine and head to my place after dinner."

"That works for me," Emma said, already looking forward to a laid-back wine-and-chat fest with her friends. She'd been at it hard work-wise for the past week and hadn't had time to do much more than see to the dogs after work and then crash. It had been grueling, so she was ready for something fun.

Though she had the idea an inquisition was upcoming. Not that she minded. She wanted to talk to her friends about her and Luke.

So they ate and caught up on mundane things, like their work lives.

"Hi, Emma. How are you and that handsome Luke Mc-Cormack doing?" This was asked by Mrs. Claire Reasor, eighty-two, and accompanied by her granddaughter Samantha Reasor, the owner of the flower shop in town. Samantha gave her an apologetic look.

Chelsea stifled a grin and Jane looked down at the bill

that Anita had just presented them with, while Anita waited for Emma to answer.

"I'm doing just fine, Mrs. Reasor. As far as Luke, I think he's working very hard to solve that string of drug burglaries. A lot of overtime for him, I'm afraid."

Claire patted her shoulder. "That's too bad, honey. It sure puts a crimp in your budding romance, doesn't it?"

Emma had no idea what to say to that. She fumbled for a response, finally coming up with, "Well, it's definitely keeping him busy, that's for sure."

"Come on, Grandma," Samantha said, mouthing "I'm so sorry" to Emma on the way by.

Emma smiled at Samantha and then looked over at Jane and Chelsea, both with grins on their faces.

"Is my relationship with Luke in the local papers?"

"No, but you know what it's like in a small town. You can't keep a secret. One person tells another, who tells another, and then there's social media like Facebook and Twitter. You're lucky no one got photos of the two of you at the lake together." Chelsea gave Jane a look. "At least I don't think there are pictures. Have you seen any?"

"I'm not on social media as much as you. If there were, you'd likely have seen them before me."

"You two are awful friends. I don't know why I hang out with you."

"We're great friends," Chelsea said. "The kind who will share wine with you so you can unburden yourself of your deepest secrets."

Emma paid her portion of the bill and stood. "No, you're the kind who will ply me with wine so you can pry all my secrets out of me."

Chelsea shrugged. "Same thing."

They headed over to Jane's house. Chelsea was going to stop at the liquor store for wine, and Emma made a run to the grocery store to pick up cheese, crackers, and some fruit. They might not be hungry now—in fact, she was stuffed—but if they were going to be drinking, there would need to be food for later.

They converged on Jane's place. She already had the wineglasses out.

"I needed to wash them," she said, taking a towel to dry the insides of the glasses. "Will and I are beer people."

They gathered up their wineglasses and headed outside to the back deck. It was nice out, and Jane lit the citronella torches to keep the flies and mosquitoes away. Archie, Jane's new puppy, played nearby. He was so sweet, and had already become a part of the family.

Emma sipped her wine and looked up at the stars, finally able to blow the stress of the past week out of her mind.

"Tough week?" Jane asked.

"Yeah. We had to put down two dogs, one for cancer, the other for an untreatable case of heartworms."

Chelsea laid her hand on Emma's arm. "I'm sorry. That's rough."

"Yeah, it was, mainly on the families. But I always hate that part of the job. It's never easy to say good-bye to a pet that you love so much. They become a part of the family."

She studied her wineglass, melancholy washing over her as she remembered all too well the number of dogs she'd lost over the years.

"This is depressing," Chelsea said. "And now you re-minded me about Scooter, the Scottish terrier I had when I was a kid. I haven't thought about him in a long time." She took a long swallow of wine and sighed. "So let's talk about sex instead."

Emma cast a smile at Chelsea. "Sorry. I am a downer, aren't I?"

"Look, honey. I love your job. I love that you're here in Hope doing your job. But sometimes your job sucks, especially when animals die. So let's not talk about that tonight. Not when we're supposed to be having fun. And face it, talking about delicious men and hot sex is way more thrilling than talking about work."

"Agreed," Jane said. "We certainly don't want Chelsea to start talking about math. Or, God forbid, science."

Chelsea stuck out her tongue. "If we don't start getting

something moving in the let's-talk-about-Emma's-sex-life department, I'm going to hit you with a Pythagorean theorem that'll make your toes curl."

"Ugh. Help us out here, Emma."

Emma laughed. "Fine. We had a great time last weekend. Hot sex ensued."

Chelsea leveled her with a look. "I knew it. I could tell from that hot kiss in the parking lot that you two had hit the sheets."

Just thinking about the weekend they'd shared at the cabin had Emma heating up all over again. "Yes. It was a great weekend."

She sipped her wine, and it took her a few seconds to realize the conversation had come to a skidding halt. She lifted her gaze to find both Jane and Chelsea staring at her. "What?"

"That's it?" Chelsea asked.

Emma gave her a benign smile. "You wanted more?"

"Hell, yes. A lot more. Details, woman. How does he look naked?"

"I don't recall. No photos were snapped."

"Oh, right," Jane said. "Like visions of Luke naked aren't burned into your memory banks." Jane wagged a finger at her. "Don't play innocent with us. Your cheeks are already pink."

"Are they? It might be the wine."

"And it might be the afterglow, even a week later." Jane grinned.

"Okay. Despite my hellishly busy and somewhat awful week, there's been definite afterglow. But he's also had a lot on his plate, and we haven't even spoken to each other."

"Based on what we saw out in the parking lot tonight, it doesn't look like you two need to say anything at all to each other to reconnect after a week apart." Chelsea leaned back on the padded chaise, a smug smile on her face.

Just the thought of that moment when she leaned over and kissed him was enough to send her up in flames.

"Your face gives you away every time, Emma," Jane said.

"The room practically went up ten degrees as you sit there, sipping your wine with that smile on your face."

Emma shifted her gaze to Jane. "It does, doesn't it? I can't help myself. And I swore I wasn't going to get involved with Luke. With any man, for that matter."

"Why?" Chelsea asked.

"Because of the clinic. I have my hands full with my job. I just don't have time for romance."

"I think that's a crock," Chelsea came back. "Seems to me you have plenty of time for romance. Or you've been making time. And it doesn't seem to have hurt your work at the clinic any."

She didn't answer.

"Is that really the truth, Emma?" Jane asked. "Or is it something else that's been holding you back?"

She so wanted to confide in her friends. Her family never discussed her abusive relationship because they knew how hard the past had broken her. Her mother thought she was fragile.

Maybe at one time that had been true. When it had first happened, when she'd first broken away, she'd felt ancient, so brittle and unstable that if someone had looked sideways at her, she would have crumbled.

But that had been years ago. She'd grown stronger, had renewed her confidence. Getting back into school had helped. Working in her chosen field had helped to get her bearings back.

She wasn't fragile anymore, but she knew her parents felt a certain responsibility for what had happened, though she had never blamed them. Still, she couldn't talk to them about it, because they felt so guilty, and Molly hadn't been around when it had happened.

Molly had enough of her own demons to deal with, whatever those might be. If Molly didn't feel comfortable enough talking to Emma about whatever kept her away from Hope, Emma didn't want to burden her with what had happened so long ago.

Which left only Chelsea and Jane. She trusted them.

"Emma?" Chelsea asked.

"It's kind of a really long story. And an ugly one. I don't come out of it looking at all heroic, or like a strong, confident woman."

Chelsea grabbed her hand and squeezed it. "Honey, we all have something in our past we're not exactly proud of. Do you think Jane or I would judge you? We're your friends, and real friends stand by you, no matter what."

Jane nodded. "We're here for you. For the bad parts as well as the good."

It was then Emma knew she could trust them with the ugliness.

So while Jane poured them all another glass of wine, Emma started talking.

Chapter 22

LUKE WAS FRUSTRATED as hell, and tired of working on a case that was going nowhere.

Typically, he closed cases the same day they broke, but this rash of break-ins was scaring the people of his town.

He couldn't blame them. Who knew where the perpetrator—or perpetrators—would strike next. Just because they'd only been hitting local businesses so far didn't mean they wouldn't start breaking and entering people's homes next.

No avenue they'd explored had turned up any leads. The perps had left no prints, and there was no video on whoever had been hitting these businesses. Any recent parolees or those with drug-related crimes in their backgrounds had all alibied out.

Which left them at square one. And the suspect hadn't struck again in over a week. Luke supposed that was a good thing, but if they could flush this guy out, they'd have a chance at nabbing him.

Which gave him an idea. Since he was on patrol and close to the precinct, he drove to the station and went into his captain's office. Pete was at his desk on the phone but motioned for Luke to come in and take a seat. He waited, looking at the awards and certificates on Pete's wall.

Luke supposed this is what he should aspire to someday—being a captain, leading a team. But he enjoyed being out on the street with Boomer, chasing down perps. This just seemed like a damn lot of paperwork and sitting behind the desk. Maybe his priorities would change several years down the road, when he was tired of walking a beat. He'd like to be a detective someday. But a desk job? He didn't see that ever appealing to him.

The captain hung up so Luke focused his attention.

"What's up, McCormack? Aren't you supposed to be on patrol?"

"Yes, sir. But I had an idea about these drug burglaries and wanted to run it by you."

Pete slid back in his chair. "Okay, hit me."

"They've targeted places that are well stocked. What if we set them up?"

"Set them up, how?"

"Get one of the local pharmacies to agree to a massive drug restocking. If someone's casing these places, they'll know, and it'll be a prime target. We wait inside and catch them when they come in to snatch the drugs."

Pete leaned forward and steepled his fingers. "Your idea has merit, but you realize there's no guarantee they'll bust in for the drugs just because a place has been recently stocked."

"I know, sir, but we have no leads at this point, and I think it's worth a shot."

His captain seemed to consider the idea, mainly by staring intently at Luke. "All right. I'll make some calls and let you know what we can work out. Get back on the street."

"Yes, sir."

Feeling better now that he'd suggested a plan, Luke headed back out to the parking lot.

"Hey, McCormack. What are you doing here?"

He walked past Evan Ashbrook and Steve Fortran, a cou-

ple of his fellow cops. "Hey. Just stopped to talk to the
captain about something. You guys coming on duty or getting off?"

"Coming off working a double, just like you," Steve said.
"This whole burglary thing is chapping my ass. And it's
making my wife cranky."

Luke laughed. "Yeah, I can imagine she's not happy."

"Not with three kids at home who miss their dad, and
her having to juggle her job plus day care and the kids at
night. There's going to be hell to pay if we don't find this
asshole soon."

"Have you got anything?" Evan asked.

"Nothing. No leads have panned out yet."

"Shit." Steve raked his fingers through his hair. "I keep
hoping I'm going to come on duty and the captain's going
to tell me they caught him, and we can go back to life as
normal."

"This guy can't be that fucking smart," Ev said to them.
"We'll corner his ass soon enough."

Luke nodded. "I agree."

"Speaking of asses, we'd better get inside before the captain has ours. I have reports to file. See you, Luke," Steve
said.

"Later, guys." Luke headed out to his vehicle and let
Boomer out of the backseat, taking him for a walk around
the property. There was a park right next to the precinct, so
Boomer got to stretch his legs. After about fifteen minutes,
he and Boomer got back in the cruiser.

He checked his watch. It was Thursday, the night Emma
kept the clinic open late so people could bring their animals
in after work. He could stop by, see how she was doing. He
hadn't seen her in a while.

Or he could just go do his damn job and stop thinking
about Emma. She was busy, and so was he.

He drove by the clinic and her parking lot was full, so
he went past. He'd call her later.

He got called to the scene of an accident, and he forgot
all about Emma as he worked the two-car rear-end vehicle

collision. The girl who'd hit the minivan had been texting, and when he'd come on the scene she was sobbing, complaining that her dad was going to kill her since he'd already lectured her once about messing with her phone while driving.

Luke didn't have much sympathy because he saw plenty of people texting and sending e-mails instead of paying attention to the road like they should. The girl was lucky the woman driving the minivan was on her way to pick up her kids and only had a sore neck, and that her children hadn't been in the car, which was exactly what he'd told Missy Davis, teenage texter.

"You don't understand," she said, tears still streaming down her face. "My dad will take my keys away. I won't have wheels ever again. He'll probably even take my phone."

The last two words were spoken at a high decibel level, followed by another round of racking sobs. One would think Missy's entire life was over. Of course being seventeen, she probably thought it was.

When Missy's father arrived at the scene, the girl's eyes widened. Dad didn't look happy at all.

"Officer, I'm Howard Davis, Missy's father. Can you tell me what happened?"

Luke explained the accident, and Mr. Davis's face grew more grim the further Luke got into his recounting of the scene.

"I see. Thank you." Mr. Davis turned and headed toward his daughter, who appeared to have shrunk several inches as she leaned against the car. Luke kept an eye on the two of them to make sure no violence broke out. But all Mr. Davis did was hold out his hand. Missy dropped her car keys into it. He said a few more words, Missy opened her mouth as if to object, but then gave Mr. Davis her phone and dejectedly headed over to her dad's car.

Maybe she'd learn a lesson from this. Luke hoped, anyway.

By the time the wrecker came and removed both vehicles from the scene, it was past eight and Luke was dragging.

He stopped at the local convenience store for a cup of coffee, then headed down the main town highway to do a patrol.

That's when his radio started squawking. The dispatcher came on with a burglary-in-progress code, the location not too far from where he was. He got on his radio and indicated he'd be heading there, one minute out. He hit his sirens and stepped on the gas.

It was the urgent care center, just across the parking lot from Emma's vet clinic. A quick glance at the time showed that Emma should be just closing up. He hoped she and her staff were still inside. And safe.

He was the first car to arrive and reported his arrival, then slid on his bulletproof jacket and grabbed his rifle.

No alarms were going off, at least not audibly, which didn't mean a silent alarm hadn't been triggered. Backup was due to arrive in less than a minute. He hauled ass out of his car, opening the back door for Boomer. He gave Boomer the appropriate commands, indicating they were in search-and-stealth mode. Boomer stayed right by his side. The dog knew his job.

The front door of the clinic was locked since they closed at seven, so he hurried down the sidewalk of the shopping center so he could head around the back.

He could see Emma's clinic from where he stood at the side of the shopping center. And just as he shifted around the corner, she came outside, by herself, no doubt locking up.

Something must have caught her eye, at the same time Luke heard a sound from the back. Emma's gaze tracked the sound and Boomer emitted a low growl.

Luke gave him the command to silence. Now Luke hesitated, warring between wanting to shout out to Emma to go back inside and lock her door or staying quiet so he could continue to stalk the perp. Emma's safety was paramount. She stood frozen to the spot, and that's when Luke spotted the dark figure darting into the woods behind the shopping center.

He gave the Go signal to Boomer, who tore past him and into the woods at high speed. Luke called in that he was in pursuit, gave his location, and headed out after Boomer. He held up his hand, waving at Emma to go back inside. When he was sure she was going to follow direction, he took off after Boomer and the suspect.

He heard the sirens pull up at the front of the urgent care center, communicated his location as he entered the thick wooded area. Boomer barked, as he was trained, giving Luke the ability to track his whereabouts. Left, about fifty yards ahead. Breathing heavily, sweating under his Kevlar jacket as he ran like hell, Luke pushed through the dense brush, not wanting to use his flashlight in case the suspect had doubled back.

"Location, McCormack."

It was one of his fellow officers; Luke gave his best guess as to where he was. "I'm not using my flashlight. Keep an eye out in case the perp doubles back out of this brush. I have Boomer in here with me. I sent him in when we saw the guy make a break for the woods."

An hour later, there was no sign of the suspect. Luke, Boomer, and several of the Hope police force had combed the area, to no avail. The perp either had a foolproof escape plan or a car hidden nearby. Hell, maybe he'd hopped into the river and taken a boat. With all of them tramping through the woods, forensics likely wouldn't be able to get decent shoe impressions.

His captain had shown up to review the scene, inside and out. This time the perp had set off the silent alarm. With the rash of burglaries lately, the urgent care center had beefed up its security, and cutting the outside alarm system had set off a backup. So when he broke in, the silent alarm had gone off.

They'd also wired in additional video surveillance, so they'd finally have something to look at, once the tech guys were able to download it.

In the meantime, Luke told his captain about Emma standing there watching the whole thing go down.

"A potential witness?" Pete asked.

"And a former victim of this dickhead."

"Go talk to her."

Luke nodded and headed across the parking lot. He pulled on the door, which Emma had wisely locked, so he knocked. Daisy came running to the door first, followed by Emma, who unlocked the door and let him in.

She was wide-eyed and pale, just like that night when she'd been burglarized. He wanted to put his arms around her and tell her everything was going to be all right, but he was on duty and there were other cops milling about outside who could see them.

"Are you all right?" he asked as she led him into her office.

She nodded, took a seat in one of the chairs across from her desk. "Yes. How about you? I saw you and Boomer run like crazy into the woods after that guy. Did you catch him?"

He shook his head. "Unfortunately, no. But we're closing in. This is the first time we've gotten close enough to him to catch him in the act."

"Except that one time he actually burglarized my place while I was here," she reminded him.

"Yes. There was that. Too bad you're not a cop."

She laughed, clasping her hands together.

"You're shaking." He took a seat and put his hands over hers. "It's going to be all right, Emma."

She looked down at their hands, then back up at him. "I saw the guy, you know."

Luke's gut tightened. "How well did you see him?"

"Not all that well. He was wearing black pants or sweats, and a black hoodie pulled up over his head. I know he had blond hair, or maybe white hair. He paused for a fraction of a second, like maybe he heard something, and he looked my way. He saw me looking at him. Then he took off like he was running for his life and disappeared into the woods."

Luke let go of her hands and pulled his notepad out of his pocket. "Okay, let's go over this from the beginning so I can make this a part of my official report."

Emma took a deep breath and tried to quell the shaking that had seemed to settle in every bone, every nerve ending of her body, from the moment she'd stepped outside to lock up. It was when she'd turned around that she'd caught a glance, a flash of someone coming out from the back of the shopping center in the other parking lot.

And then she'd seen Luke and Boomer hugging the side of the building, illuminated in the lights. She'd known immediately what was happening. Someone was burglarizing the urgent care center, the only facility in that center that carried drugs. Her gaze immediately tracked back to the burglar.

In that split second, she'd seen him, and he'd seen her watching him. It had only taken a few seconds at most, but the image, what had happened, was burned into her memory like it had all happened in slow motion.

"He was wearing jeans, now that I think about it. Very dark jeans. Tennis shoes, I think, though I can't be positive about that. A black hoodie that he wore over his head, and he had gloves on. He carried a backpack, a black one. It was slung over his back. His hair was blond, kind of a yellow-blond, not a normal color, but maybe from some kit that bleaches hair."

She lifted her gaze to Luke's. "You have to remember this was from a distance, maybe forty or fifty yards away, so I can't be certain of anything, but he looked fairly young. Not teenager young. I'd say early twenties. Anyway, when he froze after seeing me, it was like instinct kicked in because he must have seen me slide my gaze over to you. Then he started running for the woods."

"You didn't see anyone else with him," Luke asked.

Emma shook her head. "No. Just him."

"Did you get a close enough look that you could identify him?"

"I doubt it. It was mostly a blur, and the only reason I could see hair color was because it was so yellow-blond, so unusual. But no facial features."

"Was he tall or short?"

She pondered the guy's height, stacking him up against Luke. "Tall. And slender, but not skinny like he wasn't eating. Just . . . lean, like maybe he was a runner. But his clothes were baggy, so I could be off a bit on build."

"Race?"

"I could definitely see that he was Caucasian."

"Anything else you can think of?"

She shook her head. "I think that's it."

He slipped his notebook into his pocket and squeezed her hand. "You did good, Emma. Really good. Most witnesses are so frozen with fear they can't remember anything. You did a remarkable job."

"Did I? I hope so. I want you to catch this guy."

"I want to catch him, too. You helped. This is more than we've ever had before."

She stood. "I guess I should get the dogs home."

He walked outside with her and helped her put the dogs in her truck, then radioed for one of the cruisers to come around. "Listen. I need to file this report. But I'm going to have one of our officers escort you home."

"That's not necessary. I'm fine."

"I know you are. But I'd feel a lot better if someone went with you."

She cocked her head to the side. "Luke. Your suspect doesn't know where I live."

"No, he doesn't. But we don't know how he got away, or if he had a vehicle nearby. And he doesn't know how much of him you saw, so until I'm sure you're safe, I'm going to come stay with you."

She cocked a brow. "Inviting yourself over to my house?"

"You got a problem with that?"

She had missed him. A lot. And if she were honest with herself, she was more than a little freaked out that she'd had a stare-down with the crazy guy who'd been stealing drugs from several businesses. Who knew whether he was high or not? And people on drugs did desperate things sometimes. "Okay. I'll wait up for you."

"You don't need to do that."

She so wanted to touch him, but there were still police

cars everywhere. And the sheriff's department, and now the news crews. Poor Luke had his hands full.

"I know I don't need to wait up. I want to."

A police car pulled up alongside Emma's. Luke went over and talked to the officer inside, who nodded and waved to Emma.

"Then I'll see you in a few hours," Luke said.

"All right." She locked up the clinic and climbed into her truck.

Luke was already walking across the parking lot toward the crime scene. Emma so wanted to stay there with him, but she also had a lot to do at home, and the dogs needed to be fed and let outside. They were wound up from all the activity.

She needed to do a little unwinding herself. The officer, whose name was Bill, followed her home. He even came inside with her and did a check of her house, something she thought was totally unnecessary, though she was secretly grateful. He told her he'd drive around her neighborhood a few times to make sure she was okay. She thanked him and closed the door, went into the bedroom, and changed clothes.

A part of her wanted to fall into bed and obliterate this day by falling asleep, but she had some paperwork to do. So she took some chicken out of the freezer, defrosted it, sliced some vegetables and started a pot of chicken noodle soup. She let the dogs outside to play after they ate, while she sat down at the table and worked on paying bills.

She periodically checked the simmering soup while dealing with her paperwork.

When the doorbell rang, she glanced down at her phone to check the time, not realizing so much time had passed since she'd been home. She shoved the pen in her hair and got up from the table to answer the door.

Luke was there, looking as worn out as she felt.

"How did it go?" she asked, petting Boomer when the dog came up to shove his head under her hand.

Luke dropped his duffle bag at the front door. "It went

okay. Video surveillance didn't show much more than what you said. He kept his head down and his hoodie covered his face, so we didn't get any facial recognition. Since he wore gloves, we won't have any prints, either, but there are still some leads. Oh, God, what's that smell?"

"I figured you probably hadn't eaten a decent homemade meal in a while, save what you can grab at Bert's. I made chicken noodle soup. Are you hungry?"

"I'm starving," he said as he followed her into the kitchen. "Have you eaten?"

"Actually, no. I got involved paying bills, then caught up on some paperwork. I kind of lost track of time, so I'll eat with you."

While Boomer hustled off to play with Daisy and Annie, Emma got out a couple of bowls and a plate for the bread she'd made the other day. As she was reaching into the cabinet for the plates, Luke slipped his arm around her waist and turned her around.

He tipped her chin up with his fingers and pressed a long, slow kiss to her lips that made her forget how hungry she was—for food, anyway. She slid her fingers into his hair and held on, breathing in his scent, grabbing onto the work-solid feel of his shoulders as he pinned her against the counter with his body.

She moaned against his lips as he deepened the kiss, another hunger taking over when he lifted up her tank top and covered her breast with his hand. He drew the cup of her bra down and found her nipple, making her gasp as he teased and tormented her until she wrapped one leg around him to draw him closer to her.

And when he lifted her and placed her on the counter, she shoved the dishes out of the way, no longer caring about food.

"You mind waiting for dinner?" he asked.

She was breathing so hard she felt dizzy. "No. There are other parts of me hungry right now."

A low growl tore from his throat as he gathered her hair in his hand and tilted her head back, his mouth ravaging her neck in a series of hot kisses that tore her apart. And when he made his way back to her lips, he seared her with a bone-melting kiss that left her weak and needy.

"Yeah, I need to be fed, too, Emma. But it's not soup I want right now."

He drew her shorts and panties down her legs. Her legs trembled as he ran his fingers over her skin.

"I've been thinking about you every day, about touching you, kissing you, hearing the sounds you make when you come."

Nearly out of her mind with desire, she unashamedly spread for him, leaning back as he put his mouth on her sex. She cried out, so close to orgasm she was almost embarrassed by her need for him. But he'd been all she thought about since their weekend. The way he touched her, kissed her, the way he'd broken through her defenses and made her feel his touch, made her remember what it felt like to be a woman again.

She was a woman in desperate need of an orgasm right now. And Luke was the only man who could give her exactly what she needed.

He was relentless in his pursuit of her pleasure, fixing his tongue and his mouth on every spot that was guaranteed to send her right over the edge. Not that it would take much, since she'd been pining away for him—for this—every night she lay alone in her bed, thinking about him. And when she hovered so close her whole body quaked, he gave her just what she needed. She tightened, and fell, with a cry so loud she shook with her climax.

And when he moved up her body, kissing her hipbone and her belly button to give her time to come down off that high, she lifted up on her elbows to smile at him.

He helped her off the counter, and she slung an arm around his neck to bring him in for a kiss, wanting him to feel as unraveled as she was, needing him to come apart in the same way.

So she dropped to her knees and reached for the belt buckle of his jeans.

"Oh, Em. I don't think that's a—"

She lifted her gaze to his and smiled. "You're no longer in charge here, officer. So just shut up and enjoy the ride."

Luke swallowed, hard, his throat gone dry at the sight of Emma, her hair disheveled after her wild orgasm, her tank top hanging half off, on her knees and unzipping his pants. It was every man's dream, and his undoing.

She jerked his pants to his knees and freed his cock, taking it into her soft hands. He practically vibrated as she put her mouth on him.

It had been too long since he'd touched and tasted her, since he'd been inside her. He'd be lying to himself if he didn't admit she was all he'd thought about through all those grueling double shifts.

He hadn't come there to have sex with her, though he was hoping they could end the night together in bed. He'd missed her touch and the way she tasted. Never in his wildest dreams did he picture her on her knees, her mouth a wet, hot haven, taking him to hell and back while he tried so damn hard not to let go.

But Emma was relentless, determined to drive him to the very brink.

And damn, she was good, her mouth a vortex of deep, dark pleasure. He swept his hand over her hair and mentally prayed for mercy, and when he was sure he couldn't hold back any longer, he whispered her name as a warning.

"Em."

She ignored him, and gave him even more than he thought he could take, wrapping her sweet lips around him and taking him all the way to the edge.

He hovered there, watching her sweet mouth, wishing he could last, but when she lifted those sweet, beautiful eyes to his, he let go with a wild groan and an explosive shudder that made him grasp the counter for balance, sure his knees were going to buckle as his climax ripped through him.

Emma held him tight, refusing to let go until he gave her everything.

Only then, when he was spent and his legs were shaking,

did she let him pull her up and kiss her, stroke her back and hold her in his trembling arms.

"You blew the goddamn top off my head," he whispered in her ear.

"Yes. I know that feeling. I'm pretty sure my brains were leaking out of my ears when I climaxed."

He grinned. "Good to know. Now how about some soup? I have a feeling I'm going to need some energy before round two."

She pulled away and leveled a saucy grin at him. "Yes, you're definitely going to need food."

After they cleaned up and righted their clothing, Luke ate two giant bowls of some of the best-tasting homemade chicken noodle soup he'd ever had, and he was pretty sure he ate at least half a loaf of bread.

"Are you sure you're eating during these double shifts?" Emma asked.

"When I can. We've been pretty busy. I'm hoping this latest break-in will yield some leads."

"I hope so, too."

"You helped with your description of the suspect."

"Did I? That's good."

She looked away. Luke could tell she was still nervous about that guy spotting her. "You're worried about it. About him."

She shrugged. "Not really. I mean, yes. I'm not stupid. I'd like to buy a gun."

Luke pushed his bowl to the side. "Do you know how to use a gun?"

"Some. I've fired them in the past, but haven't for a while. I looked into the licensing classes to carry a weapon. I think I'll sign up for one."

"They don't give you a lot of practice time."

"I know."

He wasn't sure how he felt about her having a gun, but she was an adult and it was her call to make. What he could be sure about was that she knew how to handle herself with one.

"I'll take you shooting."

Her gaze met his. "You would? I know you're busy, and you don't really have time for that."

"I'll make time for you, Emma. You're important."

His words crept right into her heart and warmed her from the inside out. "Thank you."

After they finished eating, Luke helped Emma clean up the dishes. They sat on the sofa for a while to watch a movie. It was late and Emma was going to pay for this in the morning when she had to drag herself out of bed, but since they'd eaten late, she couldn't go to bed on a full stomach.

It didn't take more than twenty minutes, though, for her to realize Luke was sound asleep. She smiled and poked at him.

"Hey," she said.

He shot up. "What's wrong?"

"How about we go to bed and get some sleep?"

He blinked sleepy eyes at her. "I was going to ravage you."

"We'll save the ravaging for when you've caught up on your sleep."

He gave her a lopsided grin. "I'll go let the dogs out and meet you upstairs."

She sighed as he went to the back door, realizing she could get very used to having Luke in her life, and in her house.

Which was a very dangerous thing.

Chapter 23

EMMA COULDN'T EXACTLY remember the last time she'd handled a gun, but it had likely been in college, when she and a bunch of her friends had gone out target shooting. To say she wasn't adept was an understatement.

Now that some idiot was out robbing businesses, and she was a possible witness, she needed to feel secure. There were so few instances in her life when she'd felt secure, and she was tired of being a victim. She wasn't sure she could ever shoot anyone, but at least she'd have it as a choice if it ever came down to that.

Luke took her to the outdoor gun range on a beautiful Saturday afternoon. He'd also brought a veritable arsenal of weapons and ammo for her to try out.

"There are smaller and larger guns. Some have a big kick, some not so much. Some are going to be more comfortable in your hands than others."

She perused them, but they all just looked like guns to her. She lifted her gaze to his. "Honestly? I have no idea. Recommend something."

He nodded. "I think this Glock nine millimeter is the

best choice for you. It's fairly lightweight, doesn't have a huge kick, and the trigger is easy. Try it first. If you don't like it, we'll try the twenty-two."

"Okay."

"First, you need to know how to load it, where the safety is, and the fact that you never ever—"

"Point the gun at another person. I understand. I did do some research, and I do have a certain amount of common sense, Luke. You're not dealing with a total idiot here."

He cocked a grin. "Good to know. When you aim at the target, go for the largest part of the body."

"Why not the head?"

"Amateurs always think you should aim for the head, when in reality the head is harder to hit. Go for the midsection. It's a larger area and you'll have a better chance of hitting your target that way. The smaller the area of the body, the more likely the chance is you'll miss. If you miss, the better opportunity they have to get to you before you fire off another shot."

"Oh. Good point. Midsection. Got it."

"Ear and eye protection. Always. The cartridge will eject on the right side of the gun."

He went through every instruction like three times before he allowed her to start shooting.

"Relax. Above all, relax. Bend your elbows. If you tense up, you won't hit shit."

He stood behind her. She laid the gun down and turned to face him. "You're not going to shoot?"

"I will, eventually. This is about you, not me. I know how to fire a gun."

"Oh. Of course. Okay." She picked up the Glock and aimed at the target, her palms already beginning to sweat and her hands shaking. This thing was an instrument of death. One wrong move and someone could be killed.

"Relax, Emma," Luke said, moving closer to her. "I have confidence in you. You know what you're doing."

She took a deep breath and pulled the trigger. The kick was bigger than she'd expected and it scared the hell out of her. The gun was loud, too. She laid it down and looked down the range at the target. "Did I hit anything?"

"Yeah. The dirt in front of the target."

"Oh."

"Target through the sight at the top of the barrel. And did you even open your eyes when you shot?"

"I don't remember."

"That means no. Use your sight. Take a deep breath, and squeeze the trigger gently."

She picked up the gun and tried again. It was loud—again. And it kicked—again. But at least she knew what to expect this time. She started to lay the gun down.

"No. Keep shooting. Empty the clip. If your intent is to shoot someone, you're not going to shoot them one time and lay the gun down. You're going to keep shooting them until the clip is empty."

She gave him an incredulous look. "Really?"

"Really. If you're going to own a gun, and you're going to use it for self-defense, then be prepared to defend yourself to the death, Emma. It's you or the bad guy. If you're going to shoot him, then empty the clip into him so you know he's dead. Otherwise, you might miss and think you hit him, or graze him, and he'll get up and kill you."

Empty the clip into him. Okay. This was serious business. She raised the gun and pictured a really bad guy coming after her, determined to do her great bodily harm. She used the sight and focused, took a deep breath, then fired. And fired again. And again, until the clip was empty. She set the gun down and Luke came over.

"Good job. You actually hit the paper this time."

"Yay!"

"I didn't say you hit the target, just the paper the target is printed on."

"Oh." She laughed. "Obviously I need to get better at this."

"It's okay. You did good. I told you, it takes practice. We'll work on it."

They did. Luke spent two hours showing her how to load

and reload the gun, how to flip the safety on and off, and how to adjust her aim. Fortunately, she wasn't as bad as she thought, so at the end she had actually managed to hit the bad guy on the target.

And then she watched as he took his turn. As a police officer, he was very adept at shooting. He took a wide stance, and she had to admit that seeing him with a gun in his hand expertly hitting the center of the target each time was kind of—

Sexy. Plus, as she stood behind and to the left of him, she got to look at his butt, which was never a bad thing.

Luke was formidable. Skilled, extremely good-looking, and utterly patient with her. A devastating package to her senses.

"With practice, you'll improve every time. But you have to practice," he said as they carried the gun and ammo cases to his truck.

"I hate to admit this, but that was exhilarating."

"The shooting range is always fun. It's when you have to face a real-life person that it's not so much fun."

She climbed into the truck and put on her seat belt. "Have you ever had to shoot someone?"

He paused, then looked at her. "Yeah. Not as much fun as a paper target." He started up the engine and backed out of the gravel parking lot.

Luke took her to a gun shop. He told her the dealer was reputable and wouldn't gouge her on prices. She had signed up for the licensing classes for the following week, and she'd need a gun for those anyway. In the meantime, it was legal for her to keep the gun at her house.

"Fred," Luke said as they entered the shop.

"Hey, Luke, how's it goin'?"

Fred was a tall, burly mountain-man type that Emma figured had a stockpile of guns and ammo, just waiting for Armageddon or the zombie apocalypse. He wore a flannel shirt over his bib overalls and had a very long ZZ Top kind of beard. But if Luke said he was okay, then he must be okay.

"Whatcha in the market for today?"

"My girl . . . my friend Emma here is looking to buy a gun."

Didn't quite know how to describe her, did he? Emma grinned at that.

"What kind of a gun are you looking for, Miss Emma?" Fred asked, tucking his beard inside his shirt to lean over the pistol counter.

"Uh, I have no idea." She scanned the pistols in the glass case. "A Glock nine, I guess?"

"Good choice." Fred took one out and handed it to her. It was unloaded and the trigger was locked with one of those zip-tie things, so she couldn't do any damage. She felt its weight in her hand and practiced pointing it at a wall.

Luke was right. This gun felt good to her, and since he'd also made her shoot a twenty-two, a thirty-eight, and a forty-five at the range today, she realized this one was the right fit for her.

"Okay, I'll take this one."

"She gonna use your discount, Luke?" Fred asked.

"If you wouldn't mind, I'd sure appreciate it."

"No problem. I'll ring it up while you start filling out the paperwork, Miss Emma."

He handed her a long sheet of paper to fill out and walked away.

"Discount?"

"Police officers get a discount. So do their family members."

"You didn't have to do that."

He swept his thumb over her bottom lip. "Sure I did."

She stared at him for the longest time, wishing they were alone.

"Paperwork, Miss Emma," Luke said with a wink.

"Oh, right." She filled out the paperwork, and once Fred verified her, she paid for her gun and the ammo Luke selected for her.

They were in Tulsa and decided to stop for dinner at a Mongolian place Emma had heard great things about.

"Shooting things works up an appetite," she said after they were seated.

"Your arm will be sore tomorrow. And likely your hand. You use different muscles to shoot, so you'll have to build them up. You should shoot at least once a week, until it becomes second nature to you. Most of the shooting ranges offer memberships."

"Sounds fun. Maybe I can get Jane and Chelsea to go with me and practice. We could become pistol-packin' babes."

Luke took a sip of the beer the waitress handed him. "Hmm. A pistol-packin' babe. I'll have to get a mental visual going of that. Maybe you in a holster, six shooters on each side. You'd have to be naked of course . . ."

She laughed. "Of course."

"So, now you've got your gun, and you did some shooting. Feel confident you could defend yourself?"

Did she? If threatened with certain death, could she end someone else's life?

She wasn't sure.

"Honestly? I don't know."

"It's understandable. Until you've been in a position where you feel threatened, you don't know how you'd act."

She looked away. She had been in that position before. She had been threatened. She hadn't been armed. If she had, how would she have reacted? If she'd had a gun in her hand at the time, would she have been able to fire it and end his life?

He'd certainly threatened to end hers. More than once. Sweetly and subtly, and he'd used a soft voice. But the threat had been there.

Leave me and I'll kill you.

"Emma."

Her gaze lifted. "Yes?"

"You were somewhere else just now."

"Was I? Sorry. I have a lot on my mind."

"I could tell. Do you want to talk about it?"

She gave him a small smile. "Not really."

"Did Vaughn ever threaten you?"

Sometimes it was like he was psychic. "He threatened to kill me if I ever left him."

"Christ. When was the last time you saw him?"

"When I had him fired. And he was only a bully when he had me alone. He would never have come after me while I stayed with my parents. And then I went back to school in South Carolina."

"You never saw him when you were there?"

She shook her head. "No. I haven't seen him since. I don't think he ever believed I would leave him. He liked easy targets, women he could control. Once I left, it was over."

"I hope so."

She took a drink. "You think he'd come after me?"

"I doubt it. It's been a lot of years. If he was going to come after you, he would have done it right away. Besides, I'm here to protect you now, so you don't have to worry."

She always worried, always had, ever since the day she escaped from Vaughn.

He, too, had once promised to protect her. Only his protection had turned into threats and near imprisonment, to the point she hadn't known the difference, hadn't trusted her own instincts, hadn't been able to believe it when others told her that he didn't love her, that he was trying to own her, that he was abusing her.

"I'm learning to protect myself." She'd already experienced someone "protecting" her, and she didn't care to go through that again.

Luke leaned back and gave her a smile. "Yeah, you are. And you'll be kick-ass at it."

And that's where he and Vaughn differed. Because he didn't mind at all that she wanted to be in charge of her own protection.

She needed to keep reminding herself that Luke and Vaughn were night-and-day different. And Luke wasn't going to hurt her like Vaughn did.

Because Luke shouldn't have to pay for what Vaughn had done to her.

And she needed to move on with her life. She deserved that happiness.

Chapter 24

FORENSICS HAD FINALLY come through for them with the latest break-in. The perp had trampled in some dirt and left footprints, no doubt from making his entrance through the woods.

He might have been wearing gloves, but there was nothing he could do to disguise those footprints. The perp's shoes were different from the ones all the cops wore, so it had been easy to isolate them. Now law enforcement was tracking the size and type of shoe he wore, at least narrowing the field.

Luke's captain had agreed that setting a trap was the best way to go. They were going to make a big deal out of a drug delivery to one of the small pharmacies on the north end of town. If the perp was casing any of these places, he'd notice. They had it organized for the coming Thursday night. Luke and his team would be inside, the rest of the team forming a perimeter around the outside of the pharmacy, out of sight.

Of course, there was no guarantee this would work. The dumbass might not even be paying attention to the pharmacy, might not hit it at all, and their efforts would be wasted. But if he was interested in hitting a drug gold mine, then Hastings Drugstore would be the mother lode, and he wouldn't be able to resist.

Luke and Boomer were still hanging out at Emma's house. She hadn't yet thrown him out, and until this guy was caught, Luke wasn't comfortable leaving her alone. She didn't seem to mind sharing her bed with him, and he sure liked being in bed with her.

They had a routine going, and even their dogs were compatible. They both got up around the same time in the morning, and Emma never asked him for anything or put any strings on him, like wanting to know when he'd be home or giving him shit when he was late. This relationship wasn't as scary as Luke thought it might be.

Huh. He was in a relationship with Emma. He supposed he should just acknowledge that, at least to himself. He and Emma hadn't talked about it. He stayed at her house and slept in her bed, and they saw each other as often as they could, considering their schedules. But neither of them had said the *R* word.

Or the *L* word, for that matter. The thought of either twisted him up inside. He'd made such a mess of his marriage to Becca. The last thing he'd ever wanted was to go down that road again, preferring his carefree bachelor lifestyle, as commitment-phobic as any guy could get.

And now he had his toothbrush and deodorant in Emma's bathroom, and she'd cleaned out a couple of drawers in her dresser for his stuff, without either of them ever having a conversation about where they were headed.

That was just fucked-up. They needed to start communicating with each other. He needed to tell her his fears about commitment, and she needed to rely on him a little more instead of feeling like she had to hold the responsibility for her entire life on her own shoulders. He got the independence thing. After what she went through with her ex, he understood it. But leaning on him a little every now and then wouldn't break her. He just didn't know how to broach the subject without her turning tail and running. Tiptoeing around each other was only going to end in disaster.

And he didn't like the thought of their relationship ending.

He sat in her living room with his feet propped up on the coffee table, Boomer and Daisy snuggled up together on the dog bed in the living room. Annie, on the other hand, had made a bed out of his lap. When Emma opened the front door, Annie leaped off his lap, causing him to wince, since she'd used his balls as a launching point.

"Hi, kids," she said, her voice affectionate and warm as she greeted all the dogs. "Did you have a good night?" She petted all of them, and Luke loved watching her with them.

Someday she was going to make an incredible mother.

And didn't that thought tighten his gut even more?

"How did it go?" he asked as she plopped down on the sofa to plant a kiss on his lips.

She grinned. "I passed with flying colors, of course. I even placed all my bullets on the bad guy in the target. I'll have my gun license as soon as all the paperwork is processed and the required fees are paid."

He pulled her onto his lap. "Congratulations. I knew you could do it."

"The rules and law part of the class was pretty interesting. Dry at times, but interesting nonetheless. And how did you guys do tonight?"

"We watched a baseball game and then played catch in the backyard. Annie ate part of a tennis ball."

"Of course she did." Emma glared at Annie, who leaped on the sofa to launch herself onto both their laps.

"Annie. Off." Emma shooed her off the sofa. "I don't know where she developed such a bad habit."

"Huh. No idea."

Emma gave him a dubious look. "Tell me you're not letting her up on the sofa."

"Okay. I won't tell you."

She shook her head. "I need a pop. Would you like something?"

"Kitchen sex would be great, thanks."

She laughed and got up. "Wasn't what I was offering. I'm just going for the pop for now. You'll get sex later."

He grinned. She grabbed something to drink, then filled him in on the class, while he told her about his day and the sting operation they were setting up for the robbery suspect.

"That sounds intriguing. And dangerous."

"It won't be dangerous. Except maybe for the suspect. For obvious reasons, you can't repeat this to anyone. Not even Jane and Chelsea."

"Obviously. I won't tell a soul. I do want you to be careful. I never saw the guy with a gun, but that doesn't mean he doesn't have one."

"And I won't be the only one inside the pharmacy. Trust me, we'll be well protected."

She laid her head on his chest. "I hope so. I've kind of grown accustomed to seeing you here every day."

He put his arm around her and stared at the TV. "Yeah, I've kind of gotten used to being here."

And once again, the conversation stopped, neither of them willing to have that oh-so-important talk about oh-so-important things.

One of these days, though, all those critical topics were going to get discussed.

Chapter 25

EMMA WAS SCHEDULED to have a late girls' night with Jane and Chelsea on Thursday, but she was a nervous wreck. She knew all she'd be thinking about was Luke, holed up at the pharmacy, lying in wait for the suspect, and she wouldn't be able to concentrate on anything Jane and Chelsea said. Then they'd ask her what was wrong, and she'd have to lie.

She hated lying. So she called them up and . . . basically lied, telling them she had a lot of paperwork to catch up on, so they'd have to reschedule. After the clinic closed at eight, she came home and snuggled with the dogs, trying to concentrate on television, though she found herself repeatedly getting up to pace. So she decided to read a book, but she couldn't concentrate and kept reading the same paragraph over and over, which ended up frustrating her. Putting the book aside, she took the dogs outside and let them run off some energy, which did nothing for her own stress level.

She knew she wouldn't hear from Luke for a while yet. He wouldn't call while they staked out the place. And if they did manage to catch the guy, he might not call, because he'd be too busy wrapping up the case.

Which meant she had nothing to do but sit at home and . . . stress.

Ugh.

When her phone rang, she ran to answer it.

It wasn't Luke. It was Ellen Andrews, whose poodle, Nina, had gotten attacked by a much larger dog. Ellen was hysterical because Nina was bleeding and weak.

"I'll meet you at the clinic in ten minutes, Ellen. Do what you can to stop the bleeding by putting towels or bandages on the wounds and compressing on them. Do you have someone to drive you?"

"Y-yes. My husband Zane will drive."

"I'll see you there shortly."

She slid into her shoes and grabbed her keys, then ran out the door to her truck. Within less than ten minutes she was at the clinic. Ellen and Zane were there with Nina a few minutes later.

Ellen looked a wreck, her cheeks streaked with tears. She was shaking as they brought Nina to the exam room. Emma gloved up and removed the towels Ellen had wrapped her in so she could examine her.

Yeah, some dog had bitten Nina pretty badly.

"I'm going to clean her up and get her stitched," Emma explained. "Why don't the two of you go out to the waiting room. There's a coffeepot out there, and water in the nearby kitchen off to the right. You can make yourself a pot if you'd like."

Zane put his arm around Ellen. "I'll take care of that. Thanks, Dr. Emma."

Emma scooped up Nina and took her into the OR, anesthetized her, then started prepping her. Once Nina was out, she shaved the areas that needed suturing and got those spots cleaned up, much easier now that the poodle wasn't quivering in pain.

"Poor baby," Emma said, running her gloved hands over the dog. "Some dogs are just mean, aren't they?"

Emma got Nina sewed up, checked her for any other signs of injury, then gave her a shot to ward off infection.

She went out to the waiting area. "She's going to be fine, but she's still anesthetized, and I've got her hooked up to fluids. I'd like to keep her here overnight."

"We've warned the neighbors about their dog, but they ignored us," Zane said. "We called the police, and the dog has been confiscated. At least he's updated on shots so we don't have to worry about rabies."

"That's good news. And don't worry about Nina. She's going to be okay. She'll sleep all night, and you can come by in the morning to pick her up."

Ellen took her hands. "Thank you for saving her life."

"You're welcome. Now both of you, go home and get some sleep. Your baby will be okay here."

After Ellen and Zane left, Emma stretched and looked up at the clock over the reception desk.

Ten thirty. She blew out a breath and went to check on Nina. In her cage, she was asleep, her vitals normal. She went into the OR to start cleaning up the mess from the surgery, not wanting to leave it for Leanne to deal with in the morning.

When she heard the bumping noise, she thought maybe it was Nina waking up and fighting the anesthesia, so she went to investigate.

And came face-to-face with her worst nightmare. Someone she'd hoped to never see again.

Vaughn.

Chapter 26

SITTING IN THE dark in a tiny pharmacy for hours was boring as hell. At least Luke wasn't alone. Evan was on the inside with him, and they had the four guys staked out on the outside in constant communication.

They couldn't even get up and wander around. The pharmacy was well lit from the outside lights, and they'd cast shadows if anyone was looking inside. They wouldn't want the suspect to peer inside and see movement, which meant they either had to crouch and move, or crawl around on the floor.

Damned uncomfortable. And they'd been there for two and a half hours already.

"Anything?" he asked.

"Nothing here," Steve said. "Someone just sped down the highway. Clocked him doing twenty miles over the limit. Too bad we can't go after him."

Luke looked over at Evan, who rolled his eyes. "Steve lives for writing tickets."

"Who the hell likes to write tickets? It's a pain in the ass."

"Steve does," Evan said, unwrapping a candy bar he'd stuffed into his pocket. "Don't ask me why."

"We have movement out here."

"What kind of movement?" Luke shot back.

"He came from behind the housing addition. Skulking up the street. Wearing a backpack, staying in the shadows, hands in his pockets. He's heading for the back of the shopping center."

Tensing, Luke was on full alert now. He looked at Evan. "Let's head to the back of the store."

Evan gave a short nod and they crouched low, staying out of sight of the windows.

Evan took up position just inside the drug-supply area, while Luke stood right by the counter, ready to surprise the would-be burglar. Boomer was with him, staying right by his side, not making a sound.

"Oh. False alarm. He's just walking past the store."

Defeated, Luke's shoulders slumped. He gave Boomer the stand down command, and Boomer lay down.

"Well, that was a letdown," Evan said.

"No shit."

An hour later, they decided to call it a night. The suspect's typical MO was to hit early, and it was almost eleven.

"Sorry, guys. I thought this one would pan out," Luke said on his mic.

"We'll get him at some point," Steve said.

Luke wrapped everything up, locked up and rearmed the store, then headed to his cruiser. He drove to Emma's, surprised to see all her lights still on.

Daisy greeted him at the door, and Annie was out of her cage. Boomer greeted the other dogs.

"Where is she, girls?" he said, petting them both and heading to the bedroom.

"Emma?"

No answer. He went into the bathroom, but she wasn't there.

Huh. She wasn't in the house, but the dogs were. That was unusual. He took out his phone to call her, but it rang, and she didn't answer.

She must have gotten an emergency call at the clinic. Still, she would answer if he called.

He shouldn't worry about her. She was fine.

Still, it was late. Maybe if she had a call, she'd be tired. And maybe hungry. He was sure hungry.

He let the dogs out, put Annie in her crate for the night, then changed clothes, and headed for the clinic.

He'd talk Emma into going to Tulsa and eating at Denny's. A late breakfast sounded great to him about now, and if she'd worked late, he knew she'd be hungry, too.

EMMA STARED AT Vaughn for what seemed like hours. He looked . . . older. But still vital. Still as powerful as he always had. Tall and lean, but with sharp dark eyes and salt-and-pepper hair, with a goatee.

She'd once found him so handsome. Now? Now he just represented misery. Fear. Mistakes. Horror.

He took a step forward. She took a step back. He halted.

"You're not supposed to be here," she said, hearing the crack in her voice. He'd use that against her.

He held up his hands. "I just want to talk."

"We have nothing to say to each other. And you need to leave." Her heart hammered in her chest, that old fear resurfacing. She'd fought so hard to get past it—to get past him—and now it all came rushing back.

Why was he here?

"I just wanted to apologize for . . . for everything."

His words were empty, devoid of any real emotion. How could she have ever believed anything he said to her? Had she really been that naïve? The man had no heart, no real feelings for anything or anyone other than what made him happy, what suited his purposes.

She kept moving backward, needing the safety of the reception counter, a barrier between the two of them. "Vaughn. You need to leave. Now."

"Not until you listen to what I have to say."

There was something in his eyes, something she'd never noticed before. A disconnect, as if he wasn't really even speaking to her, or even seeing her.

"I thought you had moved out of Oklahoma."

He looked past her and let out a short laugh. "Yeah, after I lost my job, I did for a while." Then he lifted his gaze to hers. "Did you know that you cost me my job, Emma?"

He would blame her for that. For what he'd done. He'd always blamed her. And for so long, she'd accepted the blame. Not anymore. She straightened, refusing to cower in front of him.

Never again.

"You didn't lose your job at the university because of me, Vaughn. You have to take responsibility for what you did."

He moved suddenly and the reception desk was blocked. She backed toward her office, where her purse was. Where her gun was. She needed to get to her gun. Vaughn wasn't being reasonable. Had he ever been reasonable? Had she ever been able to stop him when he was determined to have—to take—whatever he wanted?

She wasn't the person she was back then. She wasn't under his thumb, under his control, any longer. And she'd never be again.

She took a deep breath, centering herself to find the calm balance she needed to confront him. "Let's go sit down, have something cold to drink. Then you can tell me whatever it is you want to tell me."

He tilted his head to the side and studied her, and once again she was struck by that faraway look in his eyes.

"Okay."

She waited while he caught up to her, and it took everything in her not to run from him. Just being this close to him made her nauseous as the past rushed back to her. She forced it away, staying in the here and now.

"So you work here?"

"Yes."

"It's what you always wanted to do."

"Yes, it is." She had to fight to keep her voice under control, not to tremble because he was so close to her.

She opened the door to her office. He walked in and looked around. Picked up a few files, then walked to the window before turning around to face her, his hands clasped behind his back. It reminded her so much of him standing at the front of the classroom. He'd been so commanding back when she was a lovestruck freshman. She'd hung on his every word, and he'd hooked her like a starving fish.

"So . . . you have an office. You've really come up in the world, Emma. You're a success."

"I'm just starting out."

"Still, you're on your own. Do you think you can make it without someone to take care of you?" He came around the desk and this time, she refused to cower or step back. "You always needed someone to look after you. You liked it when I did."

No, she hadn't, but she had no idea of his current state of mind, so she kept her opinions to herself.

She tilted her head back, met his gaze. "How about we have something to drink?"

"I don't suppose you have wine in that mini fridge of yours," he said, taking a seat.

She managed a smile. "No. Soda or water."

"Maybe we can go back to your place. I stopped there first looking for you, but you weren't home, so I came here."

He knew where she lived. She wondered how long he'd been stalking her. "So . . . soda or water?"

"You're not inviting me back to your home. Is your boyfriend there?"

She shifted past him and reached into the refrigerator for a bottle of water, unscrewed the top and held on to the bottle to keep her hands from shaking. Now she was next to her desk, inches away from the drawer that held her purse. And her gun. "That's none of your business. Just like my life is none of your business anymore."

"You're brave now, Emma. Braver than you used to be. You used to let me control everything."

She took a seat at her desk, using her knee to nudge the drawer. "That was a long time ago." She took a sip of water.

"Not so long ago. What changed between us?"

"I think you know what happened."

"Yes. You betrayed me."

"I didn't betray you, Vaughn. I ended our relationship. Now I'd like you to leave." She nudged the drawer open farther.

He laughed, his tone growing more menacing. She didn't want to have to take out the gun, but so help her she would if he made one move out of that chair.

"That didn't work out too well for you before, little girl. You trying to tell me what to do. What makes you think it'll work out so well for you now?"

"Because I'm here to back her up. Now get the hell up out of that chair before I kick your ass."

Emma's gaze shot to the doorway.

Luke.

Chapter 27

LUKE DIDN'T KNOW what the hell was going on, or who this guy was making threats against Emma, but based on the bits of conversation he'd picked up as he walked down the hall, he'd already figured out two things. One, Emma knew the guy, and two, she didn't like him and wanted him out of her clinic. That was enough information for him to know he had to get this guy out of there in a hurry.

Seemingly unconcerned about Luke's arrival, the guy stood. He was tall and lean, with a graying goatee. Looked like an academic type to Luke, and he had a sneaking suspicion it might be Vaughn, which sent his radar up to high. He laid his hand on the butt of his gun.

"You must be the boyfriend. I'm Vaughn Castille." Vaughn extended a hand that Luke ignored.

"I'm pretty sure Emma asked you to leave."

Vaughn resumed his seat with a smirk. "Emma doesn't always know what she wants."

"I know exactly what I want, just like I knew exactly what I wanted six years ago when I took out a restraining order against you to get you out of my life."

Luke pulled out his gun and pointed it at Vaughn.

Seemingly unconcerned by the gun pointed at him, Vaughn laughed. "I don't think that's necessary."

Ignoring him, Luke held the gun on Vaughn, pulled out his phone, and punched a button. "This is McCormack. I'm off duty, and I need a black-and-white at the Hope Small Animal Hospital on the highway. Violation of a restraining order . . . Yeah, I've got it under control until you send someone here."

He hung up and kept the gun trained on Vaughn, who wouldn't look at him, his gaze fixed on Emma, who in turn couldn't seem to tear her gaze away from Vaughn.

"Emma," Luke said. "Come over here with me."

She didn't respond.

"Emma," he said again. She finally dragged her gaze to his. "Come over here."

She nodded, grabbed her purse out of the drawer, and went over to Luke.

"See how she obeys you? You haven't changed much at all in that respect, have you, Emma?"

That seemed to pull her out of whatever trance she'd been in. She narrowed her gaze and made a move toward him. "Screw you, Vaughn."

Luke grasped her arm and shoved her behind him. "Emma. Stay there."

He heard the sirens, and Blake Howard came in.

"This your guy?" Blake asked.

"Yeah. Dr. Emma Burnett has a restraining order against him. Vaughn Castille."

Blake jerked Vaughn toward him, flipped him around and cuffed him, then did a pat down to check for weapons. Once he was secured, Blake looked over at Luke. "I'll take care of him."

Luke nodded. "Thanks."

"I'll see you again, Emma," Vaughn said.

Luke leaned toward him. "No, asshole, you won't."

Vaughn smirked. "I'll definitely see you again."

Emma turned away as Blake took Vaughn outside.

"Wait here. I'll be right back."

Emma nodded, and Luke went outside to talk to Blake. "Make sure that bastard stays locked up."

"No problem. If he's violated a restraining order, he won't get out tonight. Or hopefully anytime soon."

After Blake drove away, Luke went back inside. Emma was still leaning against the hallway wall, clutching her purse against her chest.

"Emma."

Her gaze shot to his. "Thanks. I'm fine."

"I know you are. Let's go home."

He followed her home, staying on her bumper the entire time. She drove slowly, really slowly, and he knew she was in shock. He should have left her truck and put her in his cruiser, but it wasn't a long drive to the house, so he figured she could handle it. Plus, doing something routine would make her focus.

She pulled into the driveway, and he drove up next to her, got out, and was right there when she got out of the truck.

"I'm fine," she said as she fumbled in her purse for the keys. He saw the gun in her purse.

"You could have shot him," he said as he pulled his set of keys out of his pocket and unlocked the front door.

"That's why I invited him into my office. My purse was there, in the drawer. The gun is in my purse." As they stepped inside and Luke shut the door, she lifted her gaze to his. "I thought about whether or not I could shoot him."

"If he tried to attack you, I'm sure you could have done it."

He took her into the living room and sat her on the sofa. Boomer and Daisy came over to her, and she absently petted them.

"How about a beer?"

"That sounds like a really great idea."

As he grabbed two beers, he forced himself to calm down, but he was really damned pissed off about Vaughn showing up where Emma worked. He sat next to her and handed her the beer. She gulped down two or three swallows, then held the beer between both her hands.

She looked at him for the longest time, then let out a sigh. "He came here first. And he knows about you. He asked about my boyfriend at my house."

"So he's been stalking you."

"Apparently."

She took several more swallows of beer, emptying the bottle before placing it on the table. She took a deep breath, then let it out. He'd never seen her look more defeated than when she gazed up at him. "I'm tired."

"He's locked up, Emma."

"But for how long? I know how the system works. He'll be out on bail tomorrow. And then what?"

"Then . . . we'll figure out a way to get him out of your life."

"We?" She shook her head. "I don't think so. He's my problem to deal with."

"No. He's our problem to deal with."

"Not tonight. I don't even want to think about him tonight."

He wished they could continue to talk this out, but he understood she'd just gone through a lot. "Okay. Let's go to bed."

They stood, but she laid a hand on his chest. "I don't want to upset you or make you angry, but would you mind . . . I need to be alone tonight."

He frowned. "I don't understand."

"I just need to be in my own head, to think some things through."

In other words, she was pushing him away at a time when what she really needed was someone to hold on to, to be close to. But yeah, he got the hint loud and clear. "Sure. Come on, Boomer."

Boomer, who was curled up next to Daisy, lifted his head. When he saw Luke head to the front door, he followed.

Emma leaned against the doorway. "I hope you understand. It's nothing you've done. I just need some space right now."

"I understand." He opened the front door. "Good night, Emma."

"Good night, Luke."

The door locking behind him had a note of finality to it. He'd been there for her when she'd needed him.

But maybe that was the thing—she didn't need him, or want him. Maybe she'd already had a guy in her life who was there for her way more than she'd ever wanted, and maybe she never wanted to go down that relationship road ever again. He knew she was afraid—of men, of relationships, and what that meant. Hell, so was he. But he was taking the steps.

Emma just didn't want to.

Fine with him. He'd never wanted a relationship in the first place. He and Boomer had been doing just fine as single guys.

He started up the truck and backed out of the driveway. He made a call to one of the guys on duty to keep watch over Emma's house during the night.

Like it or not, he was still going to make sure she stayed safe, even if she didn't want him in her life.

"To the single life again, Boom," he said as he drove away.

Chapter 28

EMMA HAD RECEIVED a call from one of the sergeants on duty at the Hope Police Department the next day. She needed to go in and file a report. Fortunately, or maybe unfortunately, Luke was nowhere around in the precinct.

She'd spoken to her lawyer, who told her Vaughn's violating the restraining order could send him to jail, for a short or possibly long time. That was up to the judge. But he would make bail today, and there was nothing Emma could do about that other than be on guard.

She wouldn't be caught off guard again, that was for certain. Him showing up at the clinic last night freaked her out and reminded her how hard she'd worked to become independent and gain back her self-esteem. It had taken years of therapy and dragging her ass back to school, starting over when she had allowed herself to get so far behind, to get where she was now.

And she had almost taken a step back again, had almost allowed herself to fall in love again, to put her heart in the hands of a man who could possibly break it. Where had her vow gone to never fall in love, to never have a relationship, to never trust a man again?

Luke had made it so easy. He'd been there for her time and time again, including last night. He'd walked in just in time to save her from Vaughn, who would have done God only knew what if he hadn't stepped in.

But what if Luke hadn't shown up at the clinic? What might have happened? Maybe . . . just maybe, Emma could have handled the situation.

She'd never know now.

Well, goddammit, she didn't need any man to protect her. She had a gun, she had a license, she had taken self-defense classes. She was a grown woman, a business owner, and she could damn well take care of herself. She didn't need some knight in shining armor to show up on his white horse and rescue her, then tie her down and make her fall in love and forget all her carefully orchestrated plans for her future.

And it might have stung like crazy when she'd kicked Luke out of her house last night, and she might have lain awake the rest of the night because she realized she'd been so wrapped up in herself and her own misery that she hadn't bothered to ask him about the sting operation at the pharmacy, which made her realize she was a terrible girlfriend, and he should have been the one breaking up with her.

That revelation had made her toss and turn and feel even more miserable. Even worse, she missed him in her bed, but she'd just have to get used to that because independent women like her didn't need a man and didn't need love. And even if she had realized she was in love with Luke, she once thought she was in love with Vaughn, too, so she wasn't exactly the best judge of that whole love thing, was she?

"Are you all right, Dr. Emma?" Leanne asked as they dealt with a particularly ornery chow who didn't want to have his shots or his temperature taken or his ears inspected.

Emma fought back the tears that had been threatening all day long. "I'm fine. Allergies or something."

"Oh, those are the worst. Do you need to take something?"

Yeah. A vacation. On some deserted tropical island. "No, I'm good. Let's just take care of Barney here so the poor guy can go home."

Work was an endless day of dogs, cats, birds, a snake and, for a fun change of pace, a lemur with a diarrhea problem. After that, she went home, fed the dogs, then grabbed a glass of wine and sat on her sofa, determined to do nothing but watch mindless television all night.

Until her doorbell rang. Immediately tensing, she looked over to the table where her purse lay. Deciding to check and see who it was first, she looked out the peephole, then smiled and opened the door.

"Hey, Chelsea. I didn't know we had plans."

"We don't. I just popped by on the chance you'd be home. And you are."

"Well, come on in. I'm having a glass of wine."

"Which just so happens to be my favorite pastime."

Emma poured a glass for Chelsea, who had tossed her purse on the end table and was sitting cross-legged on the floor playing with Daisy and Annie.

"I love Annie. I wish I could have dogs in my apartment. I'd have adopted her in a heartbeat if I could."

Emma laughed as Annie slurped one side of Chelsea's face. "She loves you."

"Yeah, I'm just a lovable sort." She climbed up on the sofa and took the glass of wine, then sipped. "Oh, nice. What's the occasion?"

"No occasion. Just unwinding."

"Always a good excuse. And where's the hotshot stud who's been sharing your bed lately?"

She took a sip of wine. "I sent him back home."

"Uh-oh. This could be a two-bottle night. Spill. What happened? Did you two have a fight?"

"No. Vaughn showed up at the clinic last night."

Chelsea's eyes widened. "Oh my God. Are you all right? Did he try to hurt you?"

"I'm fine. He tried to intimidate me, but he never did anything. And then Luke showed up, and Vaughn was arrested for violating the restraining order."

"Thank God." Chelsea frowned. "Okay, so somewhere in there you kicked Luke to the curb?"

"Yes." She finished her glass of wine, went into the kitchen, and brought out the bottle, refilling her glass. Chelsea was still working on hers.

"You'll have to explain," Chelsea said. "Because I'm not understanding how Luke coming to your rescue resulted in you breaking up with him."

"It's . . . complicated." She avoided making eye contact with Chelsea as she took another sip of wine.

"I can do complicated. I'm a math teacher."

"I was handling Vaughn. He was just . . . talking. Trying his typical intimidation tactics. And I had my gun in my purse, which was in my desk in case he tried something. And then Luke showed up and did the whole macho thing by arresting him."

"That bastard."

Emma rolled her eyes. "I told you. It's complicated."

Chelsea laughed. "Honey. You have to see it from my viewpoint. Hot stuff comes in and intercedes between you and the guy you told me terrified you enough that you had to get a restraining order. So instead of being grateful, you broke up with him?"

Clearly she wasn't getting her point across. "I didn't need to be rescued. I was doing okay handling Vaughn."

"So when Vaughn showed up at the clinic, you weren't freaked out in the least. You said, 'Oh, how great to see you. Let's go get some nachos and rehash old times.'"

Emma narrowed her gaze at her friend. "You are not helping."

Chelsea shrugged. "Sorry. But I'm having a difficult time wrapping my head around the fact that the guy you are more afraid of than anything in this life shows up where you work, Luke comes in and helps you out, and then you thank him by dumping him."

"Obviously I'm having a hard time clarifying the situation."

Chelsea took a sip of wine, then said, "Obviously. So why don't you tell me what's really going on?"

"I don't know. I guess I'm just scared."

"Well, no shit, Shirley. You should be scared. I would have been. After the way you described the hell that Vaughn put you through, I would have been terrified the minute he walked through my door."

"I was. I never expected to see him again."

"He thinks he owns you. Do you really think something like a restraining order is going to stop him?"

"I did. After all these years of no contact, I thought he was over it. Over me."

"He was just lying in wait, waiting for you to show up back here."

She pondered that over a couple swallows of wine. "And now I'm back."

"And so is he."

"But he violated the restraining order. They arrested him. He could go to jail."

Chelsea waved her hand. "He thinks of you as his property, Emma. The man is obviously demented. You don't think a piece of paper is going to stop him, do you?"

She sighed. "I don't know. I didn't think beyond getting him the hell out of my clinic last night."

"Which you should thank Luke for. I still don't understand what's going on between the two of you."

"I'm in love with him."

"Ohhh," Chelsea said. "And the light dawns. You love him, and that scares you. Because in your beautifully confused head, you think he's going to turn into some raving maniac like Vaughn who's going to chain you in the basement and beat you if you raise your voice to him."

Tears pricked her eyes. "I don't know. Maybe. I fought so hard to get away from Vaughn, spent years getting my sense of self and my independence back. I don't want to turn all that over to some guy again just because I might think I'm in love with him."

"Honey. Luke isn't just some guy. And do you really think he's anything at all like Vaughn?"

"The logical part of me says no. The scared part of me says I don't have any idea what any man is capable of once you give your heart to him."

Chelsea put her wineglass down and scooted over to pull Emma into her arms. "None of us knows what any man is capable of down the road. That's what trust is about. Not only do you have to trust him, you have to trust in yourself that you chose the right man."

She sighed. "I didn't do such a good job of that the first time."

"That was his fault, not yours."

"No, it was mine, too. I stayed with him and let him have that power over me because I was too afraid to walk away, too embarrassed by what I'd become."

"No, that was abuse, and you need to recognize the difference. And you did make a choice to get away. A lot of women never do. You should be proud of yourself for all the positive changes you've made in your life since you left him."

She pulled away and looked at Chelsea. "I am. I'm damn proud of all I've done. Which is why I'm also damn scared of chasing down that rabbit hole again. Love scares me, Chelse."

"Love scares all of us, Emma. It's probably the scariest thing any of us will ever do. To hand your heart over to someone who could crush it in their hands is the biggest step we'll ever take. But when you do take that step, you have to know it's for all the right reasons and for the right guy. The only guy. The one you trust completely, the one you know would never hurt you."

Emma stared into the wineglass, the red liquid answering none of her questions. "I just don't know what to do."

"It'll come to you. In the meantime, watch your back. And keep your gun close in case that crazy person is lurking around."

She leaned back against the sofa. "As far as Vaughn is concerned, my eyes are wide open."

EMMA MIGHT NOT want him in her life anymore, but Luke was still going to watch over her. Between running leads on the drug burglaries, he drove past her clinic and made periodic drive-by checks on her house at night.

Vaughn had made bail, with a court date set up for the next month. Which meant he'd need to stick around, though Luke would bet the bastard was lurking nearby anyway. He asked his fellow cops to keep an eye out for him and to let Luke know if they spotted the guy anywhere near Emma. They promised they would.

Since there'd been no break-ins for the past week, they were all working single shifts again. Which meant Luke could get in some gym time. He hit the basketball court with Will and Carter and a few other guys, some of them cops, some of them friends from school.

He needed the stress release. Too much had been going on lately, and he was wound tight.

"Hey, princess. You gonna hold the ball and daydream all night, or are we going to play some basketball?"

He looked at Carter, then dribbled around him and shot into the basket.

"Asshole," Carter said with a grin.

"You called me a princess. You're lucky I didn't knee you in the balls on my way around you to the basket."

"You ladies gonna stand around and gossip all night, or are we gonna play ball?"

Carter and Luke turned to Evan, who waited on the other side of the court.

Carter laughed. "Let's go break a sweat."

In an hour, Luke was drenched in sweat and more than ready for a water break.

"You're out of shape, McCormack," Evan said as he downed a bottle of water. "I can't believe you missed that layup."

"I can't believe you were picking your butt and missed that pass," Luke shot back. "Maybe you need a haircut. Or are you bucking for the town police calendar, so you're letting it grow out in hopes some of the ladies will vote you in?"

"It sure can't be based on his physique," Deacon, one of the other cops playing, shot back. "He's got more of a one-pack."

Evan lifted up his shirt to show off what even Luke had to admit was a mighty impressive eight-pack.

"I'm not the one sucking down all the beer after work, Deacon. You can kiss my ass. And they couldn't pay me to do that calendar."

"So maybe it's a lady you're doing all those crunches for," Carter said.

Evan went to the cooler for another water. "I've got no comment."

"So . . . no lady," Deacon said. "Otherwise he'd be bragging about it. That must mean he's spending all his time at the gym because he's only got his right hand for company."

Evan frowned. "Are we gonna play ball here or what?"

"See?" Deacon said. "It's the only thing he knows. Playing with his balls."

Luke let out a snort. Trash-talking was always the best part of playing basketball. Fortunately, they all genuinely liked each other or there would have been bloodletting by the end of the game.

"How's it going with your girl?" Carter asked him during a break as they swiped sweat from their faces with their towels.

"It's not."

"That didn't last long. Did Emma give you the heave-ho?"

"We're on a temporary break."

Carter laughed. "That means she gave you the heave-ho. She find another guy?"

"I don't want to talk about it."

"Sure you do. You're just playing the man card. Even guys want to talk about it with other guys. We just like to pretend we can man up and deal."

Luke gave Carter a look. "You never talked about it. You and Molly."

There was that look again, that shadow that always crossed Carter's face whenever Molly's name was mentioned. "Yeah, well, I wasn't a man back then, and that's ancient history. So let's man up, and after the game we'll go out for a beer and you can tell me about Emma."

Luke nodded. When the game was done, they showered and dressed, and Carter met him at No Hope At All, a bar run by Logan's best friend, Bash, and one of their favorite places to play pool.

"You wanna rack 'em?" Carter asked.

"Definitely."

They played the first game in virtual silence, shooting the appropriate balls into the appropriate pockets and drinking a few beers. By the second game, Luke knew Carter was going to ask.

"So what happened with you and Emma?"

"She had a problem with an ex-boyfriend who came back in her life."

"Someone she still liked?"

"No. Someone she had a restraining order on."

Carter's brows lifted. "Oh. Bad news. So what happened?"

"I interceded, and I don't think she cared much for that. She's got an independent streak, and I think she wanted to handle it herself."

Beer in hand, pool cue in the other, Carter nodded. "Women are a damn mystery sometimes."

Luke took his shot, then took a long swallow of beer. "Tell me about it. Anyway, I think the whole ex-coming-back thing just freaked her out, and she asked for some distance. So I'm giving it to her."

"But you're still watching over her because of the crazy ex-boyfriend, right?"

"Yeah. He's out on bail, and I don't trust that he'll leave her alone."

"I hope he does. And I hope that the two of you figure it out."

"Yeah?"

"Yeah." Carter took a swallow. "Not all of us get second chances with people we love. Don't let her get away if she's the one you want."

Luke wasn't sure if Carter, who usually wasn't one to get profound, had just told Luke what he needed to hear, or if what Carter had told him was what he'd wished had happened with Molly all those years ago.

Either way, he was right. He wasn't about to let Emma go. Things between them had been perfect before Vaughn showed up. And he knew she was scared, but just because someone pushed you away didn't mean you had to go away.

He'd walked away from one relationship. It had been the right thing to do because it was what they both wanted.

Deep down he knew neither he nor Emma wanted their relationship to end. So he was going to make sure it didn't. He just had to make sure it was on Emma's terms. Because he wasn't going to be like Vaughn and make her come around to his way of thinking, or try to overpower her. Emma had to choose him and come to him of her own free will.

He just had to be there for her when she was ready.

And in the meantime, linger nearby and keep her safe.

When he got out to his truck, he decided to give Boomer some exercise, so he drove by his apartment, got Boomer, and they went to the park for a walk. It was late, but Boomer, like his owner, didn't keep regular hours.

They walked for a bit and Luke cleared his head, then they got back into the truck and he drove past Emma's house.

It appeared he wasn't the only one up late. Emma was outside walking the dogs. Too late for him to back up the street so she wouldn't notice him.

He pulled over to the curb and rolled down the window as she came over.

"Hey, Luke," she said. "What brings you by here?"

"Just . . . driving past. You're outside late tonight."

She shrugged. "Couldn't sleep, so I thought a walk would help."

"Yeah. I took Boomer to the park for a walk."

She laughed. "It does help, you know. So . . . again, what brings you by here? Checking on me?"

Since her house wasn't on his way home, he had to admit it. "Old habits die hard, Emma."

"Well . . . thanks for that. I'm sure we'll be okay, but I do appreciate it."

"You're welcome."

He was about to lean away to put his truck back in gear, but Emma lingered next to the vehicle for a moment.

"So . . . how are things going?" she asked.

"Fine."

"Staying busy?"

"Yeah. How about you?"

"Oh yes. Lots of work at the clinic lately."

This was incredibly awkward. They'd always been able to talk. Things between them had been so easy before. He hated this.

His cell rang. He thought about ignoring it, but saw it was the station. "Excuse me, Emma." He picked up the phone, unable to believe what he was hearing.

"I'll be there right now." He hung up and looked at Emma. "Someone's breaking into Dorson's Pharmacy. I've gotta go."

"Go, hurry," she said. "Be careful."

He nodded and slammed on the gas. Though he wasn't on duty, he wanted to be there in case they caught the son-ofabitch. And since Dorson's was only a couple of blocks away, he should be able to make it in time.

He flipped on his scanner.

"On foot, the corner of Fifth and Scanlon," the dispatcher relayed.

Huh. Luke was on Scanlon, right at Fourth street. He turned right toward Fifth and saw a dark-clad figure hopping a fence. He picked up his phone and dialed it in. "I've got this guy. On foot, I'm in pursuit with Boomer, though I'm not in uniform, so don't shoot me."

He kept his phone on, pulled out his gun, and slid his badge on, then parked.

"Let's go, Boomer." He gave the command to Boomer that they were in pursuit. Boomer took off and easily jumped the fence. Luke ran like hell after the guy, hurdling the fence the suspect had just leaped over. When Luke caught sight of him, he dug in, increasing his speed.

Not this time, asshole. He wasn't getting away. "He's running through backyards on Sunshine Street, just west of Fourth," Luke said to his dispatcher. "I'm still in pursuit on foot."

The suspect tripped over something and fell, slowing him down.

Boomer was on him. He heard the growls and the howls of pain from the suspect.

Luke had him now. He leaped over the last fence and saw the suspect down, Boomer holding him by the arm.

Luke gave the command to release the suspect, then notified dispatch that he'd caught the perp. He gave their location so dispatch could notify the rest of the team in pursuit.

"Sonofabitch. Your dog bit me," the suspect said.

"Cry me a river. You're done, dickhead," Luke said, grabbing the guy and pulling his arms behind him. He heard the sirens and the slamming of doors. "We're back here!" he hollered.

Several uniforms ran back, and Luke got off the suspect so the uniforms could cuff him. Winded, he leaned over and laid his hands on his knees to suck in some oxygen.

"Good job, Boomer," Luke said, giving him lavish praise. Boomer ate it up. It wasn't often they could do a chase like this, but Luke loved being the one to take this bastard down.

"Need a ride back to your truck, old man?" Evan asked, patting him on the back.

"Fuck off," Luke said, laughing and coughing. "And yeah, a ride would be great. My legs feel like Jell-o right now. This kid can run like an Olympic sprinter."

They pulled the hoodie off the suspect. Bright yellow hair. Though he wasn't a kid. Early twenties, maybe. Fit the description Emma had given from the night she'd seen him. And he had a backpack filled with drugs that he'd just ripped off from Dorson's Pharmacy.

After they processed the scene, Luke drove to the precinct to give his statement.

"Good damn job, McCormack," his captain said, patting him on the back.

"Thanks. But Boomer took him down. I just got lucky spotting him when I was driving down the street."

"Great job, Boomer," the captain said, scratching Boomer's head.

Boomer loved the kudos he got from all the cops. Luke was glad the asshole was off the streets. Now they could figure out who the hell he was and find his drug stash.

After Luke finished at the precinct, he went to his apartment.

"Boomer," he said, petting his dog and crouching down to give him a good ear scratch. "You did so good tonight. I'm so proud of you."

Boomer knew he'd done well. Luke could see the pride in the way he held his ears erect and the way he sat.

After a treat and some water, the two of them went to bed. Luke, at least, was exhausted.

The next day Luke went in to work follow-up on the case. They'd interviewed the suspect, who of course had lawyered up, but they'd fingerprinted him, and one Bobby Tinter had a record that went all the way back to his juvvie days. Drugs, breaking and entering, auto theft—he was a real prize. He was also connected to some very big drug rings out of state, which was likely why he was hitting the pharmacies.

They hadn't pinned him earlier because he had an Arkansas address. Turned out Bobby was staying with a cousin in the Hope area. Luke figured Bobby had conned his cousin into letting him stay there, and then targeted a small town like Hope to make inroads into the drug ring by organizing several hits on businesses that carried drugs on their premises. With no one to connect him to the burglaries, he would shimmy out of town in a month or so with the booty and work his way up the ladder of the organization.

Too bad he'd gotten caught. There were stashes of drugs in the cousin's house, though the cousin had clammed up and said he had no idea what Bobby had been doing.

Ah, family loyalty. Whether the cousin had been in on it or not remained to be seen until they investigated further. Either way, Bobby was going away for a long time. Luke was satisfied they had a solid case against him.

It was great to at least get something resolved.

Now if he could get his personal life settled, he'd be happy.

Though he didn't think that situation was going to tie itself up with a bow and resolve itself as easily as Bobby had last night.

Some things required more work.

But some things were worth it.

Emma was. He just had to figure out how to make that work, how to get past her fears and the awkwardness that had settled between them.

And again, his hands were tied because it wasn't his call to make.

So right now, there was nothing he could do.

Except wait. And for a guy who was a man of action, that was damn hard to do.

On his break he went to Bert's for some coffee and something to eat.

"Hey, hero," Anita said, sliding a cup of coffee in front of him. "We heard you solved the burglary case."

Bert himself came out to pat him on the back.

"I didn't do it. Boomer took him down."

"I'll have to make Boomer a special treat, then," Bert said.

"A special cinnamon roll, just for you." Anita grinned as she placed the whopper of a roll in front of him.

He was going to be miserable in his cruiser for the rest of the day after eating that cinnamon roll.

And didn't it just figure that Emma stopped in just as everyone asked him to tell them about the bust last night.

"Hey," Emma said. "I heard you caught the guy. Congratulations."

"Thanks. Boomer did most of the heavy work."

She laughed. "Good for Boomer. But I have a feeling you did your part, too."

At that point, he wasn't sure if everyone in the diner was more interested in the story about chasing down and busting the suspect or watching the way he and Emma circled each other.

"So? Tell us how it all went down?" someone asked. "Did Boomer leap fences? Did you leap fences? I heard it all took place in backyards."

After taking a sip of coffee, Luke told his story, giving Boomer all the credit. "Then I just showed up, called Boomer off, and the rest of Hope's finest came in and cuffed him."

A round of applause followed. "He was a shifty fellow and hard to catch," Bert said, giving Luke a paper bag. "That's for Boomer."

"Thanks. He'll appreciate it."

Everyone went back to their own tables, except Emma, who took a seat at his. "I know you must be really happy to have caught the guy."

She looked so cute in her scrubs, her hair pulled into a high ponytail. He wanted to grab her and kiss her, which only frustrated him more because of where they currently were in their non-relationship.

"Yeah. It's a big relief for the entire department."

"I'm glad you're okay, and that Boomer's okay. Did the guy have a weapon on him?"

"He had a gun in his backpack, but he never pulled it during the pursuit. I think he was too busy running."

"Thank God. You're like the town hero today."

Luke laughed and took another swallow of coffee. "I think Boomer's the town hero this morning. And he's eating up all the attention."

"Deservedly so." She looked down at her phone. "I should get back to work. Congratulations again, Luke."

"Thanks, Em." She didn't seem to be in a hurry to leave, so he asked, "Are you doing all right?"

"Yes, I'm . . . fine. Thanks for asking. I guess I'll see you around."

"I'm sure you will."

She stood.

"Em?"

She looked down at him. "Yes?"

"If you need anything. Call me."

There was a sadness in her eyes. "I'll do that."

He really hated watching her walk away.

But he didn't know what to do about it.

Chapter 29

"OH, EMMA, WHY didn't you tell us this had happened?"

"That's it. I'm moving into your house tonight," her father said.

She'd resisted having this conversation for days. She knew telling her parents about Vaughn would worry her mother and kick her father's protective instincts into overdrive.

"Dad. You're not moving into my house. And I didn't tell you right when it happened precisely for this reason. Because, Mom, your ulcer would start acting up and you'd stop sleeping, and, Dad, you'd want to camp outside my door."

Her dad ran his fingers through his hair. "Well, dammit. What do you expect me to do? He threatened you before. Hell, he did worse than that. I told you what I'd do to that sonofabitch if he ever came near you again."

She sighed and placed her hand on her father's arm. "I know, Dad. And I appreciate it. But he's been arrested for violating the restraining order. He's going to have to go to court and answer for that."

"And you think that's going to stop him?" Her mother's

tone had gone high-pitched, and Emma knew hysteria wasn't too far behind that.

"It's going to deter him because if he comes anywhere near me again, they're going to revoke his bail and he stays in jail."

Her dad pursed his lips and glared at her, though she knew it wasn't her he was mad at. "I don't like this, Emma. Why don't you come stay with us until this is over."

"No. I'm not going to run from him again. I'm not going to let him drive me out of my house. I'm staying put. I'm going to get up every morning and go to work just like I always do, and I'm going to go home and sleep in my bed every night just like I always do."

"What about Luke?" her mother asked.

Just the mention of his name caused her stomach to clench. "What about him?"

"Is he still staying at your place?"

Good Lord. Did everyone know about her personal life, including her parents? You simply could not have a private life in a small town. "No. I sent him home."

"Why?" her dad asked, then frowned. "What did *he* do?"

"He didn't do anything. I just . . . needed my space."

"What does that mean? Did he hurt you as well, Emma?"

She rolled her eyes. "No, Mom. Luke didn't hurt me. He's damn near perfect, if you want to know the truth. I just need to be by myself right now."

And be lonely. And miserable. And wish every night that Luke were still there with me.

Sometimes taking an independent stand sucked.

Her dad pushed back from the dinner table. "One guy's a certifiable nutcase, and the other's perfect so she throws him out. Sometimes my daughter makes no gosh darn sense."

She wanted to go after her father, to explain about Luke, but her mother stopped her.

"He's upset," her mom said, her hand on Emma's arm. "And worried about you. So am I."

"I'm going to be fine. And Luke's not with me right now because I have to be able to take care of myself."

"He's a cop, Emma. He could be there to help watch over you."

"I had someone watching over me once, Mom. Vaughn watched over me a little too well."

Her mother leaned back in the chair. "And because of what happened before, you're afraid of putting your heart in Luke's care."

Emma didn't say anything.

"You're in love with Luke."

"Yes. I think so. It's not a very good time for me to be in love."

Her mother laughed. "Honey, there's no such thing as a perfect time to fall in love. Love is often messy and complicated. And now you have this horrible man reentering your life at a time when you just got your life back on track. I understand you want to be independent right now, but don't fight so hard for that independence that you sacrifice your safety—or a chance at happiness with someone you love."

Was that what she was doing?

"You have a stubborn streak like your father. And often you can't see the forest for the trees."

"What does that even mean?"

"It means you're blinded by your own goals and needs and what you think is right. You know I love you, Emma. You're brilliant and well educated, and after that mess you went through, I've never known a stronger, more dedicated young woman. But you're not always right. In this case, I think what you're doing is wrong."

Leave it to her mother to be bluntly honest.

"Luke is a fine young man, and he'd be a welcome addition to our family. Sometimes it's okay to give in, just a little, and let someone take care of you. It doesn't mean you aren't capable of taking care of yourself."

Emma didn't know what to think anymore.

"Emma, you know me. I've always been goal-oriented

and have gone after whatever I wanted. I have two degrees—one in marketing and one in business, and I've been a successful businesswoman my entire life."

"I know, Mom. I've always admired you."

"And I certainly have never 'needed' your father. But I couldn't manage a day without him, because I love him. So in that way, yes, I desperately need him in my life. If you look at the love you feel for Luke in that way, maybe you can learn to give a little."

"Okay, when you put it that way, it starts to make sense."

Her mother's lips curved in a smile. "You mean you might actually agree with me?"

Emma laughed. She leaned over and threw her arms around her mother. "Yes, it means I agree with you. Thanks, Mom."

"Anytime."

After having dinner with her parents, and, more important, talking with them, Emma had a lot to think about.

She'd been awful to Luke, pushing him away when he'd been there for her.

Fear had made her do stupid things. She and Luke had settled in to what had become a perfect relationship. Until Vaughn had shown up and ruined everything.

No. That wasn't right. She couldn't even blame Vaughn for what had happened. She was the one who had ruined everything. She and her own stupid fears. Now she had to figure out how to fix it.

She opened her front door, and the dogs ran inside. Daisy started fiercely barking, followed by Annie. The hairs on the back of Emma's neck stood on end. It wasn't like the dogs to bark like that inside the house, which could mean only one thing.

Someone was in her house.

So here was her independence. Should she take out her gun and go check it out herself?

Hell, no. She was independent. Not stupid. She needed to get out of the house now.

"Oh, all right, enough with the crazy barking," she said, trying to make it sound like that was normal for her dogs. "Come on, girls. Let's go for a walk before bed."

Fortunately, they both came running and she shut the front door. She tried to act natural and headed down the block. As soon as she was out of sight of the house, she pulled her phone out of her pocket and called Luke, hoping he wasn't so angry with her that he wouldn't pick up.

"Emma, what's up?"

"I think someone's inside my house."

"Where are you?"

"I stepped outside with the dogs. We're at the corner."

"I'll be right there. And I'll have a cruiser head that way."

"Thanks."

"I'll call you right back."

He hung up and she waited, staring at the street, then at her phone. When it rang, she hit the button.

"I'm still here on the corner."

"No movement?"

"No."

"Don't move from your location. Do you have your gun on you?"

"In my purse."

She heard wind sounds, knew he was driving.

"I'm staying on the phone with you. If he comes out, take the damn gun out and point it at him and tell him you've already called the police."

"You know it's Vaughn," she said, surprised by how calm she was.

"Yeah. I know it's Vaughn."

She looked down the street, toward the house. No one was coming toward her. "I knew he wouldn't stay away."

"I'm only a few minutes from there, Emma. Stay calm, breathe, and focus on your surroundings."

She made sure to turn around and look down the other street, just in case he had sneaked out the back door and climbed the fence to head the other way.

When she saw Luke's truck coming up her street, she exhaled and hurried down the block toward her house.

He climbed out of the truck, Boomer with him. At the same time, the police car pulled up.

"You and the dogs get in my truck. Lock the doors. We'll check inside."

She nodded and put the dogs inside the truck and locked the doors while Luke and the other officer went inside.

It didn't take more than five minutes for them to come out with Vaughn, handcuffed. The officer put him in the police car, along with a black bag. Luke spoke to the officer for a few minutes, then came over to Emma, who unlocked the truck and slid out.

"He had a bag with him, Emma, with a gun and duct tape. I think his intent was clear."

"Oh, God." She started trembling and Luke pulled her into his arms, holding her tight. He stroked her hair.

"He's done for. I'm sure his bail will be revoked, and he won't get it again. He's not getting out this time. You're going to be safe."

She clutched Luke's shirt, not sure she'd ever feel safe again.

"Thank you," she mumbled against his chest. "Thank you for coming."

"I'll always be here for you, Emma."

She closed her eyes and held on to that.

"You need to come in with me and make a statement so we can do a report. Are you up for that?"

She nodded. "That's fine. Let me put the dogs up."

He took her hand and they walked inside. Nothing looked disturbed, but she still shuddered.

"I hate that he was in my house, touching my things, walking on my floors." She looked at Luke. "Where did you find him?"

"In your bedroom closet."

She shuddered again. "I should have just gone in and shot him. Then I'd be rid of him forever."

"You are rid of him forever, Emma. Do you know how

many laws he broke tonight? Not only violation of the terms of his bail plus the restraining order, but breaking and entering, attempted kidnapping. He's going away for a long time, and he's not getting bail this time."

She still didn't feel safe. But she went down to the police station and made her statement, as did Luke. She had a cup of coffee—decaf this time. Her nerves were already on edge, and she didn't think she'd need any caffeine. Her parents came down and sat with her while she finished up. Luke said he'd be a while, so her parents drove her home and stayed with her until Luke showed up. When he did, they both hugged and kissed her and left because Luke promised them he wasn't leaving her alone that night.

She took a shower and they sat on the sofa, her back to his chest. She stared at the wall in front of her, thoughts of the past coming forward to assault her.

"For so long, he controlled everything about me. How I dressed, what I ate, how I was supposed to behave. In the beginning, I confused that with love. I was young and he was older, more worldly. I thought him paying that much attention to me was love. After a while, I was just too weak to fight it. Then, at the end, I plotted ways that I would escape from him. I'd lie awake at night and think of how I could get away from him. I guess I had never really escaped. I was never really free of him."

Luke stroked her hair. "You were free the moment you walked out of his house and never looked back. Vaughn's problem was that he couldn't let you go. That was *his* problem, Emma, not yours. He's the one that's sick and twisted. There's nothing wrong with you."

What Luke said made sense. "I guess you're right. Sometimes it's just so hard to let go of the mistakes you've made, especially when they keep coming back to haunt you over and over again."

"I think we're all haunted by our pasts to some extent, until we let them go."

She turned to face him. "Are you still holding on to your past?"

He picked up her legs and wrapped them around him. "I was. I was so dejected and humiliated when Becca walked out on me and divorced me, and I was determined to show the entire town that I didn't give a shit. I convinced myself that I'd never fall in love again, that no woman would ever matter to me again. It was so easy to go through one woman after another, disregarding their feelings. In fact, it felt kind of good. Like payback, you know?"

"I'm sure it did."

"Until I met you. You were the wrong kind of woman for me, a woman who I knew was the relationship type. I knew you weren't a one-night-stand kind of girl, yet I was drawn to you anyway. It was like I couldn't help myself."

Her lips curved. "I know the feeling."

"So I threw myself heart first into this fling with you, and this fling turned into a relationship, and this relationship turned into love."

Emma's heart squeezed. "It did?"

"Yeah, it did. So here I sit with you, Emma Burnett, on your sofa, in love with you, when I didn't set out for this to happen. But it did. And I know you didn't want it, either, especially now when you just had the worst night of your life. But love isn't always convenient, and I felt it needed to be said.

"I'm laying my heart out for you, and you get to decide what happens next."

Emma's chest tightened. This was exactly what she hadn't wanted to happen. And now it had. She had not expected that declaration of love from Luke. Not after the night she'd just had.

So what was she going to do now?

She looked up at him, at the honest expression of love on his face. He'd never hidden anything from her, had never been anything other than who he was. And he had never held any expectations of her, hadn't tried to control her or tell her how she was supposed to feel. He'd laid his heart out to her, and put the ball in her court.

Night-and-day different from her past. There was no comparison.

It was time to leave the past where it belonged, and embrace her future.

She cupped the side of his face and dragged her palm over the rough stubble of beard that always intrigued her and turned her on. Her skin tingled as it always did when she touched him.

"The one thing I've learned throughout all this is that there's a bad kind of love and a good kind of love. When someone loves you in a bad way, they take away everything that's good in your life, strip you of your family and friends, and want you only to themselves. Because they're afraid to share you, afraid to share the love they have for you with anyone else. That's a love they don't trust, a love that couldn't possibly last because it's tainted with darkness.

"The good kind of love—the kind of love I feel for you, and the kind of love you feel for me, is an open and trusting kind. I sent you away because I was afraid, and yet you were still there for me when I needed you. You shared me with your family, and allowed me to share my family with you. Our kind of love is an all-encompassing kind, filled with kindness and compassion, with friendship, laughter, warmth, passion, and forgiveness. It's an endless kind of love, a kind of love I've never had before."

Luke swept the tear away that had slid down her cheek.

"I love you, Luke. I've never loved anyone the way I love you."

He pulled her onto his lap and threaded his fingers through her hair, then just looked at her.

"I've never loved anyone the way I love you, Emma." Then he kissed her, oh so thoroughly kissed her, until everything that had happened earlier in the night was utterly forgotten, and all she could think about was the way it felt to be in this man's arms, to know that he loved her and cherished her, and would protect her in the way a woman would want to be protected, and she in turn would protect him, too.

Clothes were shed in a hurry, and when he was inside her, the two of them locked together, staring at each other as he moved within her, Emma could only marvel that this hot, sexy, oh-so-honorable man was in love with her. And when he touched her and brought her right to the brink, then over, she clutched his shoulders and took him with her, both of them crying out as they climaxed together.

She laid her head on his shoulder, and he stroked her back.

"Do you think you and Boomer would like to move in here?"

He lifted his head, studied her, then smiled. "Yeah. Boomer and I would like that."

Contented, she kissed him. "Good. Daisy, Annie, and I would like that, too."

They were going to be a family. Or at least the beginning of one.

One step at a time. One day at a time. And this was a great start, with a man she loved, dogs she loved, in a home she loved.

In the town she'd always called home.